DEMONCHASER V

David Berardelli

DEMONCHASER V

"Free of Hell and still wearing great shoes"

GRAVESTONE PRESS

PART 1

THE SCENE OF THE CRIME

CHAPTER 1 - THE FIRST DEMON

Bruno Stone sensed something odd about the skinny brunette the moment she came into the crowded diner and took a seat five tables up, across the aisle.

Just a few minutes ago, Bruno finished his medium-rare, twenty-four-ounce T-bone, double fries, and a huge slice of the diner's baked apple pie, and had been in the process of sucking down the last few inches of his giant chocolate shake when he spotted the brunette coming in with a dorky redheaded dude close at her heels.

Bruno immediately began wondering why he was so fascinated. He saw weird people all the time. In Hollywood, you witnessed all sorts of fruitcakes. There were throngs of folks who would do anything under the sun for a little publicity. Other nutjobs would walk through fire just to get a glimpse of a celeb. Or touch one. Or have their picture taken touching one. Or just being seen on the same street.

Bruno just couldn't figure out what was so damned special about the brunette. She certainly wasn't anything to write home about. Here, in a place where luscious babes could be seen on any street corner and behind any register in any 7-Eleven or Walmart within fifty miles, it was common knowledge that the only female worth a moment of your time was that one special babe who could set your junk on fire with a single glance. In this area alone, starlets and bosomy mega-celebs alike could be seen crossing the street or standing at the pump in ultra-tight tank tops and bikini briefs, bending over to coax a few gallons of overpriced gas into the tank of their Lexus, or Porsche.

This broad could hardly measure up. Or find herself in the same ballpark. Or even in the same county.

For one thing, her hair wasn't perfect. It was long—which gave her a much-needed point or two in the running. But it was also straggly and windblown. Its appearance gave you the impression that she'd just run a comb through it once or twice after spending a few hot minutes knocking boots in the backseat of a pickup.

Imperfect hair just didn't push his buttons. Especially in a place where high-priced stylists ran ultra-modern salons on every block.

Small titties didn't do much at all, either. The brunette was skinny—which was okay in a place where six ounces in the wrong area could mean the difference between landing a prime spot in a cosmetic commercial or being told to hit the road.

But flat boobs? Definitely *not* okay where sensational babes with long legs, perfect hair, bodacious jugs, fat lips and a flawless face were an absolute necessity.

The brunette had a nice face. It wasn't glamorous or even unforgettable, but it was easy to tell that those big brown eyes might have the ability to turn a guy into quivering Jell-O.

Her open-toed sandals also caught his eye. He'd figured them as top-of-the-line designer originals. The diamonds glittering the sides in long, wavy rows looked real. And the bright blue streak spanning the outside of the shoe just below the gems—as if fashioned meticulously by an expert hand—told him she'd obviously spent considerable cash on them.

Since he'd been living in this neck of the woods the last seventy-five years, Bruno was familiar with just about every outlet in the city. It was important to be aware of fashions in his line of work.

Those sandals easily went for five hundred, maybe seven-fifty—more than triple that, *if* the diamonds were legit. Judging by the loose-fitting red tee shirt and snug jeans that looked like a last-minute raid of the local Goodwill box, he figured this broad couldn't afford such pricey shoes. She'd either stolen them or found them in one of the trash bins near Hollywood & Vine.

Even though she was much closer to ordinary than hot or even mildly attractive, he still found something strangely appealing about her. This fascinated him, and he found it difficult to concentrate, even with the six mouth-watering beauties sitting at tables, sipping their vanilla shakes through straws stuck in the center of their collagen-swelled lips.

7

Nowadays, he'd tailored his outward appearance to affect the look of the average big-name actor. He'd chosen Matt Damon, Hugh Jackman, and a couple of the earlier James Bond hopefuls as his template. With his lean, buffed body and tanned face, Bruno had no trouble attracting the female of his choice.

Every so often, three of the babes—the two blondes and the willowy redhead—glanced his way, giving him that familiar "love the pecs, big boy" look, while the other three—the sultry brunette, the spectacular-looking Asian, and the anorexic black woman with huge fake boobs—settled on his face.

Bruno was almost certain that he'd nailed at least two of them. The redhead looked vaguely familiar. So did the Asian. As he recalled, the blonde liked to be tied down with scarves while she gave him the hummer. One of the others also tweaked his memory, but since there had been so many, he couldn't be quite pin it down. Something about leather, or rubber.

Tinsel Town squirted out succulent babes just as fast as McDonald's chucked burgers and fries, and everyone tended to look like one another. Especially babes. Thanks to the cosmetic dudes driving around in Maserati's and living in hilltop palaces, you could have just about any face you wanted if you had the cash. The boob peddlers had been raking in ridiculous piles of jack for the last five or six decades. And, of course, you had the dudes pawning off huge, pouty lips. Then there were the facelift guys pulling in five K each time they spent a pleasant afternoon slicing up a babe's face while she sat drooling in the chair.

But since everyone turned out beautiful and happy, who really gave a shit?

Bruno gave the luscious sextet a final glance.

Sorry, babes, he wanted to tell them, *but that chick over there—the plain, flat-chested one sitting at the table with the wild-haired dork—has my interest this morning.*

No matter. He could hook up with any or all of them later on. Bruno had been considered prime babe candy the last seventy-five years, when breathtaking beauties like Gene Tierney, Rita Hayworth, Faye Emerson, Hedy Lamarr, and Ava Gardner turned the silver screen into bubbling froth.

Back in the day, he'd tailored his physical appearance to favor Errol Flynn, or Tyrone Power. Not close enough to be mistaken for either, but enough to create enough sexual attraction to satisfy his enormous appetite. He'd nailed Lamarr and Emerson a few times, even played handsies and grab-ass with Ava once or twice. But that was a lifetime ago, in another world. Women were more sophisticated and challenging back then. They demanded sweet talk—as well as flowers, candy, and the offer of a weekend of luxury and unbridled passion in the Swiss Alps. Nowadays, all you had to do was tell them you knew Spielberg or Cameron, and they were all over you, tugging at your zipper.

Bruno focused on the brunette's dorky red-headed friend. Weird dude, considering his looks and the fact that he'd just picked up something from the floor—a piece of eggshell, or potato skin—and tossed it into his mouth.

Bruno wanted to gag. A dude had to be seriously messed up to grab something right off the floor in a crowded diner and suck it down. True, this was Tinsel Town, mecca for the beautiful and glamorous, but the germs here were just as disgusting as those in any Mexican or Colombian jail.

Bruno pushed aside his chocolate shake. *Two hundred years in the Valley of Decay, avoiding disgusting things crawling out of the swamp, and now here in the mortal world, the center of society's most gorgeous creatures, a red-headed dork makes me want to puke?*

He told himself that he shouldn't worry too much about this. For one thing, he wasn't even sure the dude was a male. He saw no hint of machismo coming from the mortal—nothing that would even suggest that this dude peed standing up or even had genuine erections.

It took considerable observation to convince him that the redhead could be a guy. Bruno didn't know if it was the hand gestures, how the dork fidgeted in his seat, or the fact that he was sitting the way a dude sat—slouched, his legs spread wide under the table. Also, he scratched the back of his neck the right way, vigorously and right out there for the world to see, rather than slide his hand gently beneath that thick mat of red hair to make it look like he was massaging his neck—as a babe would.

10

This dork seemed to be the type you'd expect to see in a circus. Among the freaks—like one of those midget acrobats, or maybe someone they could refer to as a "Plant Man," since he reminded Bruno of something he'd seen behind the Castle of Demons, where Olivier kept his assortment of oddities in his rock garden. This dude was about as tall as the brunette and just as skinny. But that hair was what caught his attention right off. It was fire-engine red and looked like it had been shaped with a leaf blower into some sort of crimson palmetto bush.

He looked about twenty-five. Judging by his odd behavior—plus the fact that he selected his groceries from a dirty diner floor—this weirdo had a slew of issues any shrink would have been happy to dive into. Though the floor-scraps thing might not be enough to coax the average shrink to snatch up his notebook, Bruno suspected this dork had a boatload of other things going on that were way far from normal or even believable.

The skinny blond waitress hurried down the aisle, stopped at their table, then scribbled their order onto her notepad. Bruno wasn't certain, but even though the crowd was making more than enough racket, he thought he'd heard the red-headed dork order something that sounded like coffee grounds and eggshells.

Seriously?

After scribbling their order, the waitress turned, came over and slid his bill onto the table, then scurried up to the counter and handed the cook the new order.

Bruno decided right then that he wasn't going anywhere until he saw with his own eyes what the waitress brought back to their table.

Coffee grounds? Eggshells?

He'd seen some seriously off-the-wall diets during his time here. Hell, in the last seventy-five years, he'd seen every sort of oddball meal plan under the sun. But this one really made him scratch the back of his muscled neck in total confusion. It made him even more suspicious about what this dork was doing with the brunette.

No babe in her right mind would spend time with a skinny dork who lived on coffee grounds and eggshells—not to mention whatever he could scrape up from the floor in a crowded greasy spoon.

Bruno knew all about nutcases. As a mortal, he'd spent his teen years in correction facilities, then in and out of state penitentiaries for the next ten for grand larceny, extortion, and kidnapping before he was capped by a trigger man hired by a New York Senator for nailing the big man's sixteen-year-old daughter.

Spending considerable time in the Dark Place had given him an even closer view of insanity. He'd seen quite a bit with the supers in the Castle of Demons, the subs in the Valley of Decay, and the inferiors crawling around the slimy shores of the River of Blood. And when Balberith had called him back up into the mortal world, he'd seen and stumbled across more weirdos than there were stars in the skies.

Since then, he'd been paid to thin the herd whenever the opportunity presented itself. Working with the West Coast drug lord Lorenzo "Big Man" Stefano gave him a myriad of different ways to be creative when sending deserving mortals down to the Dark Place.

He wondered if this redheaded fruitcake would be a problem. Not knowing how the two got along, Bruno had no idea if her bud might object to his advances. If so, this just might force him to perform a quick dump job.

He kept his eye on the brunette. Yeah, there was something about her. Her hair? Her face? Her slender frame? All three were definite possibilities, of course. But there was something else about her that made him want to walk right up to her table and give her a single dose of the Bruno Stone charm before carting her off to his pad on the Strip.

Just then, she glanced his way. Bruno wondered if she'd somehow read his thoughts. Impossible. Mortals couldn't do such things. But it happened nonetheless, and in that one single moment, just as those large brown eyes fixed on him, she flashed him a half-smile.

Bruno experienced a splash of warmth.

What the hell was going on?

How could this plain-looking babe do such a number on him?

Weird. And totally bizarro.

But captivating at the same time.

There would be no problem getting her in the sack. Her half-smile said, *I see you watching me, babe, and I want you, too. You're a hot, good-looking hunk.*

True, her smile wasn't one of those gleaming numbers that showed bright, shining teeth, dimples and glittering eyes. This babe was obviously the shy, quiet type. The kind who spoke softly and smiled instead of laughed.

All he had to do was smile back, introduce himself and politely ask her to follow him to his pad.

No problem at all.

And how the hell *could* there be? Bruno Stone had been nailing any piece of tail he pleased since the mid-forties. There was not one babe he couldn't attract or seduce.

After all, he was the demon spirit Agnus. A Romeo in the mortal world. An incubus in the truest sense of the word.

And since he had the afternoon free and didn't have to concentrate on beating down Big Stefano's latest renegade coke runner until the next morning, Bruno Stone would take this doe-eyed brunette to his double bed for a hot, sudsy evening of pleasure.

The waitress rushed to their table, carrying a tray. The brunette had ordered buttered toast, three strips of bacon, and a small cup of coffee. Her weirdo friend was given a large bowl filled with what looked like burnt coffee grounds topped off with crushed eggshells, a large pitcher of water and a glass of orange juice.

This made no sense at all. The dude was skinny and obviously didn't need to follow a restricted diet. Anyone who feasted on coffee grounds and eggshells should be dead—or at least suffering

14

from IBS, colon abscesses, diverticulitis, or other similar gut problems.

But apparently he was still on his feet—even with such a weird diet.

Bruno wanted the brunette. He didn't give a rat's ass about the nutcase sitting with her, crunching eggshells and swallowing coffee grounds.

Bruno planned to enjoy himself. He wanted to take her back to his loft and hump away the afternoon and evening, until the next morning, when he would calmly cap the back-stabbing drug runner for Big Stefano, for his usual five-K fee.

***

Chip munched on an eggshell. He hadn't said much since Tiffany had changed her appearance one block down the street, while they were waiting for the light to change. That was more than twenty minutes ago. Aside from ordering his lunch, he hadn't said a word to her. He wasn't looking at her, either. He seemed to be watching the street activity.

"Anything interesting out there?" she asked.

"This place is weird. Really weird. I mean really, *really* weird."

"Why do you say that?"

"I've counted at least five people walking past."

"So? There are probably ten times that out there right now."

"You didn't let me finish."

"Sorry."

"I can't tell if they're male or female."

15

Tiffany nibbled on a piece of bacon and gave a slight shrug.

"They also have tattoos where there shouldn't be tattoos," he added.

Tiffany saw no reason to reply. This area was notorious for weirdos of all shapes and sizes. She remembered being shocked by their appearance when she'd first come here, but after a few days, she hardly noticed them at all.

Chip tilted his head. "That doesn't bother you?"

"Why should it?"

"It bothers *me*..."

"Why should it?"

He shrugged. "I don't know. It just does."

"You saw weird spirits down below, right?"

"I hate to burst your bubble, Tifferoo, but we ain't down below no more."

"I've noticed." Tiffany nibbled on some toast.

The diner was crowded. She gave the room another cautious glance. Her latest disguise would easily keep the attention away from her—especially from the male hunks with raging hormones. Which would be perfect, of course. She was obsessed about staying under the radar.

The radar, of course, came from the super demon, Breath Mint—or whatever the ugly brute called himself. He'd been after them ever since they'd snuck out of Orlando, Florida.

But even though they were now in Southern California, they were far from safe. Breath Mint had a long reach. He'd found them in Pittsburgh and would have had them brought back to Florida

16

to face their fate if they hadn't defeated the demon hunter Andras and shipped him back to Orlando on a chartered plane.

Although that was a major triumph, Tiffany knew this would enrage the super demon even more. Breath Mint would undoubtedly send someone else after them. This, of course, made her more determined than ever not to let down her guard.

Tiffany had no intention of returning to Hell. Even though she, like Chip, was dead, and had been able to maintain a lifelike appearance for the last six months, she saw no reason to return to that dark, miserable, foul-smelling place.

This would be their last stop before returning to Peoria, where her mom lived. Once they'd finished their business here, Tiffany promised herself that she'd maintain a quiet existence. And since she and Chip had already purged Peoria of two dangerous demons just a week earlier, she was confident that their future might turn out all right.

However, her business here had to be completed first. This was where the good-looking, fast-talking creep at Johnny Rock's pool party had slipped her the roofie that killed her. And until she'd settled her business with him, everything else had to wait.

But right now, she was concerned about Chip. Chip wasn't exactly the most reserved soul she'd ever known. He wasn't silent very much—which told her something was amiss. And she didn't think it had anything to do with the weird people he was watching.

"What's really wrong?" she asked.

No reply.

"I know something's wrong, so I really wish you'd tell me about it."

Chip used a spoon to scoop up some burnt coffee grounds and shoved them into his mouth. She'd always found this disgusting, but it made sense. For the last three thousand years, Chip had been a flower living in the super demon Olivier's rock garden behind the Castle of Demons in Hades City. Chip's spirit form was that of the Cypripedium Calceolus, commonly known as the Yellow Lady's Slipper. His mortal form was that of a skinny, wild-haired young guy with tiny green eyes, pointed ears, and a tongue that could, on occasion, roll out of his mouth and touch the floor.

"Why won't you talk to me? Is it because of the weird people you're watching on the street?"

"Is what because of the weird people I'm watching on the street?"

Tiffany groaned. He was becoming difficult again. "You know what I'm talking about…"

"What was that?"

"Will you *please* tell me what's wrong?"

"About what?"

"Never mind." Sometimes it was best to ignore him.

Chip washed down the coffee grounds with a slug of water from the pitcher. He put down the pitcher and belched loudly. Several people from nearby booths turned in their direction, many of them glaring. Chip never seemed to care what

18

others thought of him. He stared at her, his eyes dead-steady. "You don't look like my good buddy."

"I know. I changed my appearance."

"That's most likely why you don't look like her."

"I *am* her. You know I am. You saw me change."

"I was there, remember?"

"Yes. I remember."

"I was right there. Beside you. I had a ringside seat. I was standing, but I still had a ringside—"

"I get it."

"Your golden hair turned a drab mousey brown—"

"I know. I made it do that. On purpose."

He lowered his eyes and shook his head. "Those luscious melons… My God—"

"Oh stop…"

"They…" He looked like he was about to cry. "They just… *disappeared*!"

She was beginning to get angry. "I know. I was right there when I made them smaller."

"Non-existent."

"Whatever."

"Flat."

"Get off the subject, now."

He stared longingly at her chest, sighing deeply.

"I'm up here," she reminded.

He continued staring.

Tiffany struggled to keep from losing her calm. Men could be so ridiculous. "I had to do that to keep everyone from staring at us. You know how people—especially men—look at me when I'm me…"

No response.

"Chip? Did you hear me?"

"I know, I know…"

"Is this why you're acting so…stupid?"

"Define stupid."

"The way you're acting."

He blinked. "You just don't *look* like her—like *you*!"

"I thought you'd remember what I was forced to do in Pittsburgh, when Andras was sent after us."

"How could I forget something like that? First, you're Tifferoo, that luscious, mouth-watering babe I've been doing all sorts of mischief with since we came back up from the Bad Place." He took a breath. "Now? You look like one of those hippy babes from the sixties. The ones that got arrested for breast-feeding their kid on a crowded bus, or in front of a library."

"But this is *me*!"

"I know."

"Then why can't you get past this and stop treating me like a stranger?"

He picked up a chunk of eggshell and munched noisily. "There's a nifty reason for that."

"I imagine there is. I also imagine you're about to tell me. I just hope this explains why you're acting so weird."

"Me? Weird?"

"You. Weird."

He looked hurt. "It's like…like I don't know who I'm talking to."

20

"How can you say that?"

"Right now, you're just some icky-looking brunette chick who *sounds* like Tifferoo, but—"

"I *am* Tiffer—*Tiffany*." She forced herself to keep her voice down. "Can't you understand why I've come back to this horrible place?"

He went back to watching the street activity. He reached up to scratch his head. "That guy—or chick—just copped a feel from that fat guy in a suit when he—or she—walked by." Chip was shaking his head. "I kinda think that fat dude's wallet is in the wind."

It was getting more difficult to keep him focused.

"Chip, try to keep up."

"I'm cool." He turned. "Go 'head. Spit it out."

"What's the problem?"

"Problem?"

"Yes. Problem."

"About what?"

"Our coming back here. Why I have to change my appearance so we can stay under the radar."

"I get it."

"Then why are you so bummed out?"

"That's easy. You don't look like my good buddy."

"I thought I explained all that."

"You did, but I think I might've forgotten. Lots of distractions out here, ya know. Guys who look like chicks who look like guys—"

"These people are dangerous. They're movie people. They live well and dress well, but every one of them deals with the worst characters imaginable.

21

Mob guys. Drug runners. Politicians. And I need to tread lightly if I want to find the man responsible for killing me. Can you understand *any* of this?"

Before he could reply, she added, "And there's a reason for the no-puppies thing, too."

He was staring at her chest again. And looking pitiful. Again.

"As I just said, I don't want people noticing me. You know darned well that Breath Mint has his spies out here—as well as everywhere else."

Chip sighed tiredly. "The demon's name, Muffin, is *Braithwaite*."

"Whatever."

"Anyone would think you'd have learned that by now."

"Maybe I hate him too much to keep his name in my head. Maybe I don't want his name in my head at all. Maybe he doesn't matter to me. Maybe—"

"I get it, Honey Buns."

"I'm *so* glad."

"Well, I guess you'll be pleased to know that your efforts have not exactly been in vain. If I didn't know who you were, I wouldn't waste a moment moving these beautiful little green orbs in your direction."

"If people were watching me, we'd have a much rougher time doing this. And who knows? Breath Mint—or whatever you want to call that monster—would certainly know we're here by now."

"Good point."

She lowered her head.

"Why the sudden tragic look?"

She moved closer. "My plan hasn't worked. Not entirely."

"Whatever do you mean?"

She didn't want to draw attention to herself and hoped Chip wouldn't make the situation worse. But he had to know something was going on. "To be blunt, not everyone has been ignoring me."

"Please enlighten me with a generous dose of clear elucidation, then. Unless, of course, you're too busy wallowing in personal tragedy to indulge."

She didn't want to tell him about the guy five tables down. The muscular, good-looking guy who'd been staring at her the last five minutes. For one thing, Chip might turn around and look at him. For another, she had the strong feeling that there was something very strange and extremely dangerous about the guy. But she felt she had no choice.

"Tiffers? Some much-needed clarification? Please?"

"I really don't want to talk about it right now."

"When *would* you like to talk about it?"

"When we leave."

"Why then?"

"Because this concerns someone...in this room."

"And?"

"I don't want to point him out because you'll turn around and look at him. And then he'll know we're talking about him. And then something'll happen as things usually do whenever people are involved. And then—"

Chip lowered his voice. "You're not talking about that dark-haired dude sitting a few tables down from us, are you, pray tell? Wide shoulders? Small waist? All sorts of ugly veins squirming around on his forearms? The dude wearing the tight red tee shirt advertising California's sandy beaches?"

Tiffany stiffened. "H-How did you...how could you possibly—"

"I had this feeling. And a clear image that popped into my coconut just a few minutes ago."

"That's very peculiar."

"Tell me about it. I'm just an inferior. I'm not supposed to be able to pull crap out of the air like that. Just tricks and illusions for all ages and occasions—"

"If don't didn't know any better, I'd think your powers were actually...*growing*."

"Forget about the powers. Just produce some money so we can pay our way out of here."

"I haven't finished my toast..."

"Forget the toast. We need to get rid of that guy."

***

After the strange twosome had left the diner, Bruno Stone paid for his lunch. Then, ignoring the admiring glances from the other babes, he went out into the street. The moment he joined the slow-moving crowd, he realized that the brunette and her friend had disappeared.

Having seen them heading east, he hastened his pace, squeezing past the assorted masses of tourists, bikinis and suits hogging the sidewalk, until he caught sight of the wild shock of red hair half a block straight ahead, moving leisurely down the street.

It appeared that the redhead was alone.

Had the brunette gone off in a different direction?

He soon realized that he'd been mistaken. The redhead was not alone at all. He was walking beside a female. The two were talking to one another.

However, something was very odd.

The brunette had vanished. The chick walking with the redhead was a raven-haired babe with luscious curves and a tight, perfectly shaped ass.

Where had the redhead picked her up?

More importantly, how the hell had he grabbed her and dumped the brunette so quickly?

The raven-haired babe was wearing the same clothes as the brunette. The same shirt, the same jeans. Yet something was very different.

Her shoes.

Although the same elegant style as what the brunette had been wearing, this pair looked different. Instead of diamonds running across the sides, emeralds decorated the heels and just below each ankle, in glistening patterns.

Several important details squirmed their way into his brain.

Not right.

Wrong.

Weird.

And *so* unnatural.

If anything, *super*natural…

25

When that last morsel drifted into his consciousness, he felt his pulse racing.

Bruno Stone knew right then that he'd just encountered a shapeshifter.

***

"How's this?" Tiffany asked, her long black hair gleaming in the late morning sun. "Any better?"

Chip stopped walking and did a double take. "Wow... When did *that* happen?"

"Oh, just a moment ago."

His tiny green eyes filled the sockets as he studied her. "Why didn't you make that happen before we left the diner?"

"Would it have mattered?"

He didn't reply; he was staring at her breasts.

"I'm up here," she reminded.

"Yeah, but the really cool stuff is—"

"Oh, stop."

"I can't help it. I wasn't too wild about the Plain Jane babe."

"I could tell."

"Really?"

"You made it pretty clear."

Chip went silent as a tall, slender figure in a green bunny suit crossed the street farther down.

"Does this mean you approve?"

"About what?"

"You're not paying one bit of attention to me, are you?"

"The green bunny distracted me."

"I told you about the weird people out here."

"A *bunny* suit?"

"Stick to the subject. Did you just say you approve of me now?"

"Maybe…"

"Why maybe?"

"Your face just ain't the same, kiddo."

"It's only a *little* different…"

"Tifferoo, your face would launch a thousand ships. It would send millions of horny guys rushing to the stores for Viagra, porn flicks and all sorts of disgusting sex aids—"

"What's wrong with this one?"

"Not a damned thing. It's great. It reminds me of an actress I once saw a long time ago. She didn't exactly have black hair, and her eyes were different…and she was wearing a veil, so you couldn't really see what she looked like… And as I remember, she was riding a horse—"

"Enough."

"You asked."

She sighed and struggled to remember what they were talking about. "What is it that you don't approve of?"

"I really didn't like that bunny suit. And these people with body piercing and tattoos are really doing a job on me. I saw a guy wearing a Viking helmet earlier this morning, before we went into the—"

"About me. Me!"

"What about you?"

Tiffany ran an impatient hand through her black locks. "Think! *Please*?"

"That's a super no-brainer. It's your hair."

"What's wrong with my hair?"

"It's black."

"But it's thick and long—"

"And black."

"But what's *wrong* with it? I mean really?"

"Besides being black?"

"Yes."

"Tifferoo, your golden mane has kept me awake nights, then lulled me to sleep and gave me all sorts of naughty wet dreams—which is a really nifty trick, considering I'm just a spirit."

"But—"

"Don't say it, Honey Bunny."

"You have no idea what I was going to say."

"You were gonna say I'm silly. And that I need to get a grip. And that I need to focus more. And fully understand why you've been doing what you're doing. How's that?"

"Pretty accurate, but—"

"But what?"

"You really *are* silly."

***

Once the two were no longer in his sights, Bruno Stone snapped out of his daze.

Just a month or so earlier, he'd received word through the ranks that Super Demon Braithwaite was looking for rogue inferiors. Apparently two such rogues had sabotaged Braithwaite's billion-dollar land development scheme in Southern Florida. From what Stone had heard, the rogues had disappeared and could be making their way west. Although their actual description had not been provided, it was stated that one was female, the other male, and that the female was beautiful and much more dangerous than the male.

A beautiful, dangerous female inferior?

The image of the plain-faced brunette drifted into his head. The vision he'd seen just moments ago

(*raven-haired, with luscious curves*)

told him the worst.

The hair. The figure. Everything had happened on the street, in full view of hundreds of pedestrians and yet oblivious to everyone.

The rogue was indeed a shapeshifter. Otherwise, she wouldn't have been able to change so quickly.

The important thing was to look at this logically. Bruno had seen a male and female come into the diner. From what he'd observed, the female was obviously a demon. Bruno had no idea if they were the rogues Braithwaite was looking for. Even so, he had to act on this. This might turn out in his favor. And if Braithwaite was indeed hungry for their capture, there would no doubt be a reward.

Bruno had been looking forward to something like this ever since he'd returned to the mortal world. And since he'd been doing exceptional work on Balberith's behalf for the last seventy-five years, he believed that he deserved compensation.

Back in the forties, his task had been simple. He was to use his sexual powers to infect and impregnate every female he met. As an incubus, he regarded this work as anything but a challenge. But lately, he realized he needed a change.

He'd met Big Stefano just five years earlier. After minimal coaxing, Bruno had impregnated two of the mobster's finest prostitutes causing mayhem with several high-ranking members of the film industry. By doing so, Bruno had made it possible for Big Stefano to complete several major contracts with the studios.

Being on Big Stefano's payroll had earned him status as well as a great deal of money, but he realized long ago that he could never be totally satisfied. A shapeshifter himself, Bruno's talents were limited to mere variations of his facial features as well as his physical appearance. Convenient during times of stress, of course, but when faced with larger tasks, he couldn't help feeling inadequate.

He'd always obsessed about mind manipulation. Since he considered himself many levels above even the most exceptional mortal, he couldn't avoid disappointment when his limitations got in the way of ultimate triumph. There were many things he wanted to do to distinguish himself with the Legion of Demons. When he eventually returned to the Dark Place during the Rapture, he wanted to be placed among the elite. To be able to sit with the most powerful demons in the Castle. Balberith. Ashtaroth. Olivier. Maybe even Lucifer himself.

Braithwaite was the biggest and most important supers of them all. He was the baddest of the badasses and had always been the worst demon to cross. And all Bruno had to do was keep the twosome in his sights long enough to make his call to Florida, where Braithwaite had set up shop.

Bruno hurried down the street. Using the cover of the crowds, he kept his senses alert for the shapely black-haired babe and her weird redheaded friend.

***

Tiffany and Chip reached the end of the block and headed north, where the next block brought them to a plethora of businesses. Jewelers. A bistro. A boutique. A pawnshop. A hardware store. A small pet hospital. Two nail salons separated by a deli. Young women in shorts and tank tops strolled between small groups of well-dressed business types in thousand-dollar suits and an occasional tourist wearing a camera over a tee shirt advertising Disneyland, or Universal Studios.

Tiffany grew more panicky as they went down the street. Dozens of memories raced by, overwhelming her. Faces of nasty, unpleasant people she'd dealt with during her brief stay in this mecca of fantasy and glamour flashed before her. Memories of the street leading to her small two-room apartment, just a couple of blocks north, sent chills down her limbs. Johnny Rock's sprawling mansion awaited her less than four miles north.

Johnny Rock. The mere image of the man made her wonder how much had changed in the few months since her death. She wondered if Johnny still lived in the same place. If he still collected classic guitars, movie memorabilia, rare gems, and antique guns. If he still entertained the big boys in his pool room. If the same sort of people came to his pool parties. If the same good-looking, well-dressed monster that had poisoned her drink had done the same ghastly thing to other unsuspecting starlets. If this monster had ever been punished for what he'd done to her.

I'm going to find you, she thought wildly. *I may not know your name, where you live or where you work, but I'm going to find you. And when I do, I'm going to look you right in the eye and—*

"Tifferoo?"

She blinked out of her madness. Chip was standing close by, watching her.

Sighing deeply, she struggled back to reality and forced out a smile.

"You look kind of frazzled, Honey Bunny."

"Everything's fine. Just fine. Terrific. Dandy. Never better."

"Really?"

"I just said it was."

Chip looked doubtful. "I'll just ignore that ginormous crack you've got growing between those lovely baby blues and assume that we're both having a rollicking good ol' time here in Tinsel Town."

"A crack? Really?"

He grinned sheepishly.

When she realized what he meant, she remembered that she could never hide anything from him. "I'm sorry. I'm just…I guess I'm just anxious about—"

"I get it, Munchkin. You're seriously distracted. I can't say as I blame you."

"Well—"

"Are you gonna be all right soon?"

"I'm okay." She took in a big gulp of warm afternoon breeze. "Yes. I'm just fine."

"Cool beans. Then you can answer my question."

"Which one?"

"The one I asked just before you slipped into your fugue of torment and tragedy a few moments ago."

"Okay…"

"You can answer any time now…"

"I don't think I can."

"Why not?"

"I guess I forgot what it was."

"You asked me if I approved of your latest switcheroo. I said I didn't. Then you asked me why, and I said it was because of your hair, and you said—"

Before he could finish, her hair turned a bright, glittering honey blonde—curly, thick, and shiny.

"You were saying?"

Chip gawked at her. And grinned. And just then, before she could stop him, his ears began to twitch.

"Chip, stop that before someone—"

He stopped.

Just then, something caught her attention. Something dark and cold. Something that made her visualize the diner they'd left fifteen minutes earlier.

What is it about the diner?

She turned around. And gasped.

The dark-haired, good-looking guy from the diner was standing on the sidewalk across the street, gawking at them.

***

Bruno Stone could not move.

There they were. The same duo he'd seen in the diner. The wild-haired redhead and his friend, the plain-faced brunette who'd just turned into a shapely black-haired babe. The same babe who had transformed, before his very eyes, into a sparkling vision. Never in the last seventy-five years of living among the mortals, in a place famous for glittering beauty, had he seen such a stunning woman.

She was a vision. A smorgasbord for the senses. And he was unable to take his eyes off her.

Reality soon intervened, destroying every thought process in his head. And it was right then that he knew that he was indeed gawking at a shapeshifter—which also meant that she was quite possibly the rogue Braithwaite had been looking for. The gorgeous one. The dangerous one. The one responsible for destroying Braithwaite's billion-dollar venture in southern Florida.

It was her—it *had* to be. He knew it was because he, Bruno Stone, the subordinate demon possessing the amazing ability to attract and mesmerize women, found himself captivated by the blinding vision staring back at him from the other side of the street.

He had stumbled upon her. And he, Bruno Stone, was the only spirit on the face of the earth who knew exactly who she was.

However, the instant his mind focused on those big beautiful blue eyes, the luxurious honey-blond hair, the luscious, pouty lips—

Reality once again raised its ugly face.

He had to somehow take her back to Braithwaite. And to start the ball rolling, he had to pull out his cell, take her picture, make the call and send her image to the super demon.

Just then, his raging hormones overwhelmed him, and he knew that he had to make sure she was the one Braithwaite wanted. This would require him to cross the street and walk over to her. And look into those big blue eyes. And take in her fragrance. And bathe himself in her radiance. And, most of all, maintain control over his hormones, which had gone berserk.

But before reality could intervene, he felt his body responding. While distracted by his chaotic ponderings, he'd already moved toward the curb. And just a moment later, he felt his feet stepping down onto the street.

Before even realizing what was happening, he discovered that he was crossing the busy street.

He was so captivated by her that he was unaware of anything else. The crowds. The traffic. The screaming. The yelling. The laughter. All he saw was her face. Those bright, beautiful blue eyes. That glittering golden hair. The swelled cheekbones. The pouty lips.

Her perfect boobs.

The tight jeans.

I want you, baby...want you...

Just then, she tilted her head.

Had she picked up on his thoughts? Maybe so. She was a demon, was she not? And demons had their own special powers. Maybe hers was—

Later. He promised himself that he would learn about her later, after he'd...

After he'd what?

Introduced himself? Used his powers to mesmerize her?

Could he? Or would she be able to sense who he was? What he was? Where he'd come from?

Was it worth all this trouble to see if he could seduce her? Caress her? Get her in the sack?

And if he *did* manage to get her in the sack, would it be as terrific as he imagined?

As he drew closer, he quickly found that he could not concentrate on anything else. He could not even find the power within him to avert her eyes as she watched him crossing the street.

***

"That's him, isn't it?" Chip whispered while staring at the dark-haired figure. "The dude at the diner?"

"Yes." As she watched, she used her powers to penetrate the man's brain. It took her only a few seconds to find what she was looking for. The images stood out boldly among his other thoughts like blazing neon. And when the reality struck her, she groaned.

"Don't think I like the sound of that, Tifferoosky."

"The sound of what?"

"That groan."

"Huh?"

36

"You hardly ever groan, Tifferoo. I didn't exactly overhear you when you and that restaurant owner guy were slapping boots in Ohio, but I can imagine that when you're really in the mood, you can get down and dirty with some ginormous—"

"*Stop.*"

Chip went silent.

She'd been right all along. They were watching a demon. Since he hadn't already done anything to her or Chip to indicate his powers, she assumed that he wasn't one of the more important brutes.

Nevertheless, she was certain he was from the Dark Place. The tiny red glint in his eyes she'd noticed back in the diner confirmed this. The flags had gone up.

And now, as the dark-haired beast gawked at her from across the street, she knew she had to bring it up. The horrific images developing in the demon's brain made it necessary.

Breath Mint's image flashed brightly.

Though this beast didn't know the super demon, he'd apparently heard about what Tiffany, Chip, and Ashley had done in southern Florida and planned to call Breath Mint and tell him he'd spotted them. But at the last moment, his hormones had taken over.

I want you, baby…

Before she could read any more of his thoughts, he'd stepped down off the curb and began crossing the street.

A moment later, Tiffany noticed the delivery truck.

Her heart racing, she turned back to the man. Despite the situation, she couldn't let this happen. He was a demon. He was far from nice. In fact, he was very, very bad.

Well, he shouldn't be nice, should he? That's why he was sent to the Dark Place, wasn't it?

But she just couldn't let him be run down. Not if she could stop it. Being complacent about something like that was not who she was...

She projected the message

(Back up! Now!)

directly into the demon's skull.

The man kept walking.

The truck was now just a few yards away.

Tiffany closed her eyes. Focusing, she imagined pushing him backward, knocking him down and forcing him to roll back onto the sidewalk.

The truck roared past.

The demon lay on the sidewalk, near the curb. Moments later, he turned on his side. Then, leaning on an elbow, he gaped at her as small crowds emerging from nearby stores rushed over.

Still watching him, Tiffany injected the thought into his skull

(forget about me and my friend)

and, after one last afterthought,

(forget about what just happened)

smiled and turned to Chip. They then went down the street, to the end of the block.

***

As Bruno Stone watched the busy crowd walking down the street, he had the strange feeling

38

that he'd just woke up. Surveying his surroundings, he was suddenly aware that he was sitting on the sidewalk just a few feet from the curb. Several people were standing around him, watching him closely.

What the hell happened?

Why was he sitting here on the sidewalk?

Why was he out here in the first place?

He remembered having lunch in the diner just a few minutes ago. He'd enjoyed his usual breakfast and was going back to his pad to do something—

To do what, exactly?

Wasn't there something else he had going on? Something important? Something that had slipped his mind, causing an unpleasant void in his thought processes?

"You okay, buddy?"

"Need a doctor?"

"Want us to call nine-one-one?"

Nearly a dozen people were standing around him. Some were bent over, gawking at him, looking uncomfortable.

"I'm...fine." He pulled in his legs and started the nauseous ordeal of standing up. Two pairs of hands grabbed him by the arms to help. He wanted to tell them to get the hell away. He was very capable; he could manage on his own. He was in good shape and didn't need any help. Hell, he could squat four hundred and bench three big ones. He didn't need any of these stupid mortals helping him.

"You sure?" A well-dressed, middle-aged lady with colored red hair and red-tinted large-rimmed sunglasses seemed particularly concerned. She gripped her cell in her manicured hand and was obviously more than eager to assist him. She kept eyeing his chest and muscular arms. "I can get someone here in just—"

"I said I'm *all right*!"

A tall, skinny young guy in maroon shorts, a loose-fitting green sweatshirt, and black athletic shoes held his camera out in front of him. "Sure you're okay, buddy?"

Bruno resisted the overwhelming urge to melt the camera in the idiot's hands. *Patience*, he told himself, eyeing the iPhones aimed at him from more than half a dozen mortals standing farther back.

"I can take you to the hospital." The red-haired bitch still couldn't get the hint. "It's on my way. I can get you there in just—"

"I'm fucking fine! Just *fine*!"

The burst of anger worked. Frowning, she backed up and nearly tripped on her six-inch spikes. The others also backed away. After a moment or two of silent confusion, everyone went their separate ways, some of them mumbling.

He didn't want a damned audience. He wanted to be alone. He had to think and figure out what the hell was going on. Why his memory had suddenly gone blank when everything seemed to be working just fine while he was in the diner.

When he turned around, the street activity had resumed. No one noticed him anymore. He brushed himself off and began walking down the street.

He focused once again on the diner and struggled to remember other details.

The room had been bustling. The strong smells of bacon, hash browns, coffee, and potato pancakes drifted right back. The usual female gawkers sat a few tables down, sizing him up. The customary outdoor activity, heavy with tourists, tattooed freaks, businesspeople and wannabe celebs, passed by the tinted windows. He vaguely remembered a skinny, plain-looking babe with long brown hair sitting a few tables farther down.

Something nudged his memory.

Did it have anything to do with what the redheaded dude sitting with the plain-looking babe had ordered for breakfast?

Why would that matter?

He struggled to remember, but nothing would come. The harder he tried to visualize the past events, the quicker the images dissolved.

Maybe what had happened in the diner didn't matter. He needed to focus on what had transpired once he'd left.

He took it step by step—from the time he'd finished his meal to the time he'd left the eatery. Once he left, he was on his way to—

To do what? And why?

What the hell was going on? This was ridiculous. And frightening. His mind, for whatever reason, had gone blank.

He continued his journey down the street. A minute or so later, the cell in his pants pocket hummed. He stopped, went over to stand beneath the green awning of a lingerie store and pressed the cell to his ear.

"Stone?" The voice was low-pitched and unfamiliar.

Stone. The name vaguely rang a bell. Yes. It should. It was his name, was it not?

Stone. Yes. It's me.

More images swam sluggishly by, bringing with them important details he'd forgotten up until now.

Stone. Bruno. Yes. Bruno Stone. That's me. It's been me for a long, long time...

"Yeah?"

"Y'okay? Ya sound a little...spacey."

"I'm...fine." He took a breath. This call confused him even more than his sudden memory loss.

"You ready for that job we discussed earlier? I know we set it up for tomorrow morning, but it looks like it's gotta be done tonight. Mebbe around ten? Eleven, at the latest?"

Job? What was this guy talking about?

And just who the hell *was* this guy?

"Stone? Ya there?"

"I'm here." He struggled to remember, but once again, nothing came. It made him wonder if he'd slapped his head on the pavement when he'd fallen. Instinctively he reached up with his free hand, checking for bumps, bruising, sensitive spots.

He found nothing out of the ordinary.

"For a sec I thought ya might be tryin' to pull somethin'."

His inner gut told him to remain evasive. This caller—whoever he was—sounded angry. And dangerous.

42

"Stone?"

"I'm not…not pulling anything."

"Ya sure?"

"Why would I?"

"Why else? For more money?"

What the hell was this man talking about?

"More money?"

"Don't act stupid, now. This is America, dammit. I might just think you're workin' me, kid. An' ya know how I hate bein' worked, *capisc*?"

Capisc. That was Italian, wasn't it?

Did this mean the caller was Italian? Or was the word just a part of his vernacular?

Bruno had no idea what to say. He also had no idea who the voice belonged to or what the caller was talking about.

"Nothin' to say?"

"I honestly don't know what this is all about, but—"

"Stone, nobody crosses me. Nobody. You oughta know that by now."

"Sir, I really don't know what—"

Click.

Bruno stared at his phone. He had no idea what that call was all about.

However, he had the unsettling feeling that his caller wasn't quite finished with him.

***

"Tiffers," Chip said a little later, "now you can tell me what happened back there. I might be totally wrong, but what I saw was something I'm pretty sure you caused—"

He stopped talking.

43

A skinny teen girl walking a few yards straight ahead spoke into her cell phone while flipping her freshly washed pink hair back over her shoulder with her free hand. She wore dark-blue shorts, a turquoise tank top, and designer sneakers. The back of her left leg was covered with the tattoo of an alligator. The figure of a thick brown snake encircled her right, its long, slender tongue stopping an inch short of her ankle.

Chip seemed mesmerized by the girl.

Tiffany knew Chip had to be told what was going on; she just didn't have any idea what to say. She tapped him on the shoulder to pull him out of his trance. "You mean what just happened across the street?"

He turned away from the pink-haired girl and focused on Tiffany. "Something happened across the street? Really?"

She knew right then that being vague wouldn't work—at least, not in this case.

"You're being cute, Babykins."

"I guess you don't want me doing that right now."

"You can start lighting up my ass with all kinds of useful knowledge. Unless you've got something else more important going on right now."

"You want to know what I just did?"

He groaned. "Muffin, you're doing it again..."

"I guess you want specifics?"

"Who knows? That might work instead of your aggravating back-pedaling..."

"I'm trying to think of the best way of telling you."

44

"Let's start with that little adventure with the van. And the dude we saw in the diner suddenly yanked backward and pushed back onto the sidewalk before he could be turned into roadkill. All this while you were staring at him, no less."

"I guess that's about it, in a nutshell."

"What sort of nutshell are we talking about, angel?"

"That's exactly what happened…"

"Yepperino. That was it—everything but the reason *why*. And why it probably happened because of you. And why you're finding it impossible to tell me anything about it. And why you're getting that crack between your eyebrows once again?"

She looked up. "I'm getting it *again*?"

"Tifferoosky, *please* cut the shit."

Tiffany knew how Chip reacted whenever she mentioned Breath Mint. But since he was pressuring her to tell her… Besides, he deserved to know. "I guess you want to know…everything?"

Chip bent down and snatched up a stem of grass protruding a few inches from the sidewalk. He slipped it between his lips and kept up the pace. "Let 'er rip."

"Believe it or not, that guy was a demon."

He stopped walking. The grass stem dangled from his mouth as he stared at her. His tiny green eyes looked like they were about to pop out of his skull. Tiffany could tell that his brain had turned into serious overload.

"Chip? You all right?"

"I kind of figured that it had to be something like that."

45

"You suspected?"

"It was either that, or you were being smitten again."

"Again?"

"Like in Ohio? That restaurant owner guy?"

"Oh." She felt the familiar tug at her heart. "You mean Lou?"

"Whatever. Let's get back to the things going on right now. Okay?"

She nodded.

"I know this might sound stupid, but let me lay it out clear and simple, so even a lamebrain like myself can figure it out." He took a breath. "Tell me how you know he was a, you know."

"I saw the red glints in his eyes."

Silence.

"You know I'm right, don't you? I mean, you've seen how my powers have grown ever since we came back up. I can do stuff neither of us can explain."

"I know, dammit. I've been right beside you, watching everything. And trying really hard not to barf."

"I'm not telling you this to make you feel bad."

"Then why do I feel bad?"

"Because you're maybe, um, slightly jealous?"

He frowned. "The least you could've done was try really hard—or even just a little hard—to put it gently before you actually blurted it out like that..."

She hated it when he made her feel guilty. He knew she had no control over what had been happening to her.

"Like I just said, I'm not telling you this to make you feel bad. I'm telling you because you need to know what's happening."

"What *is* happening, Muffin?"

"As I've just said, we found another demon."

"And he knows about us?"

She nodded.

"But how would you know that he knows—"

"That's just it. I don't."

"So why would he even bother to—"

"Beats me."

"You think he was in that diner because—"

"No idea."

Chip's ears twitched again. "Tiffers, *please* do me a ginormous favor."

"What's that?"

"Let me squeeze out an occasional complete sentence, okay? I'd like to think that I didn't waste all that time in a classroom, learning how to speak."

"They had *classrooms* back then? When you were growing up?"

"No. I learned all about communicating in the cave I hatched out in. From drawings the Neanderthals made."

"I'm sorry. I didn't mean—"

"Whatever. Just get back to what you did."

"You want to know what I did?"

"All right, let's go with that, instead."

"Be serious, now…"

"Okay, then, here goes… In all seriosity, let me ask you once again. What exactly did you do?"

"To the demon?"

47

He sighed loudly. "No. To the waitress who gave us lunch. Yeah. The demon!"

They resumed walking down the street. Two cars honked as they passed. The second vehicle, a red convertible sports car, slowed down. The passenger, a young guy about twenty-five with a brush cut, bleached ponytail, and blue beads dangling from his naked torso, practically fell out of the car ogling her. "Baby, light me up! A hundred bucks!" He fumbled with his belt buckle.

"She's really a guy!" Chip yelled. "His name is Bruce, and he's dynamite with makeup!" He turned to Tiffany. "Bruce, show these guys your schlong." He turned back to the two in the convertible. "It's a little tiny, but believe me, it does the job." He turned back to Tiffany. "Go 'head, Bruce, my man, just pull down that zipper and let that little sucker dangle!"

Yelling an obscenity, the boy turned in his seat as the driver went heavy on the gas pedal.

"Thanks," she said, glaring.

"It got rid of them, didn't it?"

She nodded but made no comment.

Once they'd disappeared into the heavy flow of sidewalk traffic, Tiffany closed her eyes and instantly turned back into the same skinny, plain-faced brunette she'd been in the diner. "I have to do this, you know. I don't want to attract any more attention. Those two idiots just convinced me."

Chip nodded. "Back to the subject, then. What did you do to the demon?"

"I did a number on his brain."

"I need details."

48

Tiffany caught sight of a homeless gray-haired man sitting on a bench in front of an electronics store, watching them. For a moment she thought she recognized him. After further thought, she realized that her sudden shape-shift might have been the reason for his attention.

Had he seen her do it? Or did this have to do with her being on edge about returning to this depressing place?

"Tifferino? Still waiting…"

She decided that even if the old man had seen her change, he probably had no idea what happened. The poor man's brain was probably mostly gone. He'd no doubt just lie down on the bench and sleep off his hangover.

But she still couldn't shake that nagging ring of familiarity about him.

"And *still* waiting…"

She turned back to Chip. "He was going to tell Breath Mint about us."

As she'd expected, Chip froze and instantly paled. "You're…sure?"

"I saw his image."

"You…actually *saw* Braithwaite's image? In the dude's head?"

She nodded.

He remained frozen, not speaking. His eyes were unfocused, but she could tell what he was thinking.

The crowd veered around them.

After nearly a minute, Chip finally broke his silence.

"What did you do, then? After you saw his...the super's...image?"

"I convinced him to forget about us and go on about his business."

Chip went silent. Her explanation seemed to satisfy him, and he appeared less frightened.

"You okay now?" she asked.

"I think so."

"I guess we can try looking for Johnny Rock, then."

"That sounds like a really nifty idea."

They resumed walking.

But it wasn't long before she began to wonder about that nagging feeling that they were being watched.

And followed.

By some sort of hunter.

CHAPTER 2 - THE SECOND DEMON

The tall, fine-featured man in the dark-brown Armani suit waited until the two rogues had crossed the intersection before turning back to the incubus, Agnus.

Once he saw where the demon was going, he followed at a leisurely pace, keeping himself concealed in the street crowd. He had no idea what sort of demon Agnus was or which powers he possessed; he only knew that the demon had been overpowered by two rogues—which gave the clear message that Agnus no longer deserved to be operating in the mortal world.

He had just come out of the restaurant moments ago, having partaken an excellent meal of twelve ounces of steak tartare made from fresh raw Porterhouse, chopped onions, capers, pepper and Worcestershire sauce, as well as six raw egg yolks served on a thin slice of rye bread. It had taken him less than a minute to survey the sidewalk scene that had taken place just a hundred feet down.

As a subordinate, he'd realized almost at once that he was looking at a demon the moment the brown-haired female had shape-shifted three different times in a very short period.

He wondered what sort of demon he was facing. He hadn't received word that a new sub would be entering his territory. Her companion was obviously an inferior. The rogues he'd encountered recently were inferiors. As far as he knew, there were more than a hundred in the L.A. area, most of them disguised as illegals. Those coming up from South America were Malamores, the fighters taken from the dungeons of the Castle of Demons. They were specifically chosen by Balberith to cause mayhem with human trafficking and drug smuggling, courtesy of the cartels, which were run by Leviathan and his subs operating out of Colombia.

This didn't tell him anything about this female rogue. However, such rapid, efficient shapeshifting suggested a subordinate, since no inferior would possess such powers.

But it was essential that he find out exactly what was going on. And he knew he needed to find out very quickly.

He was known as the "Brain-Eater" in the Dark Place. As a mortal, he'd been a cannibal living in eighteenth century England, feasting on mortals to obtain their power. The more brain matter he consumed, the stronger he became. After several decades, he'd become so powerful that, once he was caught by the authorities, it had been necessary to hang him twice at his public execution. Despite a broken neck and half a dozen severed vertebrae, he'd survived the first hanging, ripping through the ropes fastening his wrists and ankles in his panic to escape. He had nearly succeeded when he was subdued by more than a dozen of the King's guards.

After his second hanging, he was sent down below and given the name Comedor De Cerebro. His master was Ashtaroth, the super demon instrumental in sending him back to the world of mortals a hundred and fifty years later, to help Balberith cause mayhem in California by feasting on the minds of the politicians, as well as actors and executives in the film industry.

His powers focused on deadening portions of the frontal lobe. Nothing could beat that area for destroying the logical reasoning of a mortal. The process proved sweet and tantalizing and always possessed an addictive quality.

The results of his efforts quickly proved successful. He'd been unbelievably busy during the last fifty-seven years.

For cover, he'd been working as a licensed real estate agent since the mid-sixties—America's rebellious decade; in which the Draft, Viet Nam, a passionate anti-establishment attitude, and a quickly growing hatred for Capitalism fueled the country.

As a realtor, he went by the name Cameron Carnes. With his tanned surfer looks and long, rangy physique, he had no trouble luring the appropriate brain into his lair of death.

His heightened sense of smell, acquired and honed to perfection during his fifty-year reign of terror in England, had immediately seized the essence

(vanilla, with a hint of lavender)

of the female rogue. It would be no trouble at all to track her down. He was also confident that his boyish good looks would make it difficult for her to reject him.

He hadn't been rejected once in the fifty-seven years he'd been living among the mortals.

Right now, his main objective was hunting down the incompetent incubus, Agnus. Once he'd dealt with the situation, he'd find the blonde and her companion.

The first thing, of course, was to send Agnus back down, where he belonged. Although he never liked interfering with other demons, he knew Braithwaite would not tolerate incompetence. This made it necessary for the unpleasant task to be done. Agnus had done the unforgiveable—there was no other way of dealing with him.

Cameron knew where the subordinate lived. He'd seen him hanging around the Sunset Strip area once or twice, usually in the company of an attentive female.

Agnus gave off an odor of testosterone with a hint of ox musk.

As he moved down the street amongst the mortals, Cameron's receptors noticed this scent growing stronger.

At this rate, it would not take him long at all to find and dispose of the incubus.

***

"This where ya wanna get off?" The cabby frowned at them in the mirror. "Ya did say ya wanted me to take ya—"

"I'm sure," Tiffany replied.

They'd picked up the cab just two blocks from where Tiffany had done the mental number on the demon from the diner. Clearly knowing her whereabouts, she wanted some privacy on the way over. Since she was certain someone else had been watching them, she didn't want them getting too close to Johnny Rock's mansion. She didn't know if they were dealing with another demon or just someone who liked the way she looked. In Hollywood, people did horrible things to each other. She didn't want to deal with any nonsense before she and Chip found Johnny Rock. Their unpleasant dealings with the demon had been more than enough. She was determined to be totally alert when she encountered Johnny. And she didn't want anything distracting her when she confronted the monster that had given her the drink that killed her.

"It won't cost ya much more than another few bucks. Or so."

"Thanks. This is just fine."

The cabby shrugged. "Whatever ya say, lady…" He put the brake on, turned in his seat and held out his hand.

Tiffany produced a couple of imaginary twenties and handed them over.

"Thanks, lady." The cabby studied the bills.

"Thank *you*," she said as they got out.

Tiffany didn't feel guilty that the money she'd given the cabby would disappear the moment he'd pocketed the bills. The man had taken three wrong turns on the way over to beef up his fare. Anyway, she was much too busy trying to deal with the memories. But just moments ago, as the cab began slowing down, she'd cringed when the past came roaring back and immediately sunk into depression. Her heart ached as she stared at the familiar sidewalks and greenery fronting the long row of estates peppering the North Hollywood countryside.

It had only been a handful of months since she'd been here, but after all that had happened, it seemed like a lifetime had zipped by. When the memories eventually slowed down, she felt herself going back in time, when she'd first shown up at the mansion.

She'd gone there for only one purpose: to jumpstart her career. Johnny Rock was the biggest promoter in the city, a man who boasted strong ties with extremely important people. CEOs. Producers. Actors. Agents. Managers. Directors. Fashion designers. Promoters. Investors. Advertisers. Major backers. Distributors. Every big name associated with the film industry. Johnny had dined with Steven Spielberg, George Lucas, John Cameron, and Peter Jackson. He personally knew Clint Eastwood. Al Pacino. Warren Beatty. Dustin Hoffman. Everyone in L.A. agreed that Johnny Rock was the biggest and most important contact a struggling young actor would ever need. He was a force to be reckoned with.

Tiffany's agent had been mercilessly insistent. He'd ordered her to go to the shindig, telling her that there was no better option if she wanted her career to take off. With her looks and charisma, she could reach a meteoric mega status. The camera loved her—her face, her eyes, her body, the way she moved, spoke, blinked, smiled, pouted. She had it all—beauty, brains, personality, magnetism—and just enough acting talent to land her small parts in many of the larger productions, which could lead to even bigger and better parts. And all she had to do was wear something flimsy, do a couple of sexy walks around the pool, maybe even accidentally fall in, then wait a few minutes for the gold to start pouring in.

As her agent had said, "You're hot, baby. And you're the right age. If you don't take the plunge now, while you still have a highly marketable commodity to bargain with, you'll end up on the short end. In less than a year, you'll be twenty-three, and after that, twenty-four. Then thirty before you know it. By then you'll be washed up as a hopeful. You'll be doomed to work fast foods for the rest of your life. Two hours of your time will be all it takes to get you up there, where you belong. Trust me."

"Tiffers? Are you, by any chance, taking another leisurely but painful stroll down Memory Lane?"

Trust me...

She snapped out of it. "Uh-huh..."

"Really? Truly? Seriously?"

She wasn't in the mood for Chip's levity. She had to stay angry—at least until this was all over. "I just said I did. Why?"

He grinned sheepishly. "Because..."

"Because what?"

"Well, I don't know if you've noticed, but ever since the cab left, we haven't been doing the deed."

"What deed?"

"In a word—or two—or three, or whatever—we need to start walking. You remember, don'tcha? One foot after the other? Up the street? As close to the mansion as we can get before we can find a nifty way of going in? That's where it's all at,

57

righterino? The pool? The hokey crowd? Maybe even the evil dude who sent you to me so we could come back up here and start doing all this neat shit?"

She suddenly felt angry with herself for turning on him. "You're right. Sorry."

"Okie-dokey, then. Let's get this show on the road."

Sighing heavily, Tiffany led the way up the walk, until they reached the end of the street. Just as she was about to cross, the afternoon breeze shifted in their direction.

She stopped cold.

Splashing and giggling resonated loudly from the pool behind Johnny Rock's mansion.

***

In just fifteen minutes, Cameron Carnes, the "Brain-Eater," tracked down Agnus in a high-rise on Larrabee Street, not far from Sunset Boulevard. He decided to wait a few minutes before going inside. He wanted to give the demon time to relax before rushing in and surprising him.

Being a natural hunter, Carnes knew to use patience and stealth to achieve the appropriate results. The hunt took longer but was well worth the extra time.

He stood at the corner, watching sidewalk activity and the heavy traffic whizzing by two streets down. A family of tourists had gathered in front of the white stucco building across the street, taking pictures of themselves. A gay couple strolled on past, hand in hand, both young men wearing tank tops, matching shorts and athletic shoes.

Carnes decided to wait ten minutes before entering the building.

A skinny kid about eighteen years old approached him. The kid was about six feet tall and weighed no more than a hundred and twenty pounds. He had the appearance of a heavy drug user—pallid skin, sores, blood-shot eyes, frequent sniffing, and shaking. "Score some oxy, dude?" the kid asked in a soft, high-pitched voice. He sniffed twice and held out his trembling hand. "Fifty bucks?"

Carnes eyed the kid's scrawny neck. It was covered with sores, pimples and burn marks. The brain would taste rancid—not exactly his preference. He couldn't understand why mortals insisted on destroying their bodies with chemicals when there were so many other ways of achieving that same end. It merely strengthened his observation that most mortals were worthless dregs—which was why the Dark Place had been witnessing a heavy influx of new inhabitants the last hundred years.

"C'mon, man." The kid was desperate. "Fifty bucks? You can afford it." *Sniff.* He eyed the Brain-Eater's outfit. "Those rags prob'ly go for at least two hundred, maybe three hundred bucks." *Sniff, sniff.* A loose shrug. "You can afford fifty for a little oxy, can't ya?"

Carnes considered sending the stupid jerk out into traffic but didn't want to attract attention. Subtlety would work much better.

"I'll meet you in the alley behind that bank building in two minutes."

The kid sniffed and blinked. "Seriously, dude? Cloak and dagger shit?"

"I don't anyone seeing me score. I'm a businessman." He raised his head proudly. "I have scruples."

"Huh?"

"Morals. Ethics."

The kid scowled in confusion.

"Um…I don't want to get caught and lose my job. Does that work for you?"

The kid grinned stupidly and winked. "Gotcha, dude." Then he turned.

"And by the way," Carnes said, "this suit goes for five *thousand*."

The kid didn't pause while shuffling hurriedly down the street.

Carnes followed, turning into the alley entrance at the end of the block. The kid was standing near the end, in front of a dumpster.

Carnes closed his eyes and imagined the kid taking his product out of his pocket and swallowing the contents, then choking himself to death. Seconds later, when he opened his eyes, the kid was choking and hacking away, his skinny arms up, his hands at his throat. His face had already turned blue.

Carnes turned and calmly went back up the street. He glanced at his watch.

It was time to check in with the incubus.

***

Tiffany closed her eyes and tried hard not to think of those sounds. Those same sounds that, to most others, were the echoes of laughter. And joy.

And fun. Those very same sounds that, for her, turned into the nightmare that had ended her life. She struggled to think of other things that could dim the horror and coax her to focus on matters that would not send her spiraling into the icy panic numbing her.

Images that weren't so dark. So cold. So horrific...

Despite the horror of dying and waking up in the strange meadow bordering the heavy wall of blackness, she'd managed to turn things around. She had not only cheated eternal despair in the dark, dismal, foul-smelling place known as Hell by escaping, she'd made things right by doing good ever since she'd returned to the mortal world.

The things she had done had been necessary. It had not only brightened her spirit, it had also convinced her that she should have never been sent down to the eternal darkness, where horrible beings prowled in hatred and disgust.

This way of thinking filled her mind with the images she'd needed, steering her away from the cold reality of what had actually happened. However, it wasn't long before she sensed her concentration waning. The dark, forbidden images thundered back. The good deeds she'd done in Raven—as well as in Orlando, Pittsburgh, and Peoria—all dimmed. The disgusting image of Gutril appeared brightly. With it, the frightening image of Breath Mint...and the hunter Andras...and finally Keenan V. Durant ...and Daniel D. Lyon...

61

The splashing and squealing resonating from the pool up the next hill amplified quickly, eclipsing everything else.

The panic building inside her grew. She could hear nothing else and began trembling. She wanted to cover her ears, but her arms suddenly weighed a ton. Gritting her teeth, she struggled anyway, until her hands reached their goal.

Her efforts turned out to be wasted. The nightmare sounds had filled her being, intensifying. She let her arms drop to her sides and then took a deep breath. Gathering courage, she decided to wait it out until the nightmare either consumed her or—

"Tifferoo?"

The splashing and squealing had ebbed into a dead silence.

Chip's voice, incredibly, had overcome the disgusting pool sounds.

She opened her eyes. She wanted to thank him for being there with her. For destroying the chaos that had slithered inside her and threatened to drive her mad.

But just then, she realized something was different.

"You okay?"

She nodded.

"You sure? No offense, but for a minute I thought you were about to have a fit."

She wanted to respond, but something prevented her from doing so. At first, she'd thought it was the dead silence. Then it dawned on her. It wasn't that at all.

Chip looked different.

"Something wrong, Tiffers?"

She studied him, taking in his hair, his eyes, his face. His manner of dress. Nothing had changed, yet he appeared different.

Less silly-looking? Or was she just getting so used to him that, in her mind's eye, he'd begun looking *normal*?

Or was she just grateful that he'd quashed her inner turmoil just by uttering her name?

"Why the furrowed brow, Dearest? Is my head on backwards? Do I have a crusty?" He gently rubbed his nostrils.

At least he was *acting* his usual silly self. "You look different…"

"Different how?"

"I don't know. Less silly?"

He crossed his eyes. "How can I possibly look less silly?"

"I know it sounds strange…"

"How's this?" His ears wiggled.

Despite that, she still found that he looked slightly less ridiculous than usual. "That was good."

"One of my many talents, Sweet Cheeks. Don't forget, I'm the best trickster you'll ever see. The bestest of the best." Then he bowed. And farted loudly. "Oops. Sorry."

She laughed. "That's more like it."

"Glad I could help."

"By the way, I would have thought that you would have at least tried to learn a little self-control by now. You've been doing things like that since we came back up here, and it's kind of old. And slightly repulsive."

63

He shrugged. "Sorry, but I'm sure you know by now that I sometimes get the gazz."

"I don't see how."

"Haven't you seen all the orange juice I drink? The coffee grounds I nibble on? The eggshells? You don't think that stuff causes the gazz? And don't forget some of the things we see on the street nowadays. Bunnies? Tattooed people with chains and rings coming out of their ears and noses? I don't know if you've noticed, but mortals have gotten kinda gross nowadays."

"I guess I should've figured that one out. But please do try and control yourself—at least occasionally."

"All righty rooty. I'll just stick a cork—"

"That's not exactly what I'd like."

"Yes, ma'am. I mean no, ma'am, I can see why that wouldn't exactly turn your crank."

Without replying, she turned and began walking up the hill.

Chip caught up to her. "What's next? I mean, do we charge our way in, guns blazing? No offense, Tifferoo, but there are only two of us, and we're both dead. We can produce blazing guns, maybe even a grenade or two, but I really don't think that would work here. We'd attract all sorts of attention, for one thing. You wouldn't like seeing me on the news, would you? I have the tendency to be downright embarrassing. And since this is Hokeywood, someone would think I'd have a mental screw loose—perish the thought."

"I know."

"So then, to repeat my question…"

"I have to change into a ravishing beauty to crash their stupid party."

"I hate to bring this up, but you're already a ravishing beauty."

She sighed. "I need to change into a *different* ravishing beauty."

"Ah. I think I understand."

"For a moment, I wondered."

"All righty rooty. You're different. Then what?"

"Play it by ear—what else?"

"By that, you mean—"

"Walking around. Mingling. Flirting. Listening. And, most of all, checking out everyone." She sighed. "To see if *he's* there."

"And what, pray tell, do you want *me* to do during all this mingling and flirting and listening and checking out stuff? I can't turn myself into a flower and wait this out inside the fence, ya know. I could, but I really don't want to. It would be kind of boring. Don't forget, I had to do the same crap down below, behind the Castle. It wasn't much of a blast down there, either."

She stopped walking. His question had taken her by surprise. Although she'd spent a lot of time thinking about coming back here and handling this, she realized only now that she'd been so absorbed with herself and her dilemma that she hadn't considered Chip's role in this.

Guilt nipped at her. Chip had never been part of what had happened to her, but he was definitely a major chunk of it now. And he had a perfect right to be in on it when she completed whatever was necessary to bring the monster to justice.

Chip knew how to blend in. He also knew how to alter his appearance. And although his powers hadn't progressed much, he was much more able to handle things now than when they'd come out of the toxic landfill in Ohio. And since he'd already demonstrated to her that he could pass as a female, she knew that things would go much easier with him at her side.

But could he appear as someone the Hollywood crowd would accept?

She suddenly found herself overcome with doubt. He'd only appeared as a female a couple of times before, as a skinny, half-witted crack whore. The crowd they would soon encounter mingled only with the Hollywood elite. Johnny Rock was a multi-millionaire with contacts all over the world. The girls invited to his gigs were celebs, models, high-fashion personalities, or up-and-coming starlets. Every female at Johnny Rock's pool parties could easily boast a cover shot in *Glamour* Magazine or land a high-paying gig in a *Victoria's Secret* commercial. These people would not tolerate anyone not top rate.

But what else could Chip do?

A waiter? Hardly.

A guard? The idea was laughable.

There had to be something he could do. Chip obviously wanted to be an active part of this. And the worst thing she could do was tell him to stay behind and wait.

But how could she tell the person who had taken her out of the Dark Place, the same guy who had been by her side ever since, that he had to stay in the shadows? That these arrogant, uppity people would not tolerate someone like him?

Her heart fluttering, Tiffany struggled for comforting words that would not offend him. Moments later, when she was somewhat confident that she had a fairly suitable message ready, she turned to tell him.

And found herself gazing at the most beautiful black-haired woman she had ever seen.

***

Confident no one was in the corridor, Cameron Carnes gently touched the doorknob.

Locked.

Regarding the peephole, he knew the incubus could be cautious about opening the door. He had the power to slip inside but decided not to enter. The element of surprise would work much better. If he slipped through the door, the incubus would know who he was. This would result in a struggle. It would be much better to coax the demon to open the door.

Since he was dealing with an incubus, Carnes knew that the simplest way to gain entrance to the apartment was to shift-change.

Using his highly developed sniffer, he did a careful probe. Satisfied that the circumstances appeared to be favorable, he decided it safe for his transformation. He closed his eyes. Moments later, he tried the buzzer.

Ten seconds later, a speck of movement flickered on the other side of the peephole.

The latch clicked. The door opened quickly.

The incubus stood in the doorway, grinning stupidly as Carnes, now a ravishing redheaded female, faced him, smiling and batting his long, dark lashes.

"Can I, um, help you, baby?" the incubus asked, grinning lecherously.

"May I come in?" Carnes asked in a low, sensuous voice.

Still grinning, the incubus pulled the door open and stepped aside. "Please." He gestured for his visitor to enter.

Carnes went in and waited until the incubus had closed the door behind him. He could tell right off that this was going to be much easier than he'd expected. Agnus was a true incubus: a spirit driven solely by his uncontrollable hormones. He stood stiffly, lips parted, his eyes filling their sockets, the tension in his crotch nauseatingly evident.

"I saw you outside, about a block down the street," Carnes said.

"I wish I could say the same." The incubus's voice sounded unsteady. "Otherwise—"

"Let me guess. You would have invited me up here?"

"You got *that* right…" Slobber had gathered on the incubus' chin.

Carnes fluttered his lashes.

After an awkward silence, the incubus asked, "Why exactly are you here? Is it because you really like this package?" The incubus held out his arms and shifted his pelvis provocatively.

Suddenly queasy, Carnes was tempted to end this charade right at that moment.

"Well?" The incubus shifted his pelvis again.

"Couldn't fool you at all, could I?"

The incubus chuckled. "When ya got it, ya gotta flaunt it...right?"

"Right."

The incubus grinned and lowered his arms.

"There's something I have to tell you before we get this thing started."

"What's that?"

"Are you sure you want to hear it?"

"Talk to me, baby." The incubus' voice had become a rough whisper. "Tell me what you want. I promise I'll deliver. Anything. I'll give you *anything*."

"You're sure about that?"

"I'm sure, baby. Talk to me. Tell me what you want. Tell me. *Please*..."

"Then I guess you won't mind if I change into something more comfortable..."

Froth had gathered at the corners of the incubus' lips. His body trembled. "Do whatever you gotta do, baby. *Please* do it. Do it *now*!"

"Thank you. I'm very glad you've given me permission to show you my best side."

"Show me, baby. *Show me*!"

"Show me yours and I'll show you mine."

With a gasp, the incubus groped frantically for his belt buckle. It only took him two seconds to get it undone. By the time his trousers lowered halfway down his thighs, Carnes had changed back into his true form.

***

The slender black-haired beauty smiled brightly. She wore a maroon tank top and a short black skirt. Her long, shapely legs were tanned; open-toed suede sandals covered her feet.

Tiffany couldn't take her eyes off the vision. This was incredible. It took her several moments to find her voice. "Chip? Is that...*you*?"

The beauty giggled. In a soft, low voice, she said, "It's me, Tifferoosky."

"It's really and truly *you*? I mean, you're *him*? You're *Chip*?"

The beauty continued smiling. "Would you like to see me do a quick head spin? Or would you prefer watching my tongue drop to the ground? The ear twitch thingy won't work very well right now—not with this long hair, anyway..."

"I can't *believe* this! Chip? It's really *you*?"

"I sincerely *hope* so..." He grinned his usual stupid grin—which looked very strange on the beautiful face he'd just morphed into. "That's what my driver's license says—oh, wait, I don't *have* one of those." He shrugged. "I really should have one, shouldn't I? Everyone who owns a car should—oh, wait, I don't *own* one of those. Maybe if I—"

"It really *is* you."

He turned toward the mansion. "Well, this *is* a kind of fancy shindig, ain't it? Waiters? Bouncers? Maybe even live entertainment? Those fancy horse ovaries—or whatever they call those gooey little salty thingys they serve with crackers on a silver tray? Champagne? The works? You wouldn't want me going there in my cheap, spaced-out hooker getup, would you, girl? I honestly don't think that would work with this snooty crowd."

Tiffany shook her head. She'd never suspected Chip could pull off something like this. But he had. And now they had a much better shot at attending the party. Tiffany couldn't imagine any man in his right mind turning away from a woman looking as sexy as Chip.

"This is so awesome! I mean *wowzer*! I just can't get over this! Just *look* at you!"

"Okie-dokie, since you're so insistent…" He brought up his left hand. A mirror with a long pink handle appeared in his fist. He held it up to his face. Then lowered it. Then brought it back up. "Yepperino. Look at that. You're right, Tifferoosky. I'm quite the babe. Almost as hot as you, dearest. No offense, of course."

"None taken."

A sleek red vehicle screeched to an abrupt stop at the intersection.

Two young men sat in a convertible sports car, grinning brightly. Both were tanned, muscular and bare-chested. They looked like they'd both spent considerable time in the gym as well as on the beach.

"Oh, goody…" Tiffany hoped this wouldn't detain them very long.

"No problem, Tifferoo. There are two of us, now."

"I know, but—"

"New in town, babes?" The sandy-haired passenger rested his elbows on the door, displaying two deeply tanned muscular forearms. He wore red-tinted shades. His bright smile showed large dimples. His nose looked like it had been meticulously sculpted by a plastic surgeon.

"Can't recall seeing you two babes before." Just as tanned as his passenger, the driver made a show of flexing his well-developed biceps and triceps while reaching up to lower his polarized shades an inch.

"We can take ya wherever ya wanna go." The passenger drooled while gazing at Tiffany.

"Thanks. We really don't need a ride." She pointed behind her. "We're going—"

"Right." The driver nodded. "The Rockster? Figures."

"How 'bout we take you two babes somewhere else?" The passenger sounded eager. "The Rockster won't give ya half the good time Brad and I can..."

"Brad." Tiffany frowned. "Figures..."

"Thanks anyway." Chip lowered his arm and made the mirror disappear. "We've gotta show up at the party. Too many producers would slit their wrists if we're not there. We're what you might call hot properties right now."

The passenger couldn't take his eyes off Chip's hand. "W-What...the mirror...there was a...what did ya just do?"

Chip looked down. "You mean *this*?" He raised his arm. The mirror reappeared. "I guess it would be kinda dorky to say it was all done with mirrors, righty-rooty?"

The driver stiffened. "You two...ladies...are ya some sorta...act?"

"Act?" Tiffany asked.

"You mean like a *magic* act?" Chip lowered his arm. The mirror disappeared again.

The driver couldn't take his eyes off Chip's hand.

The passenger blurted out, "That's really...that's cool, baby...really super bad ass. What else can ya...I mean, are both of you magicians? What else...what I mean is—"

"Are you trying to ask us what we do, but can't because you're so dazzled by our beauty and also by my talented hand that your mind automatically turns to mush every time you try using it?" Chip asked.

Both men continued staring in awe. They turned to one another, then shrugged and turned back to Tiffany and Chip.

"I think you've rendered them speechless," Tiffany whispered.

Chip turned to Tiffany. "One of my many talents, my dear lady."

"All right, then. Try using another one of your tricks to get them out of here."

"No problemo. Wanna join me in some spiffy fun?"

"I'd be happy to."

"How about the tongue thing?"

She scowled.

Chip shrugged. "We need to end this quickly—right?"

"Normally, I'd say—"

"I know, Muffin. But we need to be at that party. The sooner, the better."

Tiffany nodded.

Chip turned back to the horny duo. "We've got this sort of risqué act where we need two good-looking, half-naked young men to work on. Interested?"

Both men nodded eagerly.

"The act involves us stripping and tying down a pair of young studs, just like yourself, then licking them until they go insane. The secret is, we do it in a way no one else has ever been able to copy."

"You're bound and determined to do that tongue thing, aren't you?" Tiffany sent over mentally.

"Why not?" Chip sent back. *"It works."*

"But it's disgusting."

"The ones that work usually are."

"I really wish you hadn't included me in this..."

"Got anything better in mind?"

She thought for a moment. *"No..."*

"Then what's the problem? Afraid you can't do it?"

"Of course I can do it."

"You're sure?"

"Of course I'm sure. You just stick your tongue out and let it drop—right?"

"Then what's the problem?"

"I've already told you. It's disgusting..."

"It all depends on where your tongue ends up. This won't be bad. I don't see anything on the sidewalk that would make you double up and—"

"Enough. I said I'll do it, okay?"

"As I just said, if you've got something better—
"

"All right." There was just no reasoning with him. *"Let's get it over with…"*

"Risqué act?" the passenger asked in a soft voice. "With …with your *tongues*?"

"How do ya…do it?" asked the driver.

"We do it standing up," Chip replied.

"So?" The passenger sounded cynical.

"*Without* bending over," Tiffany added.

The two men turned to one another.

"Wanna see?" Chip asked.

Again, both nodded.

Chip glanced at Tiffany. "On three. Okay, Muffin?"

Tiffany nodded. "One…two…"

Chip grinned at the two men. "Three!"

Both he and Tiffany stuck out their tongues and let them roll down to within an inch of the pavement.

Their eyes bulging, the men watched in utter fascination. When they saw the women's tongues rolling back up into their mouths, they gasped, drowning out the passing traffic.

The passenger turned pale.

The driver snatched at the wheel. The car screeched rubber as it tore away from the curb.

***

The incubus's jaw dropped. Trembling, he took an awkward step back.

Cameron Carnes could sense the chaos going on in the incubus' head. The confusion. The fear.

This was the right time to act. If he waited any longer, the incubus might recover. He would then react, and the situation would become much more complicated.

"What is your name?" he asked the incubus.

"S-Stone. B-Bruno Stone."

"Tell me your real name. The name you used down in the Dark Place."

The incubus was hesitant. Something had apparently gone haywire in his head.

After a few moments, he muttered, "My name…is Agnus."

Carnes had been correct. Agnus was the subordinate ordered by Balberith to wreak havoc by impregnating and infecting mortal females.

"You encountered two rogues down the street," he told the incubus. "Not thirty minutes ago."

The incubus didn't respond.

"One was a male, the other, a female."

The incubus opened his mouth, but nothing came out.

"The female was brown-haired…then black-haired… then blonde."

Still no response.

"And you did nothing to overpower them."

Silence.

"You let them defeat you. You were humiliated. A crowd of inquisitive mortals approached you and took pictures of you on their cell phones. Some even offered to help you."

Trying to recover his dignity, the incubus stood straight and tall. "I don't …remember…"

Carnes began a quick probe. The demon's brain had turned foggy—a clear indication that something had clearly upset him.

"Are you an inferior?"

"I am…an incubus," came the soft, uncertain answer.

"And you know nothing about what happened to you out there on the street?"

No response.

"Tell me what you remember."

The incubus closed his eyes. "I was in a diner… having breakfast."

"I don't care what you were doing. I care only about what you saw."

"Several females were watching me. They were watching me because I am an incubus, and irresistible, and they want me—"

"I don't care about that, either. Just tell me what happened when you left the diner."

"I don't know what happened. Everything went blurry. Things…turned black. And then I…I woke up…on the sidewalk."

"And you have no idea *why* you woke up on the sidewalk?"

"Everything had gone dark… The chick I saw in the diner. She was across the street, watching me. Then…then—"

"Go on…"

"She…I thought… I *don't know!*"

Carnes walked over, reached out and placed his hand on the incubus' head. With a soft gasp, the incubus collapsed onto the carpet.

Carnes knelt before him. "*When you come to,*" he pushed into the demon's brain, "*you will feel as if you'd just awakened from a sound sleep. You will get up and walk over to the window. You will open the window. You will then stick your head out the window to enjoy the fresh air. Then you will lose your balance, and before you realize what is happening, you will fall and land on your head on the sidewalk. And when you awaken, you will find yourself in the Valley of Decay. You will realize at once that it will be in your best interest to hide because the super demons will hear how you've failed up here and will hunt you down. If they find you, they will turn you into one of the lowly creatures slithering around at the bottom of the River of Blood.*"

His message delivered, Carnes straightened, left the apartment and went out into the hall. When the elevator doors opened, he stepped inside and rode it down to the ground floor. Once he went back out into the street, he pulled his cell from his pocket.

It was time to call the super demon in Tampa.

***

Tiffany and Chip crossed the street that led to the rear of Johnny Rock's mansion. Loud splashing and excited screaming reverberated down the winding path behind the professionally trimmed bushes, where the Olympic-sized pool encompassed a large portion of the rear of the sprawling property.

Once again, the memories came blasting right back. Tiffany found that she'd become trapped in the past, when she'd been urged by her agent to parade past the oglers, the Hollywood film makers and the sleazy entrepreneurs who had been invited to the shindig. It was a buyer's market, and Tiffany, like the other starlets persuaded to flaunt their half-naked wares, presented themselves as the catch of the day.

I need to do this, she kept telling herself as she and Chip crossed the private street leading to the side entrance of the residence. *If I don't, I'll never be free.*

Will you ever *be free?* echoed that same inner voice that routinely questioned her whenever she struggled with a complicated situation.

Yes. I really and truly believe this.

What if you're wrong?

Just then, another voice, this one coming from a very different place, intervened. *You can do this. You've got the power. You need to use it.*

This voice seemed to be coming from a different source. If not from her own mind, then where?

She suddenly realized that she had run out of time. She and Chip had already crossed the street.

Two extremely large men in tight-fitting suits guarded the iron gate leading to the rear of the mansion. They stood with their huge hands clasped together in front of them and looked bored. Neither had visible necks. Their heads rested on extremely broad shoulders like golf balls sitting on top of an armored tank. Both straightened the moment they saw Tiffany and Chip making their way down the walk.

"Any ideas, Tifferoo?" Chip sent over. *"Those guys look like they hadn't had their roasted brontosaurus for lunch and are looking for a suitable snack."*

"We have to slip past them."

"And just how, pray tell, do you intend we do that?"

"How do you think?"

"We could make ourselves invisible..."

"Not practical. For one thing, they've already seen us. For another, those cameras have picked us up."

"Any ideas, then? Other than tossing some meat at them and squeezing through the fence while they're feasting?"

"Don't be silly."

"I'm listening..."

"We get in by flirting."

"Think that'll work?"

"I know it will."

"How do you know for sure?"

"By the stupid grins on their faces."

"Well, there's that, I guess..."

"I've also noticed the bulges in their slacks. You know what that means, right?"

"Since I'm really and truly a guy—deep down, under all this fluff, heavenly aroma and incredible beauty—but since I'm what you'd call a quick learner, I've got some idea. However, I'd like to hear your version."

"To make it simple, it means we shouldn't have much of a problem with these two."

"All righty. But I hope you don't mind too much if I let you do the honors."

"Not at all."

"Hi," Tiffany said, smiling.

"Ditto, dudes," Chip added, also with a smile.

The guards didn't budge. However, their expressions gave them away. Tiffany could tell that negotiations with these two wouldn't be difficult at all.

"See something interesting?" she asked the one on the left.

It took several moments for him to respond. He was obviously struggling to pull himself out of whatever disgusting fantasy he'd slipped into. He straightened. "You gotta invite?"

"You think we've come here without one?" she asked.

The big man blinked. "That still don't tell me you gotta invite..."

"You're cute," Chip told the other guard, who began fidgeting.

"Why don't you just forget about the formalities and let us through?" Tiffany asked.

"Don'tcha know you gotta have an invite?" the first guard asked.

"Hum a few bars," Chip said, grinning. "Maybe it'll nudge something loose."

The big man frowned. His partner couldn't stop staring at Chip.

"I'll bet you can do some serious damage to my petals, big boy." Chip winked and lowered his eyes.

Tiffany wanted to slap him. "*Tone it down*," she sent over. "*And keep the jokes to a minimum.*"

"*I'm trying to make him uncomfortable*," he sent back.

"*He's already there. Anything more would turn out to be embarrassing.*"

"*What can I say? I love tormenting mortals.*"

"*You're so bad...*"

"Talk about climbing some lumber!" Chip touched the guard lightly on the outside of his thigh and pulled back as if scalded. "And such seriously hard thigh muscle, too!"

"*Let's just try to keep this casual, okay?*"

Chip fluttered his lashes. "I'll bet you're solid in a lot of *other* important places—if you get my drift—"

"*Chip? Do I need to splash you with ice water?*"

"*This is much more fun than I can stand, Munchkin...*"

"*Don't make me slap you, now.*"

"*No fun at a party...*"

"Who invited ya?" the first guy asked, glancing at Chip.

"Johnny," Tiffany replied.

The guard looked surprised. "Mr. Rock...he *asked* ya here? Himself?"

"He certainly did."

"Recently?"

"No, but he did say that he'd appreciate seeing me here whenever I came to town."

"Your, um, friend, too?" The guard was looking Chip up and down.

"She's new at this," Tiffany told him.

"Then Mr. Rock don't know her?"

"Not personally. He's seen her work in a ton of swimsuit commercials."

"Thanks, Babykins."

"Just trying to make this easier."

Silence.

Chip turned and grinned at the second guy. "Honey, you didn't say how cute the guards were."

The man straightened. His cheeks reddened.

"Or how well-equipped—"

"Will you please *behave?"* Tiffany sent over. *"We don't want a problem."*

"I'm having ginormous fun, Honey Bunny," Chip sent back with a smile.

"That's what I'm afraid of."

"When was the last time a girl tied you to the bed, then took off all her clothes and got all hot and disgusting?" Chip moved closer.

The guard shivered.

"Will you please stop?" Tiffany's face had reddened. *"Don't forget those cameras."*

"What's the problem? I think I'm seriously photogenic right now."

"It's not your looks that I'm worried about!"

"A girl likes to be appreciated, you know…"

"Oh, please…"

The other guy produced a cell phone. "Mind if I call 'im and ask if it's okay to letcha through?"

"Not at all."

The moment the guard began pressing buttons, Tiffany focused on his eyes and entered the man's mind. *"Just put the cell back in your pocket and let us through. You'll feel much better. However, if you make this call, you'll definitely be embarrassed.*"

The guard abruptly stopped pressing buttons. He pocketed the cell, turned around and pushed open the gate. Then he stepped aside and gestured for Tiffany and Chip to walk through.

"Thank you," Tiffany replied, smiling.

"I'll bet you've even got handcuffs in your pocket," Chip said softly to the other guard. "One of those pockets that I'll bet you'd love me to personally rummage through."

"*Will you* please *stop this before you make that poor man wet his pants*?"

"It's been a bunch of Sundays since someone handcuffed *me* to the—"

"*Chip? Please?*"

"*Oh, all right…*" He sighed. "I'll look for you later on, big guy," he told the guard. "And be sure to practice your swing, 'kay? I'm sure the two of us can slam a few out of the park once we get the big game going!" He chuckled. "I'll bet you'd *love* to see these petals flying all over the place!" He pressed his index finger to the cleft in the big man's square chin. "Maybe we can even stretch it into extra innings!" She blew him a kiss and turned to walk away.

***

Light-headed from the two strong vodka martinis he'd had for lunch at the Gourmet House, Daniel Grove came back to his office and sat down at his desk, which faced the beautiful Gulf.

He immediately began thinking of Helena. Images of the beautiful young woman's shiny golden hair filled his brain, perking him right up. It hadn't been very long at all since they'd met. He fondly recalled the day she'd come in for her interview wearing that delicious red dress that stretched tightly over her flawless curves, stopping at a proper—but sexy—distance above the knee, showing off her long, elegant legs and sending him into a lather.

Helena had answered their ad for an executive secretary on the second day of Mr. Waiter's move to Tampa. She'd shown up precisely on time, meticulously groomed and perfumed, her hair professionally done, her makeup superb, yet understated. Although she'd been working for Waite Business Diversities & Consultations less than a month, she'd quickly become a valued asset, handling calls and whatever dictation was required of her. Though Daniel found himself helplessly enthralled, he realized that he could never completely forget Ashley Parker, and reluctantly accepted the fact that he was quite possibly using Helena as a desperate means to survive the past.

Get real, he told himself angrily. Ashley was gone and would never come back. But even though she'd left Florida, probably for good, he couldn't let himself believe that he'd never see her again.

Ashley was the only woman Daniel had ever truly loved. However, knowing as much as he did about his boss, he'd totally understood what had led to their breakup and accepted the cold fact that his personal life would never truly be his own. Knowing this, he realized that treasured memories involving Ashley and their brief relationship would always remain distant and irreparable. Even if the powers that be turned fate around, he could never hope for things to return to how they'd once been.

If only he could break away from this. If only he could somehow sneak away from his life here and find her again...

Ashley had moved to Pittsburgh and had been working for her uncle, who was big in the fashion industry. Because of this, Daniel knew that she wouldn't be difficult to find. After all, Andras, the demon from Chicago, had found her quite easily. And since Daniel was reasonably sure Ashley was still there, he shouldn't have any trouble finding her, either. Then he could—

Ask for her forgiveness? Plead with her to accompany him to a different part of the country? Maybe Europe? How did Switzerland sound? Or Australia? Scotland, perhaps? They could try and continue where they'd left off, then...

There was no way any of those things would ever happen. It just wasn't in the cards. Ashley had escaped Mr. Waite. She had her own life now. And Daniel also had a life of his own. And when he thought of the four-million-dollar beachfront mansion he'd purchased for cash, as well as the yearly seven-figure income he pulled in for doing the same things most others did for less than one-tenth the money, he knew that sacrificing all this for one woman was foolish—especially since it was obvious that he could have anyone he pleased.

Including Helena, who'd quickly proven worthy of his attentions.

Sighing, Daniel sipped some chocolate-flavored coffee from his personalized mug and felt the last remnants of the martinis fading. He sat back in his chair and, enjoying the panoramic view of the Gulf through his large tinted office window, thought about where he and Helena would have dinner this evening.

The phone rang. It was Helena's line. He picked up and smiled when he heard her soft, sensual voice.

"Mr. Grove?" she asked, making his pulse flutter, as usual, when she uttered his name, "I have a call coming in from Hollywood."

"Florida?"

"California. The caller wants to talk to Mr. Waite personally, says it's urgent."

"He? Or she?"

"It's a man."

"He didn't give you a name?"

"No, and you know how Mr. Waite hates talking to anyone who hasn't been screened. Shall I connect you? Or should I insist on more information?"

"I'll take it." He didn't like the sound of this. But since Mr. Waite dealt with all sorts of influential people, many of them politicians and CEOs, it was best to find out what was going on.

He pressed *TALK*. "This is Daniel Grove. I'm—"

"Is this the office of Waite Business Diversities & Consultations?" a low-pitched male voice asked.

"Who is calling, please?"

"You said you're a Mr. Grove?"

"I'm Mr. Waite's associate."

A pause. "Then you'll be the man who decides whether or not to transfer my call to Mr. Waite?"

"Yes…"

"I'm calling from Hollywood and have an important matter I need to discuss with Mr. Waite at his earliest convenience. Is he in his office now?"

"As far as I know, he is. What can I do for you?"

"As I just said, I have to talk with him. Will this be possible?"

"I'll require your name before I ring his line."

"My name is Comedor Cerebro." Daniel was about to jot it down on his pad when the caller added, "I believe Mr. Waite would probably recognize this name."

It didn't ring any bells. However, Daniel was familiar with these people and how they talked. Judging by how important this sounded, he assumed that this man might not be of this earth. The name itself—Comedor Cerebro—sounded very strange.

Still, he knew he should find out more.

"Can you please tell me the nature of this call?"

"As I've already said, this is an urgent matter, and I'm positive Mr. Waite should be informed of my findings immediately."

This sounded more ominous by the second. Daniel had been working with Mr. Waite for six months now and could sense that his boss would want to hear what this man had to say.

"I'll have to put you on hold while I see if I can get Mr. Waite on the line."

88

"I'll wait."

"One moment…" Daniel pressed hold and clicked Mr. Waite's extension. He only had to wait two seconds before the booming voice came on.

"What's the hell's up, Grove? I'm kind of busy here. The Governor of this stupid state is being a fucking royal pain in the ass, and I'm considering having one of my subs put him out of my misery and replace him with someone I can talk to without wanting to heave my guts. I just did that same thing in Virginia, so this wouldn't be much of a problem. But it does take considerable time, and as you well know, my main objective right now involves placing as many subs into Congressional positions as I possibly can, and this tends to become fucking aggravating."

"Sorry to bother you, sir, but there's some guy calling from Hollywood, California, about a very urgent matter."

"What's his name?"

"Does the name Comedor Cerebro ring any bells?"

A sudden silence.

Daniel could feel the tension on the other end of the line.

"You said Comedor Cerebro?"

"Yes, sir."

"Know what that means, kid?"

"No, sir, but if I can remember my education properly, it sounds like it could be Latin."

"Literally, it means Brain-Eater."

Daniel swallowed a lump in his throat. Yes, this was going to a place he did not want to go. "B-Brain-Eater?"

"That's what I said. Kid, we've got a sub on the line. Understand what I'm about to say?"

"Does it mean…could it mean…that maybe you'll—"

"Kid, in plain English, this call means two very important things. First of all, Cerebro's got something I need to know about. Get it?"

"Yes, sir…"

"The second thing is quite simple. Put him on the fucking line and do it *right now*!"

CHAPTER 3 - JOHNNY ROCK

The tall, middle-aged woman marched into the office, a cell phone gripped in her hand. She was dressed in a neat maroon business suit that fitted her slim figure nicely. As always, her thick auburn hair was professionally done. She wore a pair of silver earrings, an elegant ebony watch and a large, glittering rock on the third finger of her left hand. Her long, manicured nails were a glossy red. Their color matched her shade of lipstick.

She stopped just inches from her boss's desk and frowned. "It's Vegas calling again," she said in a soft, low-pitched voice. "That same talent agency that's called three times before. They really want to know if you've decided to book Tony Bennett for the Ankara Room next weekend."

"Dammit, I guess I forgot..." The large-boned dark-haired man sitting behind the desk placed his half-smoked $55 Arturo Fuente Opus X BBMF cigar carefully onto the glass ashtray on the desk blotter and reached for his phone with a large manicured hand. "That's all right, Fiona. I'll handle this. You can take off for lunch." He unbuttoned the top button of his dark blue Baroni jacket, sat back in his padded chair and raised the phone to his ear.

Fiona quietly left the room.

"Who am I talking to?"

"Good afternoon, Mr. Rock," chirped the breathy female voice on the other end of the line. "I'm very glad I finally got hold of—"

"Why so many calls? I thought I specifically told you people that I wasn't interested in takin' on any additional talent this month."

The caller took a moment before responding. "But Mr. Rock, we're talking Tony Bennett, here…"

The name was said reverently. Johnny wondered if the broad was actually envisioning some deity that had come down from the heavens above to cast a rainbow over the Hollywood area.

"So?"

"Tony Bennett? The singing legend?"

"I've heard of the guy once or twice before, yeah…" He had the irritating notion that this chick didn't know who she was dealing with. She was either too young to know better, too new at her job, or just stone stupid.

"One of the original members of the Rat Pack? The same celebrity who does a week in any of the Vegas casinos after just one phone call? He's over eighty, and commands more than a hundred and—"

"Actually, he's closer to ninety, girl, but then, who gives a rat's ass?" He hated having to explain himself. To anyone. He'd been handling two major casinos in the Vegas area for the last five years and, aside from the usual headaches, hadn't had much trouble at all. But whenever someone mentioned a famous fossil, everyone was expected to drop to his knees while experiencing some sort of instant Nirvana.

No matter where you lived or operated in this country, big names always meant big money. However, *ancient* names, although guaranteeing

92

huge profits in some circles, slowed down the flow and prevented the newer, perkier acts from coming in. Newer, perkier acts most always attracted large crowds and younger fans, thus increasing the cashflow. And if the acts were any good, they resulted in staying power—which meant months of increased profits.

In Johnny Rock's view, a relic from Vegas' heyday didn't amount to much at all in the New Millennium. Not when the Millennials and the tekkies were heavy into graphic comics, CGI, hip hop, and rap—and anything else that looked new…or ultra-modern…or anything other than Old World.

"Mr. Rock, I was told by one of your associates that you would be open to anything that might—"

"Girl, listen to me and see if you can try just for a second to let this sink in. I could care less about some relic who left a fuckin' fart in San Francisco sixty years ago. I wasn't even born sixty years ago, so why should I care about booking some ancient artefact that spends more on rugs than I do on my imported cigars?"

"But Mr. Rock, if you'll just hear me out—"

"I know we're talking about a fellow *paisano* here, but when we're dealing with house profits, that's where the *amico* bullshit stops."

"Mr. Bennett pulls in an impressive audience wherever he goes, even at his age…"

"Lady, if you did your homework, you'd see that my places have been doin' newer acts for the last couple years. And just in case that confuses ya, we're talkin' the last twenty-four months. We've moved onto current stuff, now. You know, like the finalists from those stupid reality shows? The latest stand-up comics? Acts that'll actually *work* nowadays? Comedy Club shit, in case you're still havin' trouble keepin' up with what I'm sayin'. As far as singers go? I'm talkin' American Idol winners, or the top finalists. Taylor Swift, Kelly Clarkson, Carrie Underwood. *That* kinda talent. Get it?"

"But if you'll just—"

"You got anything for me that wasn't conceived during the Roarin' Twenties? If so, get your sweet ass off the pot and start up your search. If not, call me back when you do manage to find somethin'. *Capisc*?"

A silence.

"Hello?"

"Yes, sir."

Johnny hung up.

His intercom buzzed only a moment later.

"Who is it?"

"It's me, Johnny." Fiona again.

"I thought you were goin' to lunch."

"I heard from Security just as I was about to leave. They said two unannounced females had just snuck in through the rear gate."

Crap. What the hell were those two slabs of beef doing out there? Playing with themselves?

"Two broads got past those two apes?"

"Apparently…"

"And no one knows who they are?"

"Apparently not."

94

"Guess I'll need to check the monitors. In the meantime, you take your lunch. Bianca will handle things."

"Thanks, Johnny."

He hung up, swiveled his chair around and turned on the screen that covered the opposite wall. And instantly saw what was going on three stories below.

He sincerely hoped he wouldn't have to resort to some of the old-fashioned tactics when he, using his given name as Guglielmo John LaRocco, a street punk growing up in the tough streets of Brooklyn more than forty years ago, did errands and small favors for the Giacomo Family.

That was a lifetime ago, in a different world. Back then, everyone was dirty and borderline psychotic. Even with Hollywood glamorizing the Cosa Nostra with movies like *Godfather* and *Valachi Papers*, the System had been cracking down on Organized Crime and implementing raids for decades.

This was California, dammit. Hollywood. Tinsel Town. Glamor City. The place where many of the world's most beautiful people lived and worked. You had to be careful in this town. You also had to be subtle. Tactful, too. Above all, you had to stay clean—especially when you weren't. You couldn't just pull some lowlife out of a bar, drag his worthless ass behind the building and pump a couple of shots into his lame brain. Here, you used other people—security guards, out-of-town hitters, politicians, CEOs, even dirty cops needing extra money—to do your wet work. Five K went much farther than a hot snub-nosed .38. It was much cleaner, too. Here, "clean" was the only way to do business.

In many ways, the old days just didn't measure up to the sophistication and technology of the New Millennium.

Besides, Johnny had become a much different person. Educated. Worldly. And infinitely more successful.

At 47, he had done many things since leaving Brooklyn, when he and his neighborhood buds struggled to make money peddling pot, hash and cocaine, as well as placing bets, before they were all rounded up, brought to trial, sentenced, and sent to Attica for the next ten years.

When Johnny got out, he was twenty-eight and chafing at the bit to become an entrepreneur. His own man. Someone people looked up to. For the next five years, he washed dishes and bused tables at his Uncle Gino's Brooklyn restaurant, the "*Serata Romantica*," until the old man died and left him a quarter interest in the restaurant.

Cashing in on his share, Johnny took his money to Vegas. Using his natural good luck at the gaming tables, he doubled his money at Blackjack and Texas Hold'em, then drove his beat-up '74 El Camino to Hollywood. Hiring himself out as a bodyguard for the town's biggest and most upcoming stars, he was able to bankroll a slice or two of Hollywood's future blockbusters, which put him on the map.

Known professionally as "Johnny Rock," Guglielmo John LaRocco had been living in North

Hollywood for the last five years. A seven-million-dollar mansion in the North Hollywood hills, along with bragging rights with five of the city's top film producers and a ten-year contract as promoter and talent scout for the latest models, starlets, and actresses, had become his legacy.

It was a dream come true. And all he had to do was organize a pool party once a week for forty weeks a year, where the most luscious babes in the country would come in and parade their wares for the wealthiest and most successful clients in the country, and he could pocket ten percent of whatever transaction had transpired as a result of the event.

Now, as he watched the festivities on the huge hundred-and-twenty-inch widescreen covering the wall of his study, Johnny took a deep puff of his Arturo Fuente, slipped on his reading glasses and began to examine everyone taking up space at his poolside event. Since the cameras had been placed at a twenty-foot height, he was somewhat limited in the details. However, the high-resolution of the $50,000 surveillance system made everything reasonably clear.

He sat back in his chair. For the next fifteen minutes, he studied each face and body. Taking in body language, facial expressions, and even reading lips. It was relatively easy for him to recognize most of the bodies present. However, there were several—perhaps half a dozen or so—he hadn't seen before. He attributed them as new recruits brought in by one or two of the dozens of talent agencies he did business with.

Just then, the two beauties sashaying across the walk behind the pool immediately grabbed his attention. He focused on one of them. His heart sputtered, and he sat bolt upright in his chair.

***

"Brett Waite speaking. Is this Cerebro?"

The booming voice made the Brain-Eater's hand tremble. He nearly dropped his cell phone.

Taking a deep breath, he lowered his butt to the park bench. Ignoring the street traffic as well as the throngs of pedestrians, he concentrated on staying calm. He was, after all, a subordinate demon. With powers. And he'd been up here long enough to boast a long list of achievements. He'd been responsible for the demise of more than five hundred mortals and had never been caught or even placed under suspicion.

But now he suddenly realized how difficult the simple task of maintaining control had become. The voice on the other end of the line belonged to one of the most powerful and feared super demons of Hell. Braithwaite was infamously known for his volatile temperament as well as his frightening powers.

Watch what you say, his mind warned him. *If you don't, this demon is liable to send a bolt of lightning through the phone line and turn you into a puddle of goo sizzling on the sidewalk.*

He cleared his throat. He'd been up here much too long to slip up by doing something stupid. He certainly didn't want to be sent back down. After all, he had just done away with an errant sub less than half an hour ago, and it took only a few minutes to do it. If *that* wasn't clear proof of serious clout…

"Anyone there, dammit?" The booming voice had become louder.

Get a grip! he ordered himself. *Otherwise…*

"Y-Yes, sir."

"What took you so fucking long to answer?"

"Sorry about that, sir. I just had a problem with my cell—"

"You're Cerebro?"

"Y-Yes, sir. Up here, my name is Cameron Carnes."

"You know who I am?"

"Yes, sir."

"Then you must know my reputation."

"Yes, sir. Of course I do."

"Then you must also know that I don't like bullshit. I don't like it and don't put up with it because I don't have to. Whenever I see bullshit, I get really ugly and do some radical things, and a lot of mortals end up dead. Know what I'm talking about?"

"Yes, sir—"

"And I insist on hearing news—especially news that pertains to me, personally—as quickly as possible."

"Yes—"

"All right, then. Why the call?"

"Sir, I'm calling to inform you of an urgent matter."

"I'm listening."

"An incubus has been living in this area for quite a while."

"I'm still listening. And in case you haven't already figured it out, I'm getting fucking tired of listening to you not getting to the point. That's another thing I don't like. In other words, I hate it. When I hate something, a lot of really bad things tend to happen."

"I understand, sir."

"Then cut the bullshit and tell me what the fuck is on your mind!"

"Well, sir, to make this simple, I was forced to send this incubus back down."

"On your own? I haven't heard a word from the Legion for some time. They certainly would have told me to have someone watching out for whatever's going on."

"I personally saw him being overpowered by two rogues about forty-five minutes ago."

"Overpowered how? And tell me about these two rogues."

Carnes told the super what he'd seen. Then what he'd done after tracking down the incubus.

"Any idea what the name of this incompetent is?"

"Agnus. I probed him just before I sent him back down. His mortal name was Bruno Stone, and he was apparently doing strong-arm work and assassinations for a local mobster in the Hollywood area."

"Shit. Now it sounds like that place will need a goddamned replacement." Braithwaite groaned. "And you say these two rogues were responsible for this?"

"I'm sure it was some sort of manipulation."

"We're talking two rogue subs, then?"

"I'd guess as much."

"This means I'll have to contact Balberith or Asmodeus and tell them they're gonna have to find that incubus and turn him back into an inferior, or swamp scum. Can't have a sub wandering around down there without any visible working brain cells, can we?"

"No, sir…"

"Tell me more about these two rogues."

"I just saw them not half an hour ago, on the streets—"

"And you're sure they're rogues?"

"I'd never seen them before, sir."

"You're telling me you know every sub and inferior in that area?"

"No, sir."

"If you had, I'd know you were lying. That state alone has more subs and inferiors walking around than any other, including New York. The inferiors are disguised as illegals, the subs as politicians. They're supposed to be working together, but as you well know, we demons tend to fall into the selective hearing mode and zone out so we can do our work on our own."

"I understand, sir."

"Getting back to these two. Have you seen them shift?"

"One of them…"

"But not both?"

"No, sir."

"Both male?"

"No, sir."

"Which one of them shifted?"

"The female."

"You're sure?"

"Yes, sir."

"Tell me about this female."

"She's a looker, sir. A blonde. Slender and stunningly beautiful. That says a lot. Out here, there are more beautiful females than cosmetic surgeons."

"You're saying she's special?"

"There were probably two or three dozen other beauties walking down the street, but my attention was drawn directly to her."

A sudden silence.

"Sir?"

"Tell me more about this blonde."

"Well, sir, as I just said, she's obviously a shift-changer, so I'm pretty sure she's got to be a sub."

"Tell me about the other rogue."

"He's kind of strange."

"Strange how?"

"First of all, he's got the wildest red hair, and—"

"Wild red hair?"

"Yes, sir…"

A pause. "Is he puny? Small? Stupid looking?"

"Yes, sir—"

"About the same height as the blonde?"

"I'd say so…"

Another pause.

"What else?"

102

"Well, he just doesn't seem to go with the blonde."

"What the fuck do you mean?"

"They don't look like an actual *couple*…"

"You're not making any sense."

"It would be like pairing a Ferrari with one of those little rides you see at an amusement park ride. Does that make any sense?"

"Unfortunately, it does. And you're sure she's a shifter?"

"I saw her change from a dark-haired brunette to a blonde in a split second."

"And the other rogue—the weird, puny redhead—he didn't shift at all?"

"I saw no evidence of it."

Silence.

"Sir, what do you want me to do about this?"

"Do you think you can find her again?"

"I know I can, sir."

"That's right, you've got one first-class honker."

"They say my sense of smell is on par with that of a bloodhound. Or wolf."

"All right, then. Find them. The sooner, the better."

Silence.

Carnes waited, but the silence continued.

"Sir?"

"I gave you your instructions. What the fuck are you waiting for?"

"I was just wondering what you want me to do once I find them…"

"Find them first. Then make damned sure the same goddamned thing doesn't happen to you that happened to that pathetic incubus."

"I'm a sub, sir. And I'm an outstanding hunter. My senses are superbly developed. I can always tell when someone is trying to sneak up on—"

"I don't care how superbly fucking developed your senses are. If the blonde we're talking about is the same bitch I've been trying to find for the last six months, she'll do a number on you and send you back down long before you can even guess which way is up."

"But sir, since both she and I are subs—"

"She's better."

Carnes resented that remark. For one thing, it was insulting. Braithwaite needed to know that he wasn't talking to an amateur. "Sir, no offense, but my reputation—"

"I don't give a wet fart about your fucking reputation. This blonde has powers that none of us seems to know about. No one even knows where she got them. Or when. Or how. Or even why. She's sent four subs back down, and one of them was a much better hunter than you'll ever be. He was directly responsible for that wet work business in Dallas nearly sixty years ago, dammit. Don't give me any shit about what you can do, and don't think for a moment that you're a match for her. Just track her down and make sure you know exactly where she is. And when you do, call me."

This was beginning to sound not right. In fact, it sounded very much like something that should not even be happening. However, Carnes knew better than question the super demon. "So that's *all* you want me to do, then? Find her?"

"That's it. And believe me, that in itself will turn out to be much harder than you think."

"But if I can manipulate her?"

"Let me make this easy for you. In simple terms, you won't be able to manipulate her in a million years."

"But—"

"I've already told you about her and what she can do. The fact that she's outsmarted four subs should be more than enough for even the dumbest idiot to digest. Get the picture?"

"Yes, sir, but—"

"Just do as I say, goddammit! Find her. That's all I want. Then call me, and we'll take it from there."

"Yes, sir—"

Click!

***

Behind Johnny Rock's mansion, a half-naked starlet sat up sharply on her floating raft in the center of the large, kidney-shaped pool and reached behind her back to adjust the string of her bikini top. Her fingers slipped, and the top rolled down her back and slid into the water. Two buffed surfer types immediately dove in to retrieve it while the rest of the crowd laughed, cheered and raised their frosted glasses. Several cell phones appeared, glinting in the sun as the photo buttons feverishly clicked.

As Tiffany and Chip moved past the trimmed bushes and colorful gardens, Chip watched the commotion in fascination. "Think she did that on purpose, Tifferoo? Or did that seem more like an in-depth study in clumsiness?"

"Did you happen to notice how long it took her to cover herself once her top dropped into the water?"

"I'd say about five seconds."

"What exactly did that tell you?"

The two excited hunks grabbed the thin material and began fighting for it. After the brief struggle, the larger of the two held his prize over his head in triumph. The loser grinned sheepishly, then provided an impressive double biceps pose, nodding at the applause.

"I kinda think she ain't very clumsy."

"You catch on really quick. Being a female is actually agreeing with you."

"Nothing to it. It's merely a matter of dressing right, shaving and plucking a few things, acting interested whenever a man says anything, moving around a certain way, and looking stupid while you're doing it. Righterino?"

"Really?" She glared.

"Am I wrong?"

"Actually, no…"

"Then why the sudden mad face?"

"The way you said it. It makes us all sound so…"

"Cheap? Superficial? Narcissistic? Arrogant?"

"Yes, but—"

"But what?"

"Never mind. Just focus, okay?"

106

Once they'd reached the area between the mansion and the two-story guesthouse, Chip turned around. The two guards who had closed the gate stood close behind the iron bars, watching them. Chip smiled and blew them a kiss. Both stiffened and spun around.

Chip followed Tiffany over to the umbrella-covered bar, where the short, good-looking Hispanic barman eyed them with admiration. Chip smiled at the man and winked.

"I really wish you'd keep a close watch on your hormones," Tiffany said.

"We're dead, Princess. We don't have those pesky whatchacallits anymore."

"That's beside the point."

"But I'm having *so* much *fun*!"

"You could have fooled me."

There were at least forty people at poolside. Some men wore suits or casual attire while most others paraded around in swimming trunks. The young women wore flimsy bikinis and relaxed in lounge chairs, or in chairs at large round tables, sipping iced drinks in long, narrow frosted glasses. The guy who'd won the battle for the starlet's bikini top was talking and laughing with her as she sat on her raft, putting her top back on.

Tiffany bent over to adjust the strap on her sandal.

Chip joined her. "You'd *better* not be doing what I *think* you're doing," he whispered.

"As I told you before, I don't want anyone recognizing me."

107

"You're telling me you've seen a familiar face or two?"

"Not yet..."

"Then why change the game plan?"

"I don't want to take any unnecessary risks."

"Aren't you being just a tad over the top with this?"

"What if someone remembers me? They'll be sure to freak out."

"Princess...from what you've already told me, you didn't exactly make much of a splash while you were here last, being a mortal babe."

Chip was right. Other than just a few commercials and half a dozen other minor assignments, she hadn't exactly fashioned her place amongst the immortals.

"You know I'm right, Tifferoo."

She didn't reply.

"Doesn't this Rockster guy invite a different crowd each time?"

"Yes..."

"Then take my advice: quit fucking around with your face!"

She sighed. "I guess you could be right."

They both straightened.

"You girls new in town?"

The man facing them was dressed in a lightweight tan suit. He was about six feet tall, around forty-five and, judging by how he kept shifting his weight, slightly drunk. He wore red-tinted glasses. His reddish-brown hair was either dyed or an expensive wig. His nails were manicured. Silver rings decorated the middle finger and pinky of each hand. A small silver stud ornamented his left earlobe. He made a show of displaying his Rolex Oyster wristwatch when he raised his left arm to sip his martini. He wore a silver bracelet on the other wrist.

"That all depends on what you mean by new," Chip said, smiling impishly.

Here we go again, Tiffany thought, frowning.

The man smiled and moved closer to Chip. "I guess what I mean is, I don't ever remember seeing you lovely ladies before. I'm sure I could *never* forget such a special event."

Tiffany sighed. This was getting old…

"Tell us more," Chip said, batting his lashes.

The man stared at Chip before responding. "Actually, I don't think I could *ever* forget meeting two such beautiful young ladies."

"I'll bet you say that to *all* the beautiful young ladies." Chip touched the man gently on the shoulder.

"Watch it," Tiffany sent over.

"C'mon, Tiffers. Live a little."

"As we both know so very well—and, going by what you said to me not two minutes ago—we can't *live a little because we're dead."*

"I'm Roger Banks." The man held out his hand. "I work for Paramount Studios."

"Really?" Chip took the man's hand and squeezed it. "Have I seen you in a movie recently?"

"Hardly." Roger Banks chuckled. "I'm not exactly an actor."

"Then what exactly *are* you, pray tell?"

"Actually, I'm pretty high up in their Promotion Department. I head their advertising programs and make sure they get going when they're supposed to. Delays of any sort are extremely costly, and I've got to jump on in there and take over before any real damage can result."

"How exciting, breathtaking, and utterly fascinating!" Chip reluctantly let go of the man's hand.

"Oh, brother…" Tiffany frowned. *"You'd better tone this down. Otherwise—"*

"May I ask your name?" Roger Banks asked.

"You certainly may." Chip placed his hand on his hip and thrust out his chest. "It's not very often that Maggie and I get the chance to meet such a distinguished gentleman."

Tiffany glared.

Chip glanced at her. *"You said you don't want to be recognized. Calling you Tifferoosky—or, as your mom calls you—Tiffany—might raise a brow or two, don'tcha think?"*

"I know…but Maggie?"

"The name seems to fit—don't you think?"

"Maggie? Seriously?"

"Me? Serious?"

"Hi, Maggie." Roger Banks held out his hand.

She took it briefly.

"And your name, pretty lady?" He'd turned back to Chip.

"My name?"

Roger Banks smiled. "You have one, don't you?"

Chip chuckled. "Of course I have a name!"

110

"Then what is it, may I ask?"

"It's Persephone," Tiffany said, smiling at Chip.

"Persephone?" Chip looked confused.

"First name that came to me, actually."

"Persephone? Really? Honestly? In all seriosity?"

"Let's just say that the word phony has been ringing in my ears ever since we met up with those two guards at the gate. I just embellished it with a suitable prefix."

"Cute. Very cute."

"Her name is Persephone Sims," Tiffany said, smiling at Roger.

"That's very unusual," Roger Banks said. "But also *very* sexy."

"But sometimes confusing," Tiffany added.

"Really?" Roger Banks asked. "And why is that?"

"Whenever she puts a P.S. at the end of her emails or memos, people tend to ask her if she forgot to add anything."

Roger Banks laughed.

"Witty," Chip sent to her. *"Nauseatingly witty."*

"But your name really *is* sexy," Roger Banks said.

"You think so?"

"I've heard of a Persephone who used to do adult films many years back. She was, well, sensational."

"That's interesting."

"Now that we're on the subject, may I ask if *you've* been in any films?"

111

"*Adult* films, you mean?" Chip winked.

Roger Banks reddened. "Well—"

"She's *much* too shy for that line of work," Tiffany said.

"I'm sorry," Roger said. "I didn't mean anything by that. May I get you a drink?"

Chip fluttered his lashes. "Orange juice, please…"

"Orange juice? Nothing else with it?"

Chip smiled. "Sorry, but I'm allergic to alcohol."

"Really?"

She laughed. "It wilts the petals. And of course, I tend to do some outrageous things when I'm just a little sauced."

"Really?"

Chip nodded.

Roger Banks went silent, then smiled. "One orange juice coming right up." He turned to Tiffany. "And you, Maggie?"

Tiffany froze.

"Tifferoo? Problemo?"

"What do you think?"

Chip suddenly turned dead serious. *"We're both well beyond worrying about anyone hurting us now, don't you think?"*

Tiffany thought that over. "A screwdriver, please."

"Coming right up." Roger Banks hurried right over to the barman.

"I really wish you'd watch it." Tiffany gave Chip a glare. "This flirting stuff tends to get old very quickly."

112

"You're not getting jealous, are you, pray tell?"

"Jealous? No. A little angry? Yes, pray tell."

"Why? Because I'm having fun?"

"Because we're not doing what we're supposed to be doing."

"Which is…?"

"Blending in. Listening. Watching. Keeping in tune with what's going on."

"What do you suggest?"

"Well, I *don't* suggest seducing someone who's obviously primed to take you to the nearest motel room and pound you senseless into the mattress—"

"Here's your drinks, ladies."

"*Such* the gentleman!" Chip took the glass and downed nearly half of it in a swallow.

Roger Banks laughed. "Wow... You really love your orange juice!"

"It's *very* good for the complexion. And, of course, the petals."

Roger Banks nodded. "You really do have a beautiful complexion, Persephone. And I must say, your petals seem to be in full bloom, too," he added, his eyes lowering.

"You're *so* sweet! And naughty, as well!"

"Just calling 'em as I see 'em…"

"*You two need a room*," Tiffany sent over.

"*This orange juice…*" Chip glanced at Tiffany. "*It tastes strange.*"

"*Strange how?*"

"*Strong. Kind of sour.*"

"*Orange juice?*"

"I have a feeling that something's in it that shouldn't be."

"Can you tell what it is?"

"I'm beginning to feel a little dizzy."

Tiffany stiffened as the memories gushed back. *"And warm?"*

Chip nodded.

"Tingly?"

"Definitely."

"How about you, Tiffers?"

"Mine tastes just a tad strong, as well."

"Something wrong?" Roger looked concerned.

"Tell him you want him to take you somewhere," Tiffany sent over.

"You're sure, Tifferoo?"

"I'm sure. That is, if you can actually get him to do it."

"Sorely you jest..."

"Impress me."

"To tell you the truth, Mister Ralphie, I'm beginning to feel really relaxed...and a little giddy..."

"Can I take you somewhere?"

"Sure. Certainly. In fact—"

"Why don't you take my friend some place where she can lie down?" Tiffany suggested.

"Why don't I take both you ladies somewhere private?"

"That sounds wonderful," Chip said.

"Are you sure you'd like *both* of us to come with you?" Tiffany asked.

114

Roger Banks grinned, showing a mouthful of perfect gleaming teeth. "I can't think of anything better."

***

Cameron Carnes followed the sweet vanilla scent of the blond rogue down the street and then up the next two blocks, where the hill led to the sprawling mansions in the North Hollywood area. As he drew closer, a tall, skinny guy in a tattered tee shirt, frayed jeans and designer athletic shoes asked him for change. Carnes turned his back on him.

The guy was insistent. "Just a couple bucks, dude," he said in a whiny voice. "Ya look like you can spare it..."

"Get lost."

"Not very nice, are ya?"

"Actually, I'm much worse than you'll ever know."

"C'mon, man... Do a fellow dude a favor."

Carnes didn't have time for this nonsense. "I'm busy. Vanish. Disappear."

"Man, all I need is...*what the f--*"

The kid disappeared.

Carnes glanced at his watch. Ten seconds. At least this stupid delay hadn't taken up *too* much of his time.

He climbed the hill that led to the sprawling mansion. Dozens of top-grade trophy rides—Ferraris, Porsches, Aston Martins, Lamborghinis, Maserati's, Mercedes, BMWs—were parked along the curb.

As he remembered, this spectacular spread belonged to one of the biggest promoters in the state. Carnes had seen clips of the man's outlandish parties on the news. He'd also viewed dozens of reality shows and seen many examples of such pointless grandeur on YouTube. The biggest names in the business showed up here, along with other top-name celebs, starlets and countless other movie hopefuls.

But why would the rogues come here?

It didn't matter. Their lingering scent suggested that they'd walked up this very path.

Halfway down the block, two gorillas in ill-fitting suits guarded the premises at the side gate. One kicked a pebble down the walk while the other looked bored.

Carnes strolled down the paved walk and stopped about five feet from where the two steroid freaks stood tall and rigid, watching him closely.

"Afternoon," he said pleasantly.

No response. The men resembled two enormous pit bulls fiercely guarding their property.

"I suppose it wouldn't be to my best interests to tell you I need access to the gate," he said.

Both continued staring. After about ten seconds, the one on the left said, "Gotta invite?"

Carnes shook his head.

The guard shrugged his massive shoulders. "Ya can't get in, then."

"Really?"

The two men shook their heads solemnly.

"Nothing I can do to change your minds?"

"Not if ya don't gotta invite..."

116

Carnes chose to keep his cool. He could take care of this. "Then I guess I've got no choice."

No response.

Carnes concentrated on his finely skilled powers of manipulation. Focusing on the one on the left, he sent over, *"You will stay put, close your eyes, and think of absolutely nothing."* To the other, he sent the following command: *"Turn around, walk up to the gate, open it, wait until I walk through, then close it, come right back to your post and stand next to your partner. I will then decide when the two of you can start functioning as human beings again."*

***

The two guards opened their eyes.

They quickly discovered no one standing there in front of them. They both rubbed their eyes. It seemed as if they'd just awakened from a deep sleep.

"W-What just happened, Drew?"

"I dunno..." Drew stared at the place where the weird dude in the suit had been only a moment ago. A moment ago? Yeah. In the time it had taken Drew to blink, the dude had vanished. He was gone. Nowhere in sight. Drew glanced to his right, then to his left. He turned around. The gate was closed and latched. But the dude was gone.

"Drew, there's...there's nobody there!"

"I know, Doug. I see that."

"He was just *there*! Right *there*! A dude in a suit. He was standin' right *there*. Now he ain't!"

"I'm right beside ya, dammit. I'm seein' the same damn thing you're seein'."

"He's…he's *gone*, Drew!"

Drew pointed to his eyes. "These things work, ya know."

"Are we goin' crazy?"

"Didn't think so. Least, not before now, anyway…"

Doug turned around and studied the area. "What happens now? I mean, the cameras—"

"Yeah." Drew squinted at the security camera positioned on the metal post about fifteen feet up, tilted toward the gate. "They pick up every damn thing."

"They *saw* this, Drew?"

"They saw *somethin'*."

"Are we in trouble? I mean—"

"Nope." Drew suddenly smiled. "No trouble at all."

"Whaddya mean? That dude was standin' right there, talkin' to us. Then he wasn't. And now, we don't know *what* the fuck—"

"He disappeared."

Doug didn't reply.

"Know what that means, don'tcha?"

"What's it mean, Drew?"

"It means that if the camera didn't pick up on what happened, the boss can't nail our asses for it."

"Really?"

"Count on it."

Doug thought about that for a little while. "Ya *sure* about that?"

"How the hell can they fire us for somethin' they'll never even be able to figure out themselves?"

118

***

Cameron Carnes made his way down the winding walk that led to the pool area.

The scent of the blonde and the redheaded male grew stronger as he approached the bar, where two slender beauties in skimpy bikinis leaned against the counter, flirting with the Hispanic barman, whose silly grin suggested that he could care less about anything other than the two fresh, tanned bodies pointing their ample breasts directly at him.

The scent quickly dissipated in the other direction, where the walk curved around the other side of the pool, leading to the front of the mansion. The bar area gave off stronger traces of the two rogues. Carnes decided that the barman would provide useful information. But the bikinis were a distraction and would have to be somewhere else.

"*Drift*," he sent over to the two females. "*Take your voluptuous bodies and your drinks over to the portly dude in the orange sports shirt standing in the shade of the recreation area. He looks like he's got money—something this barman obviously lacks.*"

Just as the barman began telling them about the new Ferrari he wanted to buy from a friend, the two females abruptly walked away, heading straight for the man in the orange sports shirt.

"Got a minute?" Carnes moved closer to the counter.

The barman ignored him. The idiot was probably trying to figure out why the two babes had moved away so abruptly.

"Hey…"

119

The barman snapped out of it. Glaring, he turned to Carnes. "Yeah?" His voice was a low croak.

"Do you happen to remember two people who might have been here just a few minutes ago? One was a young blond woman, the other a redheaded guy. The guy was skinny, about the same size as the blonde, and the blonde was—"

"Sorry, bud. Don't remember."

"You didn't let me finish."

The barman's dark eyes blazed. "If I don't remember, I don't remember."

"You would have remembered the blonde I'm talking about."

"Why's that?"

"She's gorgeous."

The barman jabbed a thick brown index finger at the pool. "Take a look around, bud. This area's crawlin' with gorgeous, hot, and sexy. I see tits and ass everywhere—which is why I got this damn job in the first place. Every damn time I turn around, I gotta take a short break and get myself off in the fuckin' rest room. Blondie could be out there right now, lyin' on her back on one of the floats."

"She's not there."

"Oh well…" He gave a loose shrug. "Those be the breaks, I guess. Maybe next time, yeah? Then, maybe, if you can—"

Carnes placed a spell on the man, who suddenly stopped talking. And moving. And thinking. He just stood there, his deep-set dark eyes pointed straight ahead, toward the pool.

Carnes conducted a probe and glimpsed several beautiful young women in the barman's thoughts, including the two who had just walked away. Just then, the image of a fat, middle-aged man with thinning white hair, sitting in an armchair and whispering something into a cell phone, flared brightly.

"Anything promising there today?" the white-haired man asked.

The barman spoke into the tiny headset attached to his left ear. "Two new babes I haven't seen before. One's a blonde, the other a brunette."

"Tell me about the brunette."

"Nice. Fairly tall, thin, shapely, and hot...real hot. I mean sizzling...*"*

"Face?"

"Perfect."

"Slip her our special. Is Banks anywhere around?"

"He's already spotted her."

"Make sure he takes her someplace quiet. His penthouse suite should suffice."

"What about the blonde?"

"She's hotter. A lot *hotter."*

"Even better. Both of them, got it?"

"On it."

The man hung up. The image dimmed.

"Address?" Carnes asked the barman, who remained zombielike as he gave out the requested information.

Carnes clicked his fingers. The barman snapped out of his trance. He was looking around stupidly and scratching the back of his thick neck as

121

Carnes made his way down the walk, toward the front entrance of the estate.

***

The short black hair on the back of his thick neck bristled as Johnny Rock cautiously approached the wall screen.

After watching the activities, he decided that he needed to take a walk downstairs and check out the pool. Something about the beautiful blonde had sparked something in his memory. There was something about her face that had made his left eyelid twitch.

She was stunning. Absolutely gorgeous. One look at her and he'd experienced an instant stirring below decks. But there didn't seem to be a good reason for it. Every pool party he'd organized in the last couple of years guaranteed more than a dozen babes, each worthy of a prime spot on a *Victoria's Secret* calendar, a feature spread in *Sports Illustrated*, or a cover shot and in-depth *expose* for any of the most popular men's magazines on the market.

Yet very few of them had pressed his buttons as quickly as the blonde.

He couldn't help wondering what the hell was going on. He organized functions like this one all the time. Arranged it so the best-looking studs, the sexiest babes and the most influential filmmakers and promoters would get together and make miracles happen. He pitched it to the proper bigshots, then put on a dazzling shindig and took fifteen percent right off the top from any deal made.

So then, what was so damned special about the blonde?

Was it the way she walked? Moved those hips? Those perfect thighs?

Or was it something else?

Johnny boasted the reputation for having a remarkable memory—especially when it involved beautiful women. It was ridiculously easy for him to recall eyes. Faces. Smiles. Cheekbones. Dimples. Hair. Boobs. Ass. Legs.

Most of all, he possessed the uncanny ability to recollect the circumstances surrounding a particular woman the moment he'd first seen her. And the images filling his head in this instance reminded him of a national commercial he'd seen on TV only a year or so ago.

Was it a hair feature? Possibly. This young lady had an incredible golden mane. But what seemed prevalent in this instance was that he kept putting her image together with one of those high-end underarm spray sponsors.

Yeah. *That* was it. He'd seen her in—

No. That *couldn't* be the same woman. As he remembered, that young lady had unfortunately OD'd at one of his parties. And the horrible accident had occurred not long after she'd shown up and paraded her stuff in front of half a dozen film producers and a couple of agents, all of whom had come to him later on to ask about her.

But then the sickening aspects of the event plunged into his memory. Not long after she'd been hauled off in an ambulance, apparently from a

123

stroke, she was pronounced dead before the ambulance had reached the hospital.

Reluctantly he pushed aside the dark images and turned back to the camera, which showed the festivities going on at the pool.

The sexy twosome had walked over to Julio, who was tending bar. For one brief instant, the two faced the camera.

His pulse hastening, Johnny paused the image and zoomed it in.

And caught a full-face image.

It made him cringe.

My God... Was this really her?

How can this be?

In that next instant, the twosome turned toward Julio. And started talking to him.

Shaking a little, Johnny kept staring, waiting for them to turn around again. *Turn around, baby*, he thought, his skin turning cold. *Turn around. Just for one more second*!

But neither girl did as he wished.

He kept staring at the blond mane, the perfect ass, the tiny waist. Even though she nor her brunette friend weren't dressed provocatively, she was still light-years ahead of the rest of the pack.

But even so, that wasn't the important thing here.

She's alive.

Yes. That was the thing. The girl he remembered was dead. This one wasn't. And it didn't matter how much she resembled the other girl. This one was alive!

No. It *couldn't* be her.

Get real, he ordered himself. *This isn't like you at all.*

For a moment he feared that he might be losing his mind. Too many double martinis, obviously. Or too many blood-rare Porterhouse steaks. Or maybe that expensive Colombian weed his gardeners brought him after their families had flown it in. Or too many private lap dances in his den with some of the less inhibited babes while Sophia fed the twins lunch downstairs.

Or all the above.

Whatever it was, it didn't matter now. The blonde may have resembled the babe he'd been thinking about, but it really wasn't her at all.

This girl, he reminded himself once again, was *alive*.

I need to cut back on my drinking. Or the steaks. Or the babes—

Nope, definitely the drinking.

But he did realize that he had to find out what the hell was going on.

He went back to his desk and punched in some keys. When he logged onto the side gate monitors, he entered *rear camera back fifteen minutes*, and pressed ENTER.

The two guards were talking to a sandy-haired guy in a good suit. They were talking low, making it impossible for the audio to catch what they were saying. Johnny adjusted the volume, flipping it all the way up, but caught only one or two random words.

Then, suddenly, the guards froze. The guy in the suit waited until Patterson had turned, walked stiffly up to the gate and opened it. The stranger walked through, entering the estate. Patterson closed and locked the gate, turned around and went right back to where Sandler was standing.

What the fuck was going on?

Johnny programmed the camera option once again, this time going back thirty minutes. And once again pressed ENTER.

The two babes, the brunette and the blonde, were talking to Patterson and Sandler. The brunette was flirting with Sandler, who was grinning stupidly. Patterson then pulled his cell out of his pocket. The blonde said something to him. Patterson quickly lowered his cell, turned, and went over to the gate. He unlocked it, pulled it open and let the babes through. He locked the gate and went right back to where Sandler was standing, watching the two babes as they went down the walk leading to the pool.

What the fuck is wrong with those two oversized meatheads?

Johnny picked up his cell and buzzed his switchboard.

"Yes, sir?" Bianca asked.

"Get Security on the line. Now!"

***

It took Roger Banks less than two minutes to have one of Johnny Rock's valets bring his shiny black BMW up to the side entrance of the estate. After the tall, slender young man had opened the back door for Tiffany and Chip, Roger slipped him a twenty, then jumped behind the wheel, pulled the door shut and tore away from the curb.

126

Tiffany and Chip sat close together in the back seat, watching the man as he hurried down the block, barely slowing at the stop signs and then zipping through the yellow light without a moment's hesitation.

"He seems to be in quite a hurry," Tiffany sent over to Chip.

"I think Roger the Artful Dodger is having a major issue of extreme urgency going on in his drawers," Chip replied.

"Obviously."

"And me without any sort of heads-up on how to eradicate myself from such a predicament."

"I'm sure you'll think of something."

Roger kept watching Chip in the rearview mirror, occasionally glancing at what was happening straight ahead.

"By the way, how do you feel?" Tiffany asked. *"Still dizzy?"*

He smiled. *"That was just for show, dear girl."*

"How'd you know the buzz wasn't just the orange juice?"

"Did you ever drink orange juice, Tifferoo?"

"Of course."

"Did you ever in your entire life get a buzz from it?"

"Good point."

"Anyway, you could call me an expert. I detected something slightly odd—which just doesn't normally happen with fresh orange juice."

"I figured as much. Good thing this idiot doesn't know we're both dead, and obviously immune to drugs."

"Is this what happened with you, Honey Bunny? I mean, sipping the drink and tasting something not quite right?"

"It hit me hard really fast. As soon as I took my first sip, I could tell something wasn't right. And believe me, it wasn't a very big sip."

"I take it that the idiot who gave you the drink had no idea it was gonna hit you that hard."

"I still blame him. He obviously knew exactly what was going on. Just like our Roger the Ready boy, here."

"You took a small sip and wham? Flat on your back?"

"I didn't even make it to the hospital. "

"That definitely would be a ginormous bummer."

"Believe me, it was."

"How d'ya think he slipped it to me?"

"The barman must have dropped something into your drink."

"Then the barman's in on it?"

"It's kind of obvious—wouldn't you say?"

"You're saying he'd be the one with the easiest access to the drugs?"

"Who else could do it without anyone watching? We both saw cameras. They were everywhere."

"But how would the idiot know to do something like that? I didn't see Roger Dodger showing any sort of suspicious—"

"Didn't you see that thing the barman was wearing in his ear?"

"One of those tekkie hearing hickeymajigs?"

"Exactly."

"And that's how they got you?"

"I'm not sure. But we have to find out. And getting this idiot alone seems to be a very good place to start."

"How's everything back there, ladies?" Roger Banks asked, his eager eyes on Chip. "I've never encountered such beautiful young ladies who don't talk very much."

"It's a gift," Tiffany said.

"Still feeling dizzy, Persephone?"

"Not too bad. But I must say, I've never had a glass of orange juice with such a kick before."

He laughed. "We'll get you to my place in just a few minutes. Then you both can chill out and have a nice, relaxing drink. My place is very comfortable. I've got piped-in music, climate control—the works. What sort of music do you ladies care for?"

"I've always loved Mantovani," Chip said.

"Mantovani?"

"You've never heard of Mantovani?"

"Sure, sure."

"Then what's the problem?"

Roger Banks shrugged. "No problem. I don't think there was a problem. Did I say there was a problem?"

"You sort of insinuated that there was."

"How'd I do *that*?"

"When you said, "Mantovani?""

"I was merely asking if I heard you—"

"You said, "Mantovani," the same way other people say, "Drugs? In my purse?""

129

"Really? I actually sounded like *that*?"

"Oh, yes. Right, Maggie? Didn't he sound like that?"

"I'm sorry, I wasn't listening."

"The Mantovani thing."

"He doesn't like Mantovani?"

"He never said. But you could tell there's something about Mantovani that makes him kind of nervous and—"

"I don't have *anything* against Mantovani!" Roger Banks nearly swerved into a streetlamp.

"It sounded like you did…"

"I don't. I really and truly don't. Believe me."

"Now you sound upset. Doesn't he sound upset, Maggie? He sure sounds upset to me. In fact, he sounds almost like he's trying to convince a court of law that he didn't actually kill anyone…"

"I'm not under *any* circumstances—"

"He does sound a *little* upset," Tiffany said. "Not a lot, but maybe just a smidge?"

"Hear that?" Chip asked. "My friend Maggie says you sound—"

"I'm not." Roger Banks sighed and took a breath. "I'm really and truly not upset *at all*…"

"All right, then." Chip turned to the window and went silent as he watched the mansions they passed.

Roger Banks hunched forward and concentrated on his driving.

"You really did a number on him," Tiffany sent over.

"Seriously?"

"Seriously."

130

"Are you impressed?"

"Extremely."

"Thanks, Tifferoo. This guy's a real asshole. I'm having serious barrels of jaw-breaking fun freaking him out."

"I can tell."

"Should I make him have an accident in his drawers?"

"Maybe later."

"No problem."

Still silent and somewhat unsettled, Roger Banks pulled the BMW into the winding drive that led to the underground garage of a sprawling apartment complex.

***

Both men stood stiffly in front of Johnny's desk. Patterson kept shifting his weight, first from one foot, then the other, as a chained elephant would behave in a circus. Sandler continuously clenched and unclenched his huge fists, which he kept at his sides.

Johnny sat behind his desk, his forearms on the blotter, his hands clasped in front of him. He studied the expressions of his two employees and took his time before saying anything, letting the silence build up the tension. He'd been in this business long enough to know all about strategy and finesse. And when you found yourself facing two employees who had just acted irrationally—or, to be more accurate, stupidly—you had to resort to any psychological trick you'd acquired along the way.

In this case, it would be wise to size them up individually. Stare at one, then the other. Things would go much better this way. Judging by the weight-shifting and the fist-clenching, both were already scared. And they really should be, considering that they'd both done the unforgiveable by letting three strangers into the shindig without calling Johnny and asking him to intervene.

Still, Johnny thought it best to go for the simple and see where it went.

"Either of you know why you're here?"

No reply.

"I'll make this easy." Johnny took a breath and forced himself to keep his cool. "What the hell happened down there? And before either of you starts talking, just make sure you get everything right in your head. And talk plain. I ain't a young guy anymore. Sometimes I have trouble lettin' things sink in."

Neither spoke. Worse, neither looked like he *wanted* to speak.

"You two heard me, didn'tcha?"

Both men nodded.

"All right, then." This was going to be difficult. Since simple obviously wasn't going to make a dent in this, a different tactic would be required. "Patterson, tell me something."

"Y-Yes, sir?"

"Who were those two women you two were talking to out there?"

"Sir?"

"Women. Babes. You know. Boobs? Long hair? Long legs? They smell really good and can

132

make you forget your own name in a matter of seconds."

Two blank looks.

"Do I have to turn on the security camera and show you what I saw down there?"

Silence.

Johnny struggled to stay in control. This was not the time to lose it. These two didn't seem to be holding anything back, so at least that was a start. Those babes had obviously done a number on his men. Johnny fully understood; he'd been there himself. Many, many times. He just didn't want this happening right now.

You're gonna have to do this the hard way after all...

He picked up his remote and switched on the screen.

The men didn't budge.

Johnny wondered if these two had suffered brain damage from 'roid usage. After all, both spent most of their off time at the gym, pushing all sorts of tonnage. "You two will have to turn around if you wanna see what's goin' on."

The two glanced at one another. Then, reluctantly, they did as their boss suggested, and focused on the big screen. Neither moved.

"Ring a bell?" Johnny asked.

No response.

"Why'd you let them through without verifying who the hell they were?"

Patterson turned around and looked sheepish. "Sorry, Boss. They just...well, they just seemed like they—"

"Like they belonged at the party?"

Patterson nodded.

"What about you?" Johnny asked Sandler. "What were you and the brunette talkin' about?"

Sandler shrugged. "She was really nice, sir. She seemed, well, she, uh, had this smile, and a dimple, and she smelled *really* nice—"

"I get it." Johnny could tell the females had done a serious number on his men. But this didn't make any sense. Both Patterson and Sandler had been manning their post for more than a year. They knew better than act like two teen punks with their first hard-on. They were being paid entirely too much money to let their hormones go totally berserk.

Johnny reset the camera fifteen minutes ahead. Then switched it back on.

Once again, the two stood at their post. A moment later, a guy with sandy hair walked up to them. Words were exchanged. Patterson walked the man to the gate, unlocked and opened it, let him through, closed and locked the gate, then went back to where Sandler stood, motionless as a statue.

Johnny flicked it off and dropped the remote on his desk. "You can turn around now."

Once again, the two did as ordered.

"Well?" Johnny held out his hands. "What the fuck happened? Why'd you let that guy in? You can't tell me he had a smile, a dimple, and smelled really nice, too. Well? Can ya?"

Two more blank looks.

"Patterson?"

No response.

"Sandler?"

No response.

"C'mon, now. Tell me what the fuck happened down there."

The two men exchanged frightened looks.

"Boss," Patterson muttered after a brief silence, "I got no idea what happened…"

Sandler added, "I can't remember that happenin' at all, Boss."

Johnny sat back in his chair. This was getting way the hell out of hand. First, the two babes. Then, the guy in the suit. What the hell was going on? And, most important of all, what had happened to turn his two most trusted guards into imbeciles?

"You two. Get the hell outa here."

The two men spun around and rushed out of the office.

Johnny picked up his cell.

It was time to get in touch with someone who might be able to sort out this mess.

"Sir?" Bianca answered on the first ring.

"Get me Nathan McCormick *now*. I need to speak to him ASAP!"

***

Roger Banks escorted Tiffany and Chip into the private elevator that would take them to his penthouse suite. When he turned to face them, the huge smile covering his face made him appear dimwitted.

"He looks so silly," Tiffany sent to Chip.

"He's definitely super horny," Chip sent back.

"That's an understatement. He looks like he wants to wear your butt for a mask."

135

Chip glanced at his reflection in the metal doors. *"I can't say as I blame him. Just look at this package. I'm one seriously hot babe!"*

"You are so full of yourself..."

Chip grinned. *"And I'm getting this sudden urge to switch back to my old self—just to shake him up a tad."*

"Right here? Right now?"

"Bad idea?"

"He'll probably have a coronary."

"Now that would be entertaining—don't you think?"

"He's not exactly a good guy, you know."

"I'll bet he also knows the sparkling knight responsible for killing you."

"That's what I was thinking."

"Then please let me nail his ass, Tiffy. I promise it'll be satisfying for both of us."

"Not until we find out a few things first."

The elevator dinged. A moment later, the car slowed to a stop.

"We're here, ladies!"

The door slid open. They crossed the carpeted hall.

The man's penthouse apartment took up the entire top floor. Just beyond the doorway, a carpeted hall extended fifty feet to what appeared to be a suite of rooms. At the opposite end of the living room, the hall stretched roughly the same distance. The living room was decorated in wall-mounted artwork and various modern sculptures sitting on large marble pedestals. An oval-shaped

136

Turkish rug provided a comfortable setting for the sofa, chairs, end tables and cocktail table.

The moment Tiffany and Chip entered the enormous split-level living room overlooking the panoramic view of the sprawling hills beyond the glass wall, Roger told them to make themselves comfortable. He hurried right over to the bar, which was just as impressive and as well-stocked as any Tiffany had seen in nightclubs.

"This is so *exciting*!" Chip gazed breathlessly at the beautiful sight just beyond the tinted glass. He carefully crossed his bare legs on the comfortable L-shaped sofa, making sure the hem of his skirt was adjusted appropriately. "It just takes my breath away!"

"*I'll be so glad when you're back to your old self,*" Tiffany sent over with a scowl. "*And by the way, you're showing entirely too much thigh.*"

"*I'm having the time of my life, Shady Lady. And I'm trying to urge our host to lose his cookies faster.*"

"*Just don't get him to lose them* too *fast. We don't want him to get suspicious. He might be scared off and ruin everything.*"

"*You're beginning to sound just a teensy bit jealous again...*"

"*I just think you're much more tolerable as a guy.*"

"*You were always getting on my case about something when I was a guy...*"

"*But at least you were easier to deal with.*"

"Would you still prefer orange juice, Persephone?" Roger asked. "I've got an impressive

137

collection of other fruity drinks here, as well as in the fridge…"

"With alcohol?"

He shrugged, reddening. "Just a smidge. Not *too* much, of course…"

Chip giggled. "You wouldn't, by any chance, be trying to get me drunk now, would you, you horrible, nasty man?"

Tiffany groaned and turned away.

Roger laughed. "Can't blame a guy for trying, can you?"

Chip tilted his head. A curtain of long black hair spilled down his chest. "Can't blame a girl for not wanting to do anything to wilt her petals, can you?"

"*Touché.*" Roger winked.

"You know what they say, don'tcha? A girl's petals are her best friend…"

Roger tilted his head. "I thought diamonds were a girl's best friend…"

"For some, maybe…"

"But not for a gal like you?"

"Myself?" Chip sighed deeply. "Actually, I prefer the simpler things in life, like long walks along the beach, or a quiet afternoon watching a cloud drift gently across the sky."

"*You're being ridiculous, now…*" Tiffany glared.

"*I'm working my shtick, girl…*"

"Something for the perky petals of a beautiful, very unusual lady." Roger squatted behind the bar. A moment later he stood up, holding a small carton

138

of orange juice. He carefully poured her drink. "Orange juice it is…"

Chip smiled and batted his lashes.

"*I'm beginning to be sick to my stomach,*" Tiffany sent over.

"And you, Maggie? What will your pleasure be?"

"A gin and tonic would be lovely," she said. "Just don't make it too strong, please?"

"Coming right up."

Roger brought over the drinks on a silver tray and placed it on the polished cherry cocktail table. He handed Tiffany and Chip their drinks, picked up his martini and held out his glass. "To what pleasure do we toast to?"

"How about to the beginning of an exciting new relationship?" Chip suggested.

"That sounds sensational." Roger grinned. "How about you, Maggie? Something to add?"

"The beginning of an exciting new adventure?"

Roger's eyes grew. "And what would this new adventure be?"

Tiffany found it difficult to keep her emotions in check. *Keep cool*, she reminded herself. "Why don't we just wait and see what happens?"

"Fair enough."

They clinked glasses.

Tiffany sipped, then frowned.

"*Something, Tifferoo?*"

"*This drink is spiked.*"

"*You're sure?*"

"*I'm sure.*"

139

"Good, because my orange juice also tastes, well, icky."

"I do believe Mr. Banks, here, is about to work some sort of number on us."

"I assume you're ready to do something about this, then?"

"More than..."

"Why is everyone so quiet?" Roger lowered his glass. "We're all having fun, aren't we? I'd have my housekeeper bring us some assorted snacks, but since it's her afternoon off..." He shrugged. "If you'd like something special, I'll see what I can scrounge up in the kitchen—if that's all right."

"If you don't mind," Tiffany said softly, "we'd like to try something with you."

"Really?" His eyes grew. He squirmed in the chair. "What exactly would you like to do?"

Tiffany instantly recognized the clear signs of sexual arousal. The fidgeting. The glossy eyes. The stupid grin. The slight trembling. It wouldn't take much at all to coax the idiot into unconsciousness.

"This wouldn't be something you'd expect," Tiffany said.

"But it *would* be just as exciting," Chip added. "For us, anyway."

Tiffany deepened her gaze at the man and sent over her suggestion. *"You're about to fall into a heavy sleep, and when I start asking questions, you will—"*

Just then, she stopped.

A strange dark image interrupted her concentration. It began drifting closer and closer, and in just moments she found that it had entered her mind. When the darkness clouded the images in her thoughts, she realized something bad was about to happen.

She turned sharply toward the front entrance.

An eerie darkness lurked behind the apartment door.

***

Cameron Carnes had no trouble tracking down the blonde and her redheaded partner to a North Hollywood high-rise just one block north of Santa Monica Boulevard. As he entered the lobby, the blonde's vanilla odor had grown much stronger. So had the other scent, which reminded him of a flower. Although he hadn't seriously analyzed this second scent before, he decided that since it wasn't quite as pungent as the blonde's odor, it belonged to the redhead.

Thankfully, the lobby was deserted. This was good. When mortals were present, things became complicated very quickly.

Silver mailboxes covered much of the wall facing the glass windows overlooking the street.

He approached the wall. The name *Banks, R. C.*, printed in white lettering and attached in black stencil to the penthouse apartment box, struck his immediate attention the moment the images from the poolside barman flashed in his mind.

He pressed the UP button. About half a minute later, it came to an abrupt stop. The doors hummed open. He entered the car and pressed PH. The doors closed with a soft moan. The car began its ascent.

Less than a minute later, he crossed the carpeted hall and cautiously approached the door.

141

The peephole prompted him to veer to the right. Anonymity would be best in this case. As he leaned against the wall, he closed his eyes and brought his superb olfactory senses into play. Once again, the vanilla scent of the blonde—as well as the floral trace of the redhead—drifted prominently into his nostrils. He had successfully tracked them down.

He pressed his ear to the cool plaster wall. It took him only a few seconds to hear the voices coming from the apartment.

"If you don't mind," a muffled female voice said, "we'd like to try something…"

"Really?" This voice sounded like a man—possibly Banks. "What exactly would you like to—"

"This wouldn't exactly be something you'd expect," the female said.

"But it *would* be just as exciting," a second female voice said. "For us, anyway."

A *second* female voice?

The housekeeper?

The housekeeper wouldn't be participating in anything involving the host and his guests, would she?

What in hell was going on? As far as he knew, the blonde and the redheaded male were the only two who'd gone inside with Banks.

Then who belonged to this other voice?

Just then, Carnes heard a different voice. This one was dreamy—as if coming from someone's subconscious state. It was very close to the voice of the blonde.

"You're about to fall into a heavy sleep, and when I start asking questions—"

His instinct urged him to intervene. He had to go on in there and take care of this before things went south.

But just as he was about to use his mental powers to enter the apartment, he heard yet another voice, this one exploding in his head. It was very loud and terrifying.

He knew the moment his fingertips lightly touched the doorknob that he was about to get into serious trouble.

"Just track her down and make sure you know exactly where she is when you call me back."

It was Braithwaite's voice chilling him to the very core of his spirit.

The message was frighteningly clear. He wasn't permitted to do this on his own. The super demon had strictly forbidden him from doing anything other than what he'd already done.

He was very familiar with Braithwaite's powers as well as his malicious disposition.

Still, he wasn't one hundred percent certain of what was happening inside Banks' apartment.

His thoughts spinning, he struggled to recall his conversation with Braithwaite. One important detail that stood out was that the super demon had seemed much more interested in the blonde than the redhead.

Yes. The fact that Braithwaite had spoken almost exclusively of the blonde and very little of the redhead convinced him he was right.

The blonde had clearly proven to be the major snag in the super demon's agenda.

She was in the apartment—he was reasonably sure of it. The vanilla smell had been the dead giveaway. He'd also heard her voice.

But what about the redhead? The flower scent?

None of this told him anything. He tried analyzing the dreamy voice and decided that it belonged to the blonde and that she might have been placing a spell on someone inside.

But this told him nothing about that second female voice…

He stood perfectly still, his fingertips barely touching the doorknob. Should he just move away and make the call? Or use his special powers to slip inside to see what was going on?

Chance it?

Risk discovery?

Face Braithwaite's horrible wrath?

If the super demon had wanted things done a certain way, there had to be a good reason. If the two rogues had been responsible for sending four others back down to the Dark Place, they were obviously much more devious than anyone assumed.

He'd heard it from Braithwaite himself.

"The blonde has powers no one seems to know about. "

His mind was made up. He would do exactly what Braithwaite had ordered. Let some other poor schmuck risk everything to handle this.

144

This settled, he sighed in relief. But just as he was about to pull his fingertips away from the doorknob, he stopped cold.

***

Nate McCormick hadn't seen anything interesting come across his desk in several days.

As the owner of NMack Enterprises the last seven years, Nate was known in the Los Angeles area as the man who got things done right. A guy who showed up early, got right down to the core of the problem and saw that it was fixed completely, and in record time.

In Hollywood, this meant everything. However, as with all enterprises dealing with rich, powerful people, such a specialized business had its share of ups and downs. It wasn't uncommon to arrange for a high-profile diva to be accompanied by the appropriate escort without the constant worry of a stalker or ex-lover popping up and destroying a project amounting to six or even seven figures. At a fee of $25K per day, NMack guaranteed its services 100%.

However, such gravy jobs didn't happen nearly often enough.

The Southern California weather was certainly as close to perfect as anyone could hope for. The scenery alone—the beaches, restaurants, theme parks and movie sets—was well worth those quiet, unproductive periods. But when intervals between jobs stretched into uncomfortably long periods, it didn't make much difference if a man's office sat on prime property in Malibu or on some side street in the worst section of Watts.

But now it looked like Nate's leisure time might be in for a drastic change. Johnny Rock had just called, and his contact alone always resulted in things quickly turning chaotic—and, more importantly, highly profitable.

Johnny was seriously high-profile. The man knew a shitload of heavy-duty people. He'd hobnobbed with the last two Vice Presidents, for God's sake, and had been a major contributor to nearly half a dozen of the latest high fashion productions that had been seen on every major TV network in the country.

Johnny had called just twenty minutes ago and asked Nate to come over to his North Hollywood estate to discuss an urgent matter.

Sounded good. In fact, it sounded fantastic. The man's name alone meant big bucks. The standard local joke was that Johnny Rock didn't get out of bed in the morning for less than a hundred K. His mansion went for several mill, and everyone knew about the taxes in that neighborhood. Johnny's climate-controlled twenty-stall garage sheltered prime rides any serious classic ride fanatic would envy. A vintage Porsche. A '64 Aston Martin DB5. One of the very first '64 Mustangs ever made. A '68 Shelby, personally inspected by none other than Iacocca himself, and still in classic showroom condition. A Maserati. A Lamborghini. A '68 Jaguar XKE. A Rolls Royce Silver Phantom, for God's sake.

And he'd just called Nate to discuss a job.

146

Nate couldn't help feeling ecstatic as he took the silver Lexus up the winding drive leading to the front entrance of Johnny Rock's mansion.

**

Tiffany sat perfectly still, her senses taking in the eerie darkness lurking on the other side of the door.

"Tifferoo?" Chip's voice was barely above a whisper. "You look kinda freaked out right now. Something I should know about?"

"Not yet…"

Chip looked worried. He was about to say something else when she pressed her index finger to her lips and pointed to the front door.

She was convinced that a demon was out in the hall. Sensing the cold foulness, she somehow knew that this demon had come for her and Chip. Since she couldn't possibly know this demon's power, she thought it best to keep her thoughts vague.

She closed her eyes and concentrated on using her inner sight to view what was going on in the hall. It took only a few moments for the image to appear in her mind.

A sandy-haired man in a nice suit was leaning against the wall, his ear pressed against the plaster. Listening, obviously. Not bad looking, but his eyes were cold and dark, with a reddish glint emanating from their centers.

A demon, all right. This fiend stood there, his nostrils flared. She guessed that he was sniffing her fragrance.

147

Concentrating, she opened every sensory mechanism she could find within herself. The booming voice of Breath Mint

("track her down")

filling the demon's thoughts

("make sure you know exactly where she is when you call me back")

told her everything.

She focused even harder. In just moments, Breath Mint's voice conveyed the unmistakable message that the super demon wanted her badly, that he feared her, and that she and Chip were presently being hunted.

Her pulse racing, Tiffany opened her eyes.

"Tifferoo," Chip whispered nervously, "you look kinda scary. Sorta like how you were with the restaurant owner guy in Ohio. You know, all cockeyed, hot and messed up. Got anything to add? Or should I wait and read about it tomorrow morning in the paper?"

She got up from the couch. In a whisper, she said, "Just sit there, okay?"

Chip nodded.

"And don't move. Or talk. And try not to think about anything specific."

He gave her a subtle wink.

Tiffany silently crossed the living room and hurried to the door. As she moved, every fiber of her being had focused on the door. The demon was out there, but she strongly sensed that he might be considering walking away. It only stood to reason—especially if Breath Mint wanted her badly

148

enough to send others after them. She had to do this quickly, before the demon could slip away.

She rushed to the door. Then, holding her breath, yanked it open.

***

Bianca brought Nate McCormick a small brandy on a silver tray. He thanked her and experienced the usual sexual tension when she smiled back at him with her large doe eyes. As he watched her leave the room, he forced himself to concentrate on the powerful, well-connected man sitting behind the desk facing him. And tried to remember why he was here in the first place. It only took him moments to bring it all back into focus.

He'd been asked to come here for an urgent matter. Which meant serious money.

On the drive over, he tried hard to imagine the possible scenario. Although their phone conversation had been brief, he couldn't help forming a conclusion or two based on the few things Johnny had mentioned.

Urgent. Troublesome. Immediate attention.

It sounded like Johnny had stumbled into forbidden territory. Which stood to reason, considering how the man did business and who he dealt with.

And the moment Nate had entered the man's office, he knew he was on the right track.

Johnny sat stiffly at his desk, his elbows planted firmly on his blotter while he stared at the polished cherry box of imported cigars lying just a few inches beyond his clenched fists. Johnny was normally a laid-back type of guy. Dean Martin came into mind. Most of the time, Johnny kicked back, laughed, puffed away on a cigar and had a little wine—as if nothing could ruffle his feathers.

However, the image he projected right now suggested that he could be sitting on a live grenade and had no idea how to get up and walk away without setting it off.

Nate knew better than ask questions. Johnny was the one in control. The wisest thing Nate could do was to let Johnny do the honors. In his own way, and in his own time.

"How's the brandy?"

"Terrific, Mr. Rock."

Nodding, Johnny picked up a small glass of port wine. After all, the man was Italian; he'd been drinking wine ever since Nate had known him. Johnny had no doubt grown up with the stuff.

After a long sip, Johnny put the glass down and stared at it. He seemed deep in thought once again. Then he fixed his gaze on Nate. "I've got something for ya."

"I figured you might."

"This one could be a motherfucker."

Nate didn't respond. This could mean that they might be dealing with something way out of the park. Something Johnny obviously didn't want to face by himself. And since it was widely known that Johnny Rock prided himself on handling his own affairs, this problem, whatever it was, suggested something dangerous.

"Think you're up to it?"

Nate shrugged. Best be non-committal. "I won't know until you tell me what it is."

Johnny thought that one over.

Dealing with Johnny usually tended to be a pleasant experience. The man didn't tolerate bullshit. He talked the way he'd learned to communicate on the street and expected honesty and simplicity in return. If he suspected that you might be scamming him or leading him on, you were tossed out on your ear, no questions asked.

"Good answer," he finally said.

Nate had a sip of brandy and waited.

"When I tell you what's going on," Johnny said, "you're gonna think I'm drunk, mental, or the biggest bullshit artist on the face of the earth."

Nate knew better than respond.

Johnny had more wine. Then he got up and went over to the huge bay window facing the pool. He stood very still as he watched the activities. After nearly a minute, he took a breath. "What I'm about to tell you is gonna sound like I just went brain-dead after sitting through a damned *Twilight Zone* marathon."

"Are you trying to tell me this job will be weird?"

Johnny just sighed.

"Are you also saying that—"

"I don't know *what* the fuck I'm sayin'." Johnny spun around. His expression was a mix of fear and anger. "All I can tell you is what I know and what I've seen. I'm gonna show you what happened down there just a few hours ago, and then you can figure out for yourself what I'm dealin' with. Whatever this is, it's nothin' I ever saw

151

before. But when I tell ya what I think happened, you'll no doubt agree with me."

Nate was about to respond when Johnny went back to his desk, grabbed the remote and aimed it at the wall screen.

"What am I looking at?"

"Just watch. And then *you* tell *me*."

The screen turned bright with the pool party Johnny had already mentioned. The time and date displayed on the lower left-hand portion of the screen said that this had happened two hours and twenty-three minutes ago.

The screen displayed the usual pool activities. Splashing. Flirting. Puffing. Flexing. People and waiters wandering around the pool. Various stages of inebriation showing on the well-dressed guys standing in the shade of the recreation hall adjacent to the mansion...

The scene immediately shifted to the side gate, where two huge men in tight-fitting suits guarded their post just a few yards from the sidewalk, talking to someone in a suit.

"Sir... what's this all about?" Nate asked.

"Just keep watchin'."

A couple of minutes later, when Johnny froze the screen, Nate realized that he had no earthly idea what he had just witnessed.

***

Cameron Carnes couldn't take his eyes off the woman standing in the apartment doorway.

This lady looked nothing like the gorgeous young female rogue he'd been hunting. This woman's curly blond hair was obviously colored and a different shade. It was also not nearly as full.

However, the most important detail catching his eye was the fact that this woman was at least sixty years old. Although the right height, she was also extremely slender. She wore a loose-fitting gray sweater and maroon skirt that extended at least six inches below the knee, displaying her lean legs. Her shiny black open-toed casuals looked pricey. Carnes saw no jewelry other than a plain wristwatch on her left wrist and a sizeable rock on the third finger of her left hand. This woman was very attractive for her age and had relatively smooth skin. Other than some lipstick and just a hint of pencil work on her faint brows, she used very little makeup.

She smiled at him and said, "Yes, young man?" Her voice was very soft, somewhat high-pitched, but gentle. "And how may I help you?"

Perplexed and slightly embarrassed, Carnes found that he had nothing to say. But he knew he'd better say *some*thing, or this lady might get suspicious and call Security the moment he turned for the elevator.

"I'm sorry to bother you, ma'am, but I think I've got the wrong apartment."

"Which apartment were you looking for?"

"Well, I was looking for a man named Roger Banks—"

"Roger?" The lady's face lit up. "I'm Roger's Aunt Mildred. I met up with Roger just a few minutes ago. Just down the street, in fact. My car's parked about half a block away." She shrugged and reddened. "I'm sorry to say that I'm not very good with directions, so I have to call people to ask where I should go. I wasn't sure where my nephew lives, and I'm not at all very good with all this modern GPS stuff, but I found the right block and parked in the first available place I saw. I'm here from San Francisco, and we really don't get to see one another very much anymore. Isn't that just awful? I mean, when Roger was a little boy, he used to come and see me after school, when his family lived down the street from—"

"I'm really sorry to bother you..."

"It's no bother at all. Would you like to come in? Was Roger expecting you? Are you a business associate or something?"

Carnes risked a quick sniff but caught very little vanilla. The woman's minty perfume seemed overwhelming. "No, ma'am—"

"Roger does a lot of business, so I just assumed..." She shrugged. "But if you'd like to come in—"

"No, thank you, anyway..."

"It's no trouble at all. It's just him and myself, and also my daughter. We came to see him since a cousin of mine is arriving from London for a fashion show, so we decided to see if we could possibly—"

"No, thank you. And like I said, I'm really sorry to have bothered you."

She smiled. "I can't interest you in a cup of coffee? Or maybe some tea? Roger, the dear, isn't partial to tea, so I brought along some Earl Grey with me, and—"

154

"No, thanks again. I really do have to go."

The lady nodded.

He tried one last time to determine what was going on. Was this nice elderly woman the rogue? Had she shapeshifted?

He tried penetrating her thoughts by staring directly into her large blue eyes. Aside from an image of a man—Banks, no doubt, and a slim brunette, possibly the woman's daughter—he saw nothing, felt nothing.

"You have a very nice afternoon, young man." The woman held out her hand.

Carnes took it, flinching at its warmth. His embarrassment, most likely. He smiled back. His hand and arm remained warm and slightly tingly for several moments before returning to normal.

He boarded the elevator and struggled to figure out how he could have been so wrong about all this.

He had to tell the super demon that the two had disappeared. Since Braithwaite had told him how elusive and tricky the two were, that would be no surprise.

The car reached the lobby.

Carnes got out, pushed open the glass door, went outside and walked down to the end of the block. By the time he reached the stop sign, he realized that he had no idea who he was, where he was or what he was doing.

***

Somewhat confused, Nate McCormick sipped his brandy.

From what he had viewed on the screen, nothing about this job suggested anything weird or

155

supernatural. Yet Johnny was treating this as something snatched right out of a horror flick.

It was painfully obvious that Johnny was superstitious. The horseshoe plaque above the study door as well as one hanging over the doorway at the front entrance of the mansion substantiated this. Nate attributed this to Johnny's Italian upbringing. He'd known several successful Italians in his business dealings. Every single one of them had their own little ritual. The knocking on wood for luck. The sign of the cross when hearing of someone's passing, or when faced with some dilemma.

However, Nate had never suspected Johnny Rock, of all people, to let his irrational beliefs interfere with his business activities.

Johnny sat at his desk, staring at the remote in front of him. His lack of expression gave clear indication that he'd drifted into some sort of trance.

Nate thought it best to coax things along. "What's this really all about?" he asked. "I mean no disrespect, but what I just saw looks like a simple——"

"Nothin' simple about it," Johnny blurted out.

"But this makes no sense. I mean, this seems nothing more than——"

"Tell me what you think you saw."

Although Nate had no idea what had been spooking this man, he simply couldn't read anything sinister or mysterious about what had shown on the screen. "Your guards were talking to a well-dressed guy around forty with sandy hair.

156

Then one of them opened the gate and let him into the grounds. Case closed."

"Anything else?"

"Not that I could tell."

"Then I guess we need to turn the clock back a few minutes so you can see what went on before." Johnny picked up the remote and adjusted the time option.

Two shapely young women—one a brunette, the other a blonde—were talking to the two guards. The brunette was obviously flirting with one of the guards. The other guard pulled his cell out of his jacket pocket. The blonde said something. The guard abruptly pocketed his cell, turned and went over to the gate. He unlocked it, opened it, then let the women through.

"Well?" Johnny asked.

"Mr. Rock, if you're trying to tell me something other than what I'm seeing—"

"I'm givin' you the opportunity to shed some different light on what just happened."

"I can't—not if I just saw the same thing you saw."

Johnny Rock nodded. Then he leaned forward and reached for his wine glass.

Nate waited for the man to continue, but once again, there was a prolonged silence. Growing impatient, he said, "I wish you'd tell me why you think you need me…"

"Here's the job in a nutshell. I want ya to find those two babes. Then I want ya to find that guy. And when ya find 'em all, I want ya to bring 'em here. I need to talk to them."

"But what would make you think you'd need me when you can find out all this for yourself? All you have to do is talk to the two guards, and—"

Johnny sighed deeply. "I already had 'em up here."

"Okay…"

"They were standin' right there, in front of this desk. I asked 'em point blank why they let in three bodies that weren't invited to this shindig. Ya know what they said when I asked 'em what the hell was goin' on?"

Nate shrugged.

"I don't remember."

Nate could sense confusion and frustration in Johnny's eyes. "I don't understand. Are you saying you can't—"

"Not *me*, dammit! My *guards*! They can't remember *what* the fuck happened, even though it hadn't been long at all since they let the three bodies in. *Neither* of 'em had the time to work up a good story."

"You mean—"

"Somethin' weird's goin' on, and I wanna know what the fuck it is!"

"But—"

"It still bugs me half to death when I saw one of my guys pocket his cell right after that blonde said somethin' to him." He shrugged. "What the hell did she say? Why the hell did he pocket the damn thing when he shoulda been callin' me and askin' what should he do about this? Doesn't that bug you? It sure as hell bugs the tits off *me*!"

158

Nate didn't reply. But since Johnny had brought it up, it did seem curious.

"There's somethin'…strange…*real* strange…about that babe," Johnny said, his voice barely a whisper. "The blonde."

"Strange how?"

Johnny didn't reply. He was looking in Nate's direction but seemed to be staring at something else. Something that wasn't in the room.

"Mr. Rock?"

"I can't say. Not now, anyway…"

"But—"

"Not now, dammit…" His voice a whisper again.

Nate could tell something had spooked this man.

Johnny began staring at his wineglass once again. Nate could tell that he was trying to calm down. After nearly half a minute of silence, Johnny picked up his glass and drained it. "Here's the proposition." His voice had become louder. "This job pays ten grand. Ya in or out?"

Ten thousand dollars. For what would probably amount to a day or two of his time. Only an idiot would turn down a job that paid that much. "Well, I'm definitely in, but—"

"All right, then. I've already made a digital copy of those two little displays. Bianca will give 'em to ya when ya leave. *Capisc?*"

"Yes, sir…"

"Now do your damn job. Find 'em and bring 'em here. Then I can ask *them* what the fuck's goin' on and how they managed to turn my most loyal,

159

trusted guards into a pair of muscle heads without a brain cell between 'em!"

***

After changing back into her natural form, Tiffany went back to the sofa. Her pulse fluttering, she knew she had done well. There was no reason to feel stressed. After all, she'd just gotten rid of another demon and had done it without hurting him or anyone else.

This should have made her feel better. But somehow, it did not. She knew that nothing would satisfy her until she found the man responsible for her death. Coming back to this horrible place had been very stressful. She couldn't wait to finish her business and leave forever.

"Great catch, Tifferoosky." Chip's green eyes gleamed. "I'm impressed. And bedazzled. And taken aback. I think I've even got a lump developing in my throat area—or at least where my throat area should be—"

"Oh, stop." Tiffany wasn't in the mood for his wit. Besides, she didn't think she had done much. But it had been necessary. Dealing with another demon had interrupted their session with Roger Banks. "I couldn't let him see the real me—not if I wanted him to go away."

"What did you do this time? Is that dude anything like he was before you opened the door?"

"Well, I kind of…tweaked things. Just a little."

"Is he still in his right mind, so to speak?"

"I didn't do any permanent damage, if that's what you mean…"

160

"Hmmm... I take it you did your usual Mind-Vanishing Act, didn't you?"

"I wish you wouldn't call it that. All I did was make him forget about us once he went back outside."

"Ah. I get it. You kind of applied a little of this and a little of that, so he wouldn't remember what he was trying to do. And where he was trying to do it. Or why. Or who he was. Or where. Or why he was standing out there on the sidewalk, looking like a shithead and wondering why the sky was so blue."

"I figured that was the easiest way of handling the situation."

"So then, that's *not* mind-vanishing? Just a little mental distraction? Sort of like suggesting that the poor guy isn't really walking toward an open manhole cover? That the hole is just a black circle where someone spilled some paint onto the pavement?"

"It's not like that at all."

"I'm more than ready for the textbook version..."

"I consider it more of a gently-nudged forgetfulness than anything else."

"A gently-nudged forgetfulness. Not a gently-nudged mind sweep?"

"That sounds *so* cold-blooded."

Chip shook his head. "Not exactly something right out of Winnie the Pooh, you're saying?"

"*Must* you make something funny out of *everything*?"

161

"Tifferoo, I know I've said this to you before—
"

"Are you about to get nasty with me again?"

"*Moi*? Nasty? With *you*?"

"Yes. You. Chip. Nasty. With me. Tiffany. Every time I do something without actually *hurting* someone, you sound that way."

"Which way?"

"Nasty."

"How can I possibly be nasty with you? You're a certifiable badass."

"It's a very simple explanation. You try and make me feel guilty. You've already said that since I was in that horrible Dark Place, I must be a—"

"I know, I know. I might have said something once or twice about your being a…a…well, a demon."

"Yes. You shouldn't have, but you did." The thought of it caused the anger to come right back.

"I didn't want the neighborhood to think you didn't belong there."

"But I didn't!"

He didn't reply.

"I didn't…*did* I?"

"Not exactly…"

"What do you mean by *that*?"

"By what?"

"Don't act stupid, now…"

"You honestly think this is an *act*?"

Tiffany took a breath. Sometimes it was better not to say anything.

After a few moments, Chip said, "I haven't done it lately, have I?"

162

"No…"

"That sounds like one of those sentences with three dots after it."

"Why *haven't* you done it lately?"

"There are two—maybe three—really terrific reasons for that. First, you're *not* a demon. Second, I didn't know you at all when I first brought it up."

"What's the third?"

He shrugged. "I'm a dickhead."

Tiffany wanted to smile.

Chip nudged a thick strand of long raven hair away from his cheekbone. "The least you can do is disagree. Or at least attempt to argue…"

"But Chip…you *were* a dickhead…"

He looked hurt.

"I said *were*, didn't I?"

He grinned.

"Feel better now?"

"Good enough to do the head-spin."

She sighed, waiting for the inevitable. "Well?"

He shrugged. "Can't do that right now." He grabbed a handful of hair and held it straight out. "I'm liable to strangle myself."

"Good point. Besides, we've got more important things on our plate."

"Like Roger Dodger?"

The man remained sitting in the armchair, his eyes closed.

"Exactly. Now that we're alone and don't have to worry about further disturbances, let's work on this guy. There are things we need to find out."

"Affirmativo. I'm always game for a little fun and frolic."

Tiffany positioned herself directly in front of the sleeping man. She closed her eyes and projected her thoughts into the man's brain. *"How long have you been going to Johnny Rock's pool parties?"*

The man took a breath and said, *"Nearly a year."*

"Excellent. You will now show me the images of the people you dealt with at these parties about six months ago. You will show me these images slowly, and when I tell you to stop, you will do as I say and answer any question I ask. Do you understand?"

The man nodded.

"All right, then. Show me what's going on."

An avalanche of bleak memories immediately filled her head. Bikinis parading around the pool. Celebs in shorts and tank tops sipping umbrella drinks at the bar. She recognized three of the men who'd propositioned her openly for commercials on that fateful day. Johnny Rock in his study, watching the activities from his window while talking to a woman standing in front of his desk, holding an iPad. Another image of a celeb appeared, this one signing autographs on the street just beyond Johnny Rock's driveway. More images, this time with Roger Banks in his office, talking to two men in sports jackets.

"I'm interested only in the activities at the pool party," she reminded him.

The images vanished, replaced with more celebs and half a dozen young starlets in bikinis leaning against the bar, joking with a different barman and giggling while sipping mixed drinks and displaying their breasts.

A familiar face strolled by in a maroon bikini. A stab of ice tapped her at the base of her neck and then moved downward.

Stacy Burton. Tiffany remembered Stacy from when she'd first arrived in Hollywood. Just a week or so before Tiffany had gotten off the bus, Stacy had landed a job as an extra in a Spielberg movie and was advertising for a roommate to share living expenses. To make ends meet, Tiffany started working as a waitress in a diner on Sunset Boulevard and found an agent a couple of weeks later. Convinced her luck was about to change, she spotted Stacey's ad and agreed to share expenses while the two went pounding on doors.

This was getting dangerously close to the time frame she'd been searching for. While viewing images of Stacy, Tiffany feared that that it wouldn't be much longer before the fateful day would soon appear.

She didn't know if she could take much more of this.

Do I have a choice? she asked herself.

Why have you come here? asked another voice.

You know the answer to that, she replied to the awful voice.

But will you be able to do this?

She didn't know. But she had to try.

It took her more tense moments to gather enough courage to find her voice. She had to dig deep, but she managed. "*Do you know who that girl is?*" she finally asked Roger Banks.

165

"No, but she wasn't very nice."

"What makes you say that?"

"She didn't like me."

"Did she arrive at the party with anyone else?"

Roger was silent for a moment. *"Another blonde."*

Tiffany cringed as the ice slivers dug in deeper. This was becoming much more difficult than she ever thought possible. It took her considerable effort to ask her next question. *"Who was this...blonde?"*

"I never knew. She left the party too soon."

She had to take a few breaths to find her voice again. She was *so* close...so painfully close... *"Do you know why...why she left?"*

"She...got sick. They took her away. In an ambulance."

Tiffany sat back. Everything had quickly become intolerable. She fought down the nausea as well as the disgust. *I have to do this*, she reminded herself. *It has to be done. I've come all this way. I must find out what happened.*

"Tifferoo?" Chip sounded uneasy. "How goes the interrogation? No offense, but you look kind of messed up and—"

"I know. But I have to do this."

He said nothing.

She took another deep breath and turned back to Roger. *"This blonde. Did you see her with anyone? Before she got sick?"*

Roger went silent. Tiffany wondered if he had drifted off into a deeper trance. He finally said, *"There was a guy. One of the TV hopefuls Johnny*

166

had invited. He just wouldn't leave her alone. He wanted...you could tell he wanted to get in her pants." Roger smiled. *"I couldn't blame him. Every guy there was drooling over her."*

Tiffany felt the tension oozing back. This was difficult, but she was much too close to stop. *"What...was his name?"*

Roger went silent.

"His name? Please?"

More silence.

"Did you know him?"

Roger shook his head.

"You don't remember his name?"

Roger sighed. *"Richard, I think. Or maybe it was Richards. Something like that."*

"How about his first name?"

Roger thought about that for a few moments and shook his head.

"Any idea where he works?"

"He works out of one of the talent agencies in town."

"Any idea which one it was?"

"One of the biggies. LA Models. Or Starlight. Global One, maybe. Now that I'm thinking of it, I might have heard him or someone else mention Goldcrest."

Goldcrest. She remembered that one because it was tied in with big sponsors of reality shows.

The tension had grown unbearable, but she forced herself to continue. There could be no chance for error—not for this. This would be the toughest step of all. But it had to be done.

"Show me his face."

Roger hesitated.

"Why won't you show me?"

"Not sure...not sure..."

Tiffany went back and penetrated the man's thoughts, this time more vigorously than before. More images. Stacy again. Then Johnny Rock. Then—

The man's face popped up, filling the picture screen in Roger Banks' head.

The darkness grew, and in moments enveloped her. An intense heat came with the darkness, bringing back the nausea. Then a heavy sourness. Then more nausea. Then...

A strange pasture with colors that just didn't seem right. Colors that were all wrong. Grays and browns where greens and yellows and golds should have been. Then...a wall of blackness. And then something wrapping around her, pulling her back, until—

Surrendering to the darkness, Tiffany closed her eyes, moaned weakly...

And collapsed.

***

"Calling Tifferoosky...come out, come out, wherever you are..."

She opened her eyes. Chip had changed back into his original form. Roger Banks remained in the armchair, his body relaxed, his eyes closed. The panoramic view of the Hollywood hills just beyond the window hadn't changed. Neither had the furniture in the apartment. In fact, the room itself looked exactly the same. But everything felt different.

What *had* changed?

I went back...

She'd gone back to the past. To the pool party. And glimpsed the man who had slipped her the fatal drink. And once again experienced the cold, bleak darkness that had overwhelmed her after she'd sipped whatever poison had been put into her glass.

The darkness seemed to be the key to all this. It proved the most important—and most frightening—element of all. The darkness was significant because of what had happened right after. The fact that she'd awakened somewhere in the woods down a weed-covered hill brought the nightmare back. Every single aspect of the horror came right back with it. The strange colors in the pasture. The wall of darkness looming behind her. The bizarre sensation of being sucked toward the wall. And, despite her struggle to pull away from it, the invisible force that held her fast.

And then, the most terrifying aspect of all...

The rustling sound of someone behind her, grabbing her and pulling her closer to the wall...into the darkness...and the strange, foul-smelling woods just beyond...

Into the land of forgotten souls.

A place called the Meddaworld.

And, finally, facing the vile creature that had pulled her into that horrible, dismal, sour-smelling place. The leering, slobbering spirit she'd originally thought was the actor, Lee Van Cleef. The dark spirit who turned out to be the appalling subordinate demon known as Gutril, who'd pulled

169

her into the Meddaworld, then the Dark Place, because he was bored—and horny—and wanted to party. The same demon that had gone right into her head and yanked out images she'd kept hidden inside her consciousness all her mortal life. Images she'd never wanted anyone else to know about. Treasured thoughts that had always been close and personal to her, and meant a great deal to her...

Personal reflections she'd collected as a small child growing up in Peoria, years before her father died in the hunting accident that would destroy her childhood and forever change the rest of her life.

Treasured memories and images she'd always associated with the childhood that had been so happy when her father was alive. Things that, to her, had meant family. And love. And happiness. And togetherness. And everything that would always be good and wonderful in life.

Her life. That very same existence that had been snatched away from her in one single moment, when she'd sipped a drink from the handsome monster in the expensive suit who'd smiled brightly and told her he knew powerful, influential people, and then promised that he'd introduce her to them so they could do wonderful things for her and her career.

"Tifferoo?"

Reality again.

She rubbed her eyes and kept them closed, hoping that things would be different when she opened them again. She'd be alive again. Without memories of demons or the Dark Place. Without enduring the constant anguish of having lost her life at a very young age and facing the grim future of battling demons. Peace sounded so wonderful. Peace and tranquility, without endlessly fighting evil and hatred.

Then, once harsh reality had nudged back into her consciousness, she realized things were not nearly as bleak as they should have been. She'd escaped the Meddaworld and the Dark Place and had returned to the mortal world. She was dead, but doing good by helping people, and for some strange reason she could not possibly understand, she could instantly recognize evil and demons. And, with this knowledge, she could always triumph over them.

She had powers. All sorts of powers. Powers no mortal would ever have. And even though she could never experience a lasting romance with a mortal, she would never forget that she'd once loved one. This love had been doomed from the start, but she'd handled it very well, and if she'd done things the right way, the man she'd walked away from would be happy and content for the rest of his life.

"Calling Tifferoosky again... Where have you gone, faithful friend, luscious babe, and notorious butt-kicker?

Chip again. Her one true friend. He was concerned and obviously worried. But there was no need. Not really. Once she'd settled her account here, she'd be all right. She and Chip could leave this horrible town, go back to Peoria and take care of her mother.

She smiled at Chip. "I'm okay," she told him.

"Cool beans. For a moment I thought that maybe you'd gone back there and—"

"I did go back."

He blinked. "If you went back, you must have gone through the whole thing again. Is that what happened? Did it bring everything back?"

"Yes."

"Then it brought back the hurt."

"Yes."

"And the anger."

"Especially the anger."

"You saw him, didn't you?"

"Pardon?"

"You know what I mean, so stop pulling that dumb blonde bit. I know you, Tifferoo. You're anything *but* dumb. Besides, you shouldn't hide things from me. Not at this stage."

He was right. They'd been through too much together. It would be so very wrong to keep secrets from him.

"Tifferoosky? Come on out again, your public awaits you…"

She thought for a moment. And when the images came back, she knew right then that she had to confide in him. And when she looked at him again, she didn't see a silly-looking redheaded idiot who could spin his head around like a top, wiggle his ears, or make his tongue drop to the floor. Instead, she saw something else. Something much more important.

Chip would never let her down. And aside from his crudeness and nonsensical humor, he was

172

the best friend she could ever have in this or any other life.

The same friend she loved and respected.

The same friend who had helped her rid the mortal world of Gutril. And Andras. And Keenan V. Durant. And Daniel D. Lyon. And even though she'd singlehandedly done in the demon from the diner as well as the one known as the Brain-Eater, she knew she couldn't have done any of it all by herself.

"I saw him," she finally told him.

"You actually *saw* the dude?"

"He wasn't a *dude*. He was a monster! A fiend!"

Chip waited a few moments before speaking again. "What'd he look like?"

"Just as I remembered." The image turned her vision a bright red, blinding her with rage. She rubbed her eyes and struggled to focus. "Tall. Well-dressed. Good-looking. Impeccably groomed. Not one single disgusting brown hair out of place." She took a breath. "He looked like…like he belonged on a magazine cover."

"That doesn't sound like a monster—or fiend—to me, anyway. In fact, he sounds more like one of those stars on those sappy lawyer TV shows. Or one of those guys they use to sell pricey cars—"

"He *killed* me, Chip!" She knew that if she weren't dead already, the nausea and vertigo exploding through her would have given her a heart attack. She took a few more breaths. "He wanted me in the sack, so he got whatever he needed to drug me so he could—so he could—"

173

"I getcha."

She sighed. Feeling drained, she lay back on the sofa and closed her eyes. She had to send the fury away. To release every drop of negativity and hatred from her spirit. She didn't want anything ruining her plan or distracting her.

All I need now, she thought as her nerves settled down, *is some idea of where this monster lives.*

"So what's next, Babykins?"

She shrugged. "It's very simple. I have to find him."

"*Finding* this guy? In *this* town? *Simple*?"

"I said what we do next will be simple. I didn't say finding him will be."

"Ah. Some irritating philosophy from the golden-haired kickass."

"*Please* don't call me that."

"That's what you are."

"I just don't like thinking of myself like that."

"Then why do I think of you like that?"

"Because you're crazy?"

"That's kind of harsh, ya know..."

"Did I speak inappropriately?"

"I guess not...not really..."

"Then why was that harsh?"

"You want an answer now? Or can I have a little time to think up a really crackerjack reply?"

"No. You can't."

"All righty-rooty, then. Let's get back to what we're doing. I have the strangest feeling that I've somehow lost the thread of our exchange."

"I don't."

174

"My…we really *are* harsh, aren't we?"

She took a breath. This senseless banter was getting them nowhere. "Listen… I only know that we're a lot closer than we were before."

"And?"

"I have absolutely no idea what I'll do when I actually find the guy."

"I thought you were gonna—"

"Like I said, I have no idea."

"All righty, but don't forget, I'm in this, too. Five-oh, five-oh—all that sort of all-for-one-and-one-for-all cuddly bullshit."

"I haven't forgotten." She got up and took one last look at the panoramic view. The sun was still bright, and the hills in the distance shined like glittering gems beneath the clear blue sky.

"What about Roger Rabbit over here?" Chip jabbed a thumb at the zoned-out man in the chair.

She regarded him for a few moments. "I guess I'd better snap him out of it."

"Or at least make sure you arrange to have the maid come in every few days to dust him off."

She sat back down. Roger's expression was blank. Any other person would have considered him dead or comatose.

"You're not gonna kill him, are ya? Turn him into worm food? Or some tasteless pillow arrangement?"

"You're not serious."

He shrugged. "The mood you're in right now? I wouldn't put anything—"

"I don't *kill* people, Chip. I don't even hurt them if I can help it. You more than anyone should

175

know that by now. I'm just gonna bring him back. But I'm also gonna make sure he doesn't remember us."

"That's *it*?" He sounded disappointed.

She gave him a half smile. "I might coax him to donate most of his earnings to St. Jude—or maybe the Shriners, or the Humane Society."

Chip just shook his head.

"Something wrong about that?"

"Well?"

"You don't want extra money helping puppies find a home?"

"I *love* puppies."

"Then what's the problem?"

"Just that a demon wouldn't—"

"Are you by any chance calling me a *demon*?"

He stiffened. "Sorry, Tifferoo. A slip of the tongue. You know me. A trickster for all occasions, but not exactly someone known for carrying around an overabundance of actual finesse."

"Good answer."

PART 2

JUSTICE

CHAPTER 4 - THE THIRD DEMON

Dressed in his street garb—sunglasses, shorts, athletic shoes and tank top—Jose Bribon wandered down Hollywood & Vine, past the homeless and the stone heads lurking in doorways and alleys, as he searched for his next victim.

In his view, suckering mortals was much more entertaining here than down in the Dark Place, when he was known as Nequam, or, "The Rascal." Mortals were much less formidable—or vengeful—than demons. Although every bit as nasty as doomed spirits, mortals had no powers, making retaliation minimal and, in many case, laughable. In the Dark Place, it was much more difficult to do a nasty trick to a demon. But since there were less of them down there than up here, finding an idiot mortal to torment always turned out to be endless fun. And after spending three hundred years as an inferior in the Dark Place, Nequam had been more than happy to take his place up here to help Balberith turn this mecca of flesh, fantasy and broken dreams into a breeding ground for sin, pain and degradation.

At the next intersection, a skinny redheaded young babe in a short skirt, bikini top, and six-inch wedgies waited at the light. Her head was turned as she tried ignoring two buzz cuts at the curb, yelling obscene suggestions from a copper convertible.

Jose wanted to laugh. Mortals loved setting themselves up. It was all he could do to keep up with the busywork.

He moved over to the redhead and stopped about a foot away. While she tried her best to ignore the horny morons in the convertible, he used his special mental talents to loosen the strap of her handbag. About ten seconds later, the bag dropped to the pavement, snapping open and spilling its contents. Gasping, she bent over to retrieve her belongings. In the process, her pink laced panties were exposed.

A symphony of whistling and catcalls followed. The two buzz cuts applauded and howled laughter. Jose turned toward them and applied a strong mental suggestion. The driver's foot immediately slipped from the brake. The convertible lurched forward, slamming into a passing tour bus. The bus jerked to a stop just as a crossing pedestrian tried zigzagging out of the way, bumping into the white Lexus stopped behind the convertible. Jose focused on the pedestrian. Seconds later, the youngish man dropped his briefcase. It bounced off the bumper of the Lexus and cracked open. Papers and brown folders flew upward, sailing in the air, fluttering back down to the pavement like dying birds and sliding quietly beneath the convertible and the bus.

Grinning, Jose dodged the gathering crowd and crossed at the light. He stepped up to the curb and

178

glanced at his watch. 2:30. Time for coffee and a sweet roll or two before heading down to the Barrio for more interesting challenges. Perhaps a nasty coffee spill at one of the outside cafes. Or an oldster breaking her hip after falling on a blot of icing smeared on the pavement outside a bodega.

Jose chuckled when he thought of all the business he'd sent to the local hospitals and emergency wards in the last seventy years.

Down the block, Paco's Pastries & Refreshments seemed just the place for a quick respite. The Hispanic-run eatery was well-known for its goodies—as well as its known connection with one or two of the local gangs. While inside, he could tune up one of the *turistas* for an added giggle. Or have one of the cooks sneeze at the wrong moment and hurl a hot pan of freshly-baked rolls at a bunch of unsuspecting customers.

Mortals were fun to torment.

His cell buzzed. He pulled it out of his side pocket and checked the display.

And cringed.

The number was the special exchange Balberith had assigned him when the super gave him his cell a decade or so earlier. But although Balberith had gone back down, Jose's direct line to HELL 9-9-9, connected from *6, plus his own personal four-digit code, was still valid. This call was from Tampa, Florida, where Balberith's successor was now living.

Dios mio, he thought with a shudder. Was this indeed him? The Big Man? *Numero uno*?

Braithwaite the Horrible? The monster of terror, who was notorious for explosions and mass murder?

His logic came into play, prompting his inner voice to step right in. *If this truly is Braithwaite, this voice said, you'd better answer right now. You really don't want to get on his bad side...*

His hands trembled as he pressed *TALK* and lifted the cell to his right ear. "This is...this is Nequam," he said in a soft, trembling voice.

"This is Daniel Grove calling from Tampa." It was a calm, understated voice. Definitely not Braithwaite. Jose could feel the chill easing up. "I'm calling on behalf of my employer, Mr. Brett Waite, who wishes to talk to you as soon as possible. Am I speaking to the right individual?"

Brett Waite. The mortal name Braithwaite had picked for his hundred-year reign.

"Y-Yes..." The chill returned, as well as the trembling. *Pull it together. You've been doing your job ever since you were brought back up. A damned fine job—and you've been doing it for seventy years. You've got nothing to worry about. Nothing! Pull yourself together and get those cojones working again!* Jose took a breath and struggled to chill. "This is...this is...yes...I am...I'm Nequam."

"Mr., er, Nequam, I'm about to put Mr. Waite on the line. Are you able to talk freely?"

Jose pressed his back to the brick building and waited for his nerves to calm down. This was scary, no matter how you sliced the pie. But he had to do it.

Get those cojones working!

180

"*Si*. Yes. I can talk."

Click!

Jose felt the cheeks of his buttocks tightening when he heard the loud click. He was about to yell at himself again when the booming voice invaded his head.

"This is Brett Waite. What the hell are you calling yourself up here?"

Jose took another breath. He wanted to reply but immediately discovered that his voice was nowhere to be found.

"You still there? I can't hear you worth a shit!"

"Y-Yes, sir! I-I-I'm here!" *C'mon, man! Get a grip!* "B-Bad connection, sir. I've got it covered now."

"Fucking cell phones... I told Asmodeus and those other assholes down there in Hades City that random scraps of cheap plastic would be worthless. I've got a hundred years to destroy things up here, and I don't want this goddamned technology shit to interfere with my fun." He paused to noisily clear his throat. Jose jerked the cell away from his ear. "All right, then. Let's get back to business. Answer my goddamn question."

Jose nearly panicked when he discovered that he was suffering a sudden memory loss. *Answer my goddamn question.* What the hell *was* the question?

Once again, his inner voice came into play. *Your name, you idiot! He asked your mortal name!*

"B-Bribon, sir. My mortal name is Jose Bribon."

"Bribon? How the hell do you spell that?"

Jose spelled it for him.

181

"What the hell *is* that? Spanish?"

"Yes, sir."

"What's it mean?"

"Rascal."

"Ah. Like Nequam."

"Yes, sir."

"I take it you're one of the illegals fucking up that state?"

"Yes, sir."

"Working with anyone at the moment?"

"No, sir."

"What the hell *are* you doing, then?"

"Right now?"

"No, dammit. Twenty years from now. Of course, right now!"

Jose swallowed a lump and forced himself to struggle through this. "Collecting Social Security, Unemployment checks, Food Stamps, and all that other good shit this government loves tossing at their illegals."

"Sounds good."

"It's easy work, sir."

"What did you do before you were sent down below?"

"I was in Mexico, tormenting the Catholics."

"Interesting work?"

"Yes, sir. I was playing tricks and pranks on them for years before Carlos III, the King of Spain at the time, ordered an entire congregation of us to be gathered up, lined up in front of a wall, and shot. Apparently they thought I was a member, but all I did was supply the drinking water for the pastors of the church."

182

"That's *all* you did?"

"Well, I added stuff to the drinking water to make them sick. Sometimes things I found growing wild in the fields made them crazy. I had a lot of fun doing it."

"And now you're working on Californians?"

"Yes, sir."

"You did say Carlos III?"

"Yes, sir."

"I believe he's been a sub down there for some time."

"Yes, sir."

"He recognize you?"

"No, sir. I stayed clear."

"Good strategy. I've heard that he's still looking for Catholics down there but has been having some trouble. Seems most of the Catholics have been sent to the other side."

"I've heard that, too."

"Anyway, I've got an important job for you."

"I'm up to it, sir."

"Don't be so goddamned cocksure of yourself. This won't be easy. In fact, it'll probably be the hardest thing you've ever done. I want you to find two rogues roaming around your area."

"Two rogues, sir?"

"That's what I just said."

"Inferiors?"

"One of them is. I'm not quite sure about the other."

"I...I don't think I understand."

"How are you with the ladies?"

"They like me, sir."

"You like them?"

"Very much."

"How about blondes?"

Jose grinned. "*Love* blondes."

"All right, then. But like I just said, this won't be easy. This blonde and her stinkweed partner have already sent at least four subs back down to Hades, and I just got word that two more working in your area were also sent down in the last couple of hours."

"Two *subs*?"

"Seems like it. This blond bitch has been a thorn in my side ever since I came up here. I won't rest until she's caught and sent back down. Actually, I know of at least eight subs and three or four supers who would salivate over this bitch. As I've already said, this job will possibly be your most difficult. If you accomplish it, I'll be grateful. This'll mean a lot—especially if you decide somewhere down the line that you'd like more powers. Get the pic?"

He couldn't help feeling the excitement. Impressing Braithwaite would be the ultimate triumph.

"I *said*, got it?"

"Yes, sir."

"All right, then. I'm about to give you the details. Make sure you listen to every word I say. You've no doubt already heard that I hate repeating myself."

"Yes, sir…"

"Okay. Now listen carefully…"

***

Tiffany and Chip entered the glittering glass-covered twenty-story building on Santa Monica Boulevard. The floor of the lobby consisted of large squares of ceramic tile. Potted plants and several pieces of modern sculpture of birds in flight lined the wall facing the street. The directory covered a large section of the wall next to the elevators.

"Why are we here, Tifferoo?"

"Guess."

He glanced at the sculpture. "You brought us here because these birds remind you of how we got rid of that asshole Andras in Pittsburgh?"

"Not exactly."

"Remember how we got the birds to shit on his head? How pissed he was when—"

"Of course I do…"

"And how I was able to nail his ass when the bird shit got in his eyes and he couldn't see much of anything—"

"Yes…but that's *not* why we're here."

"Let me see… You brought us here because this building brings back a shitload of fond memories about—"

"Nope."

He shrugged. "I guess I'm plumb out of ideas."

"*There's* a first."

"Be patient with me, Honey Bunny. I have issues."

"Now *there's* an understatement."

"Are you gonna stand here and insult me all day? Or are you gonna tell me why I'm standing here with you when I could've been back there with Roger Dodger, tormenting the crap out of—"

185

"Goldcrest Talents."

"What about it?"

Tiffany scanned the columns of business firms on the wall. The firm's name, listed under G, was the third entry in the second row, about halfway down. The number 812 next to it suggested that it was located on the eighth floor.

Tiffany felt a stab of anger. "Roger didn't know Richards' first name, but he did have an idea where the man worked. He mentioned four agencies he thought would be our best bet. This was one of them. I remember coming here when I first came to town, so I decided to try it first. It specializes in reality shows, so…"

"How'd you do? When you came here, I mean."

"They wouldn't even talk to me."

"Why the hell not?"

"They said they were too busy to take on any unknown talent."

"Did you look like you do now?"

"Of course."

"And they didn't get all turned on and stupid? We're talking *guys*, here, aren't we?"

"The receptionist was a female."

"Figures."

"Whaddya mean?"

"Go find a handy mirror, Tifferoo. We just stepped in rabid jealousy territory—in case you don't know what I'm talking about."

"But the agents were all guys."

"You didn't get to meet any of them?"

"No."

"What did the receptionist look like?"

"Pretty. Young. Well-dressed."

"Like I just said. Jealousy territory. She was probably intimidated."

"I don't think it would've mattered even if I *had* seen them."

"We're still talking guys, right?"

"Yes."

"You don't think they would have salivated? Or at least started breathing funny? Fidgeting? Squirming around?"

"Why would they?"

Chip blinked. "Honey Bunny....how would you explain *my* behavior?"

"You're silly. Ridiculous. Funny, but also nasty and insulting. And so totally weird sometimes that I—"

"I think that just about does it. And thanks for the character analysis."

"You asked."

Chip frowned.

"Am I wrong?"

"Well, no..."

"Then what are we talking about? And why are you looking so hurt? I only said what you already know..."

"Yeah, you did."

"You *are* getting better, though..."

"A lot?"

"Maybe. But forget all that for right now and focus." Tiffany was getting tired of this. It was time to move on. "We need to find that monster. The sooner, the better."

"I know."

"I'm *so* glad you're on board."

He was silent as he followed her to the elevator.

***

The Goldcrest offices took up the entire eighth floor of the building. The reception area was visible through the glass wall at the far end of the hall.

Chip pushed open the heavy glass door and followed Tiffany in. A well-dressed, brown-haired receptionist in her forties smelling of lilacs smiled at Tiffany as they approached her desk.

"Hello," she said brightly. "Welcome to Goldcrest Talents. How might I help you?"

It took Tiffany a few moments to collect herself. Although it had only been three years since she had come here for the first time, it seemed like a lifetime had passed. "I'm looking for someone who uses this agency. He's an actor. He's around thirty-five, good-looking—"

"That describes most of the gentlemen who have been retained by our agency." The woman gave a slight shrug. "Could you please be just a pinch more specific?"

Tiffany forced herself to stay composed. "About six months ago, this man…was chosen…to be a contestant on a reality show. As I remember him telling me, the show was "Pick a Bachelor," or something like that. He's about six feet tall, with reddish-brown hair, blue eyes—"

"That sounds like Alan Richards," the receptionist said after a moment or two.

Alan Richards. The mere utterance of the name brought about another stab of hot anger. Roger Banks had been right. And the name seemed to fit the face. The face of the man who had calmly destroyed her life grew even clearer in her mind.

The more she thought of it, the more ironic it sounded. It was a quiet, unassuming name. A very common name.

Not the sort of moniker you'd associate with someone responsible for killing you.

Names really meant nothing. Not when it came to murder. Many of the most notorious murderers in history had quiet, common names. John. Lee. Ted. Charles. Jeffrey. Timothy.

"A-Alan R-Richards?" Tiffany could barely get it out of her throat without choking.

The receptionist smiled. "I believe Mr. Richards could be the gentleman you're looking for." Her forehead quickly wrinkled up. "Unfortunately, our contract with Mr. Richards didn't pan out, and our agency cancelled him and severed ties."

"Just like that?"

"This is an extremely competitive business. Our contract, I believe, was limited to his run with the show. And since the program chose not to further utilize his talents—"

"You're telling me he is no longer among your list of clients?"

"I'm sorry, but Mr. Richards hasn't been with us for at least five months."

Tiffany felt a sharp twinge of disappointment. "He…he just *left*?"

189

"Yes."

"Can you tell me *why* the show severed ties with him?"

"I'm sorry, but I really don't know the details. From what I've been told, he apparently experienced some sort of personal setback, which forced him to bow out of the competition and future projects, as well."

That made her feel somewhat better. A "setback." To Tiffany, this meant that they might know where he was.

"Do you know if he's coming back?"

"I'm very sorry, but the matter was kept quiet. I honestly hope you haven't been inconvenienced in any way. Is there something else I can help you with?"

Inconvenienced. Tiffany wanted to smile and scream at the same time. Being murdered could certainly be considered an inconvenience. But this lady hadn't been involved, so there was no reason to put her through any unnecessary torment.

Chill. And stay focused. "Would it be possible for me to talk to someone else working here, then?" she asked.

The receptionist opened the large leather-bound black book lying in front of her. "And what would this be about, if I may ask? Mr. Richards? Or some other matter?"

"I'm—that is, we—" she gestured to Chip "—specialize in magic, and I was told Goldcrest might be interested in our act."

"Magic?" The woman slipped on her tiny reading glasses and consulted her book. She turned

190

a page, then another page. "I'm very sorry, but it doesn't look like any of our agents are presently available to—"

"*Someone will be available right now*," Tiffany sent over to the woman.

She abruptly stopped scanning the list. "Excuse me, but I stand corrected. Actually, I do believe Mr. Roland might be available to talk to you for a few minutes. He has a three o'clock, but I'm sure he might be able to squeeze you in."

"Mr. Roland?"

"He's our General Manager, but he also handles a small list of special clients. And it looks like he'll be free in a few minutes."

"Does he know Mr. Richards?"

"I'm sure he does. Mr. Roland started up this firm nine years ago, and he personally discovered Mr. Richards, so—"

"So then, we can see Mr. Roland very shortly?"

"I'll send him a text. What is the name of your act?"

"Well, we've been in the process of selecting one."

She closed her book, took off her glasses and frowned. "In other words, you're not exactly an *established* act?"

"Well, no, but we did perform a highly successful routine in a children's hospital in Peoria a little while ago…"

"I'm very sorry. This firm handles only established—"

"We're really terrificoso," Chip said, stepping up beside Tiffany.

191

The receptionist looked him over as if noticing him for the first time. Then she scowled.

"*You might have to win her over*," Tiffany sent over to him.

"*Does it matter how?*" he asked.

"*Just make it good. We don't want to stay here any longer than we have to.*"

"*All righty rooty. One dynamite, very effective trick coming right up!*" He grinned at the receptionist. "You'll definitely be impressed."

"As I just said, uh, sir, this firm represents only—"

Chip immediately elevated himself until he was suspended two feet from the floor.

The receptionist sat back sharply as if she'd been shoved. Her eyes bulged. Her jaw dropped. She turned pale. A strange squeal trickled out of her throat.

"Wow…" Chip was staring at the ceiling fan positioned directly above the woman's desk. "You can really see things better up here. One bad thingy, though… I can tell that the cleaning crew doesn't really care much for dusting off the fan blades."

"Do we get to see Mr. Roland?" Tiffany asked. "Or do you want my partner to make his head pop off and roll down the hall? Believe me, you don't want to see something like that. The last time it happened, it took us nearly half an hour to find it and put it back on right so he wouldn't throw up each time he sneezed. Take my word on this, it isn't a pretty sight. It also gets a tad messy—especially if he's eaten something soft."

Chip chuckled, glanced at Tiffany and winked. Then he lowered himself slowly to the carpet.

Still very pale, the receptionist clumsily snatched up her phone.

***

Nate McCormick left Johnny Rock's estate feeling both confused and exhilarated. Ten grand for just a few hours of his time was something he'd never expected. Other than the big jobs, those using his most trusted men to protect divas and celebs, the most he'd ever earned for something he'd handled solo was five K, which took several days and involved getting dangerously close to one of Colombia's drug cartels.

This, however, felt totally different. As far as he knew, it had nothing whatsoever to do with the cartel or any other illegal association. Judging by the information Johnny had provided, this involved finding and bringing three people who had crashed Johnny Rock's pool party back to the mansion.

Nate was confident that he could handle this one without too much difficulty. He'd have to employ a couple of his strongarms to help him, but they could easily be brought into this for five hundred apiece. He might even have to rely on one of his street CI's to ask around, but that only meant another two or three hundred.

In this case, he decided to try one of his own personal assets to get the ball rolling and save time. This, of course, required him to contact the detective agency he had helped set up for his brother-in-law, Robert Sothern. Sothern, the stupid shit, had bailed on Nate's sister less than a year after the wedding. Sothern had decided to spend his early retirement in beautiful Belize with a couple of the local hookers rather than share a productive life in Hollywood with Andrea. But even so, the agency had been doing quite well the last three years.

Nate entered the offices of Caldwell Investigative Services a little after three o'clock. After a brief but very pleasant exchange with Alana, the attractive blond receptionist, he was invited to the office of Bill Caldwell, the agency's President & CEO.

Blue-eyed and wearing a blond brush cut, Caldwell, standing at a towering six-five, looked ten years younger than his fifty years. Grinning widely, he welcomed Nate with a vigorous handshake. "Nate, my man! How's life been treating ya and why the hell are you here?"

Nate laughed. Caldwell had always been the in-your-face type. He pulled no punches and would not tolerate being lied to. It was no wonder the agency had been doing so well.

"Life's just fine, Billy. I'm here to see if you can still deliver what your ads promise."

"Figured this wasn't social. Or a clumsy ploy just to get in my secretary's pants. Have a seat." He gestured. "Take the load off and give me the poop."

Nate sat. "It's like this. I've just been handed this gravy job, but I think I might need a helping hand from one of your boys to help me work my way through it."

Caldwell sat back. "What's this involve?"

"Maybe an hour or so of street surveillance."

"For what?"

194

"A blond beauty and her brunette friend—also a beauty."

"Rough work," Caldwell said with a slight grin.

"Yeah, but someone's got to do it."

"What exactly are we talking about? Extortion? Hookers? Fugitives?"

"I'm not quite sure. Neither is my employer."

"Then let's make this simple so my aging mind can come to grips with the picture. Just tell me who's handling the money and I'll take it from there."

"I wouldn't normally consider divulging that information."

"You sound like you're dying to tell me."

"I am." He shrugged. "Ethics, ya know…"

"Fuck ethics. We're talking money here. Probably *big* money. Besides, we're friends, aren't we? And if this is gonna be a joint venture, I should know just what I'm getting into."

"That's right. You should."

"Then tell me what the hell's going on."

"Johnny Rock's the client."

Caldwell regarded his friend in total silence. Nate could tell what he was thinking. Money. Influence. Babes and celebs. Publicity. Also, corruption and high-profile extortion.

"I can hear those heavy-duty gears grinding," Nate said.

"I've been working on fixing that, but at my age, things don't move as smoothly as they once did."

"Any questions you'd like to ask right off?"

195

"Several. But at least now I can assume what you meant by a gravy job."

"I hear ya."

"And with Johnny Rock, it always comes down to big money."

"Five figures for just a day or so of my time."

Caldwell nodded. "Then I must also assume that this blonde and her friend might have ruffled a few of the big man's feathers."

"Apparently they pissed off Johnny by showing up uninvited at his latest shindig."

Caldwell didn't speak right off. Then he shrugged. "And he's footing this hefty bill just for a simple gate crash?"

"That's what I've gathered."

"Well, everyone knows how possessive he is about his parties."

"He's been paying a small fortune just for security, software and hardware for the last several years."

"Well, since this entire county knows about him, I must also assume that these two females were also aware of his policy."

"No doubt."

"What else have you gathered? That is, from what he *hasn't* told you?"

"He's obviously hiding things from me, but since he's footing the bill for this job, I don't want to upset the works by questioning him about what it is he clearly doesn't want to share."

"Nothing else, then?"

"Just one, but it's something I can't put my finger on."

"Go ahead and spill it anyway."

"Something about one of the women has got the man spooked."

"Spooked how?"

"I'm not sure, but it's one of those things that made Mr. Rock look like he'd seen something he regretted seeing."

"Seriously?"

Nate nodded. "If I'm not mistaken, the man looked like he'd actually seen a ghost."

"That's it?"

"That's it."

Caldwell went silent again. Nate could tell the man was assessing the situation. Caldwell finally said, "So what you're telling me is that you want me in on this so I can put eyes on them? And then provide you with some way of tracking them for you to deliver them later on? Or do you want us to find them and deliver them to you as well?"

"I'd be happy as a pig in shit if you can just get eyes on them. If there's a problem, we'll work things from there. But if you can just get a bead on them for now, that should be all we'll need."

"And if they turn slippery?"

Nate shrugged. "Then I guess we'll need some strongarm stuff after all."

"Well, as you already know, we monitor close to seventy-five percent of the street traffic in the immediate twenty-block area, plus a fairly large percentage of East L.A. traffic. I can put out an alert for the two of them within the hour. If they're in the area, we'll be able to find them very quickly."

"There's also a third party involved. It's a man around thirty-five or so, and he also seems to have pissed off Mr. Rock by going in uninvited as well."

"I assume you're going to provide me with the information I'll need?"

Nate dug into his jacket pocket and pulled out a thumb drive. "This is a dupe from Johnny's monitoring system. It's a twenty-minute copy of the digital he has of the three people he's interested in."

Caldwell inserted the drive into his laptop. "How's the quality?"

"Excellent."

"I'll have one of my men look at this, dupe it, then clean it up for clear scans." He flicked on his computer and punched keys. After about ten seconds, he said, "Is Rock interested in anything the guards are talking about?"

"If you want to do a voice analysis on that, feel free. But as far as I know, he's interested only in the two females and the guy in the suit."

Caldwell picked up his phone. "I'll get with one of my scanners and let you know what we find."

***

The man sitting behind the desk was about forty. His brass nameplate said: *CHARLES D. ROLAND.* He was broad-shouldered and had obviously spent considerable time and money on his hair. It was professionally cut and styled. Not one dark brown hair was out of place, and it complemented his boyishly handsome face perfectly. He was dressed in a custom-tailored, dark

198

blue suit. Tiffany guessed that the outfit easily passed the five-thousand-dollar range.

"*This boy looks like the poster child for rich and pampered,*" Chip sent over as he followed Tiffany into the spacious office.

"*It's the profession,*" she sent back. "*These people deal with celebrities. They can't afford to look anything but obscenely rich. And, of course, perfect in every way.*"

The man stood up and held out his hand for Tiffany. "I'm Charles Roland," he said in a soft, low-pitched voice. He beamed while gazing at Tiffany. His thoughts rang loud and clear. She had to force herself from frowning. *Nice. She looks vaguely familiar, but most females out here look similar. She looks like one of those babes Ralph Steiner handled last year for Revlon and Dove. Wouldn't mind seeing this one naked. Those tits are fantastic. And that hair! Shame she's part of some stupid magic act. She looks more like she should be doing hair and makeup, or maybe swimsuit promos. But since Cynthia sent her in here, I might as well see what the fuss is all about…*

Tiffany remembered Ralph Steiner well. He'd been her agent at the time. The one who'd urged her to attend Johnny Rock's party.

Despite her efforts, the anger crept back.

Steady, girl…

Tiffany shook Charles Roland's hand and immediately pulled away. It felt greasy and cold. She couldn't help thinking that even if she hadn't known how this man earned his living, she would have guessed that he was not someone she would have chosen for a friend.

"Your name, please?"

"My name is…" *Easy*, she reminded herself. *You're much too close to blow it now.* "My name is Maggie Lawson."

"Hello, Maggie Lawson. Please. Have a seat."

"My partner's name is—"

"Chad," Chip quickly tossed in, holding out his hand. "Chad Floss."

"Floss?" Tiffany glared.

"I was thinking of my teeth at the time."

"Your teeth?"

He gave her a quick grin. *"These little white Chicklet-looking things sticking out of my gums. I always had a thing for them—especially when I was young and stupid, and liked chewing on things. Problem?"*

"Never mind."

Charles Roland obviously didn't want to shake Chip's hand. He did it reluctantly, making the action very brief. "Hello."

"Can I have a seat, too?" Chip pointed to the second chair. "Or is that one reserved for a colleague you'll want to bring in to chat with once we dazzle you with our act?"

Tiffany wanted to smile.

The man gestured.

Charles Roland sat behind his desk, rested his shiny golden cuff links on the desk blotter and clasped his manicured nails together. He was obviously irritated by the interruption and kept thinking of some appointment he didn't want to be late for. "Cynthia tells me you have a potentially dynamite magic act. And that I should see a sample of it for myself."

"Yes. We do."

"Yes. You should," Chip added.

The man sighed. "Cynthia usually isn't impressed by much these days. Neither am I, I'm afraid. We've both been in this business much too long to let ourselves get starry-eyed over anything anymore."

Tiffany didn't like being in this room and wanted to end this meeting. However, she realized she had to find out a few things first. After all, this man had known Richards. They'd probably even gone out for drinks, maybe even went out together in the evenings to hunt for women. This sealed this man's doom in her eyes. But she knew to tread lightly.

"In other words," Roland added, "you must have done something to impress her."

"It was what *I* did," Chip said.

Roland glanced coolly at him but didn't respond.

"We're the best that money can buy," Tiffany said.

"What she means is, money can't buy what we do," Chip added.

The man ignored Chip. "And the name of your act?"

"Chad and Maggie's Golden Magic," Tiffany said.

"*Not bad,*" Chip sent over.

"*Best I could do for now.*"

"You actually gave me top billing?"

"'Maggie and Chad' doesn't roll off the tongue quite as easily."

"Touché."

"I don't believe I've caught your act. Are you local? If so, why haven't I heard of you?"

"No," she replied.

Roland blinked. "No?"

"Yes. No."

Confusion wrinkled his fine features. "You're not local, then?"

"You could say that."

Roland regarded them in silence before speaking. "I'm sure that, being in this business, you can understand how difficult it is to sell an act that hasn't been proven locally."

"Want a demonstration?" Chip asked.

Roland glanced at Chip. "That really won't be—"

"You're willing to dismiss us without even a glimpse of our act?" Tiffany asked.

"It's not *that*…"

"What *is* it, then?"

"Well, our agency isn't presently booking new acts. Even if we were, we're not looking for magic."

"What *are* you looking for?" she asked.

He shrugged. "The usual proven moneymakers. Actors. Models. Music. Stand-up comedy. That sort of thing."

"Time for us to show off again, Tifferoo?" Chip sent over.

202

"Go for it," she replied. *"This idiot has no idea what he's up against."*

"How about something like this?" Chip quickly turned himself into the striking black-haired beauty once again. He got up from his chair and did a sexy walk to the door, turned and came right back.

Gasping, Roland sat bolt upright. His eyes filled their sockets.

"Still doubtful?" Tiffany asked.

Roland could not speak.

"How about this?" Tiffany stood up and turned invisible.

Roland jumped up from his chair and trembled, gawking first at Chip, then at the empty chair facing him.

"Cool, eh?" Chip grinned, pushing a thick strand of long black hair away from his cheek and thrusting out his hip.

Tiffany reappeared, standing at the desk just inches away, facing him. "Now that you've just seen what we can do, how about if we do something completely different? Something even more challenging?"

"D-Different? M-*More* challenging?"

"How about a little mind manipulation, for starters?"

The man paled. "M-Mind manipulation?"

Tiffany nodded.

The man swallowed. "I-I don't understand…"

Tiffany moved closer to the man and sent her next thoughts directly into his brain. "*Let me make myself slightly clearer. Why don't we start off with you telling me everything you know about Alan Richards?"*

***

Jose Bribon had a fairly good idea of the number of blond babes walking the streets in Hollywood. Being up here the last seventy years had made this observation kind of easy. However, when it came down to the matter of finding a *specific* blonde—especially in a place where all young babes tended to pop up from the same mold—that's when it registered to him that this job might not be nearly as simple as it sounded.

The Hollywood "dream world" was known for many things. Beauty. Perfection. Youth. Sensuality. Tits. Ass. Pouty lips. Tanned skin. Agelessness. Flawlessness. The one place in the mortal world that defied time, as well as reality.

Braithwaite wanted Jose to find a certain blonde. In Hollywood. And, to make matters worse, this blonde was, in Braithwaite's own words, the "best-looking piece of tail" anyone would ever see.

Terrific.

Just as the disappointment and frustration began to build up, something else popped up in his head regarding this job. Something that would take a portion of the edge off in the equation.

The blonde, according to Braithwaite, was running around with a redheaded male the super demon called a "stinkweed."

"Stinkweed" could mean several things. But since the big man hadn't elaborated, Jose realized that he'd have to think this out and form his own conclusion.

Since these two had once been in the Dark Place and had obviously not been given specific instructions for their function up here, Jose had to assume both were inferiors. Inferiors knew how to hide. And blend in. And become totally invisible. This state alone, for example, boasted thousands of them. And although the big man had told him precious little about the two rogues, Jose figured he could deduct a thing or two about the redhead. The term "stinkweed" told Jose that they were probably dealing with a low-ranking inferior, perhaps of the vegetation variety.

Down below, he'd encountered inferiors stagnating in the Valley of Decay as well as countless species slithering around the slimy banks of the River of Blood. He had seen many inferiors that could easily be placed in the "stinkweed" category. But since he had not been given specifics, anything he'd come up with would amount to nothing more than conjecture.

Jose had spent his entire demonic existence living and working in this town. He figured he knew just about everything that was important to know.

His gut told him he had to act fast. If he tried milking this in any way, Braithwaite would be on him like flies feasting on rotting meat. But if he did his job, he'd be sitting pretty.

Jose was determined to make this good.

Blondie, he thought, a big grin lighting up his dark features, *you're about to do me a world of good.*

And with that thought urging him on, he headed down the street, searching for the best-looking piece of tail he would ever see.

***

"What did that guy tell you, Tifferoo?"

"What guy?"

They faced one another at a strip mall on Santa Monica Boulevard, in front of a FedEx store, as the wandering street crowd veered around them.

Chip rolled his eyes. "The guy you were just talking to. Perfect hair? Pricey suit? Smelled of clean sheets and lilacs? Wanted to throw up—or drop a huge load—when I shook his hand?" He shrugged. "*That* guy."

When she didn't reply right off, he said, "C'mon, now. This is me—remember? We're supposed to be a team. I saw you pull your mind thingy on that guy."

The instant Tiffany opened her mouth to reply, Chip said, "And don't try that dumb blonde act again, okay? I know what you did. And if I'm right, you probably pulled everything out of that asshole's head, including his Social Security number, blood type, and sperm count."

"I didn't need his Social Security number, blood type, or sperm count."

"Then tell me what you found out and I'll quit bugging you."

She glanced at the passing crowd and lowered her voice. "He told me he hasn't seen or heard from Alan Richards in at least three months."

"And?"

"He said something about Richards going through some sort of personal crisis. He'd heard Richards had started drinking again and was involved in some legal matter."

"Like what?"

"Some nasty business about Richards hitting someone with his car. He was arrested and charged with hit-and-run."

"The poor schmuck he hit... Was there a death?"

"The victim lived to sue Goldcrest for more than five million dollars. The suit hasn't been settled yet, but Mr. Roland told me they planned to settle out of court in a few weeks."

"So then, this leaves us where?"

"He told me where he thinks Alan went to live while all this went on."

"Do we know where to look?"

"Yes. Unfortunately."

"Unfortunately?"

"It's not exactly in the best section of town."

"No offense, Tifferoo, but I haven't exactly seen anything I could call the best section of town. I see people covered with tatts, chains and all sorts of piercings wandering around, looking like they were just dumped here from another planet. I also see all sorts of creatures standing in alleys and storefronts, peeing or worse on the pavement. If you want my opinion, Hokeywood isn't much different from the Dark Place. The only difference is that everyone here is alive—so to speak."

"Even so, the area we need to see is much worse."

"Would we be talking about a place where disgusting dregs slither around like the inferiors in the River of Blood?"

"Most likely."

"Then I guess I'm in."

"You're sure?"

"Honey Buns, I haven't been sure of anything since we first arrived here."

"You know what I have to say about that?"

"Go ahead, lay it on me."

"Welcome to Hollywood."

**

Ralph Sykes, a former munitions expert who had worked in Iraq with Owen Willis, President of S&J Monitor Systems, Ltd., was assigned the task of locating the three individuals Nate McCormick had been looking for.

Slim and fit at 38, Sykes had the eyes of a hawk and a gut instinct that had saved his life in mortal combat on more than one occasion. Using the digital photo pinned to the shelf directly above his desktop, he didn't need much time at all to zero in on the shapely blond woman and a skinny redheaded guy standing in front of the FedEx store on Santa Monica Boulevard, engaged in heavy conversation.

The instant Sykes sited the pair, he made the call to his boss, Owen Willis. "Sir? I've spotted one of them."

"Which?"

"The blonde."

"Is she alone?"

"She's talking to a redheaded guy, and they're standing in front of the FedEx store on Santa Monica Boulevard."

"They're there right now?"

"Yes, sir. Not far from Tindle's Hair Studio on the next block. The cameras across the street at Electronics R Us are picking them up."

"And you're sure this is the blonde?"

"Yes, sir."

"But no sign of the brunette?"

"No, sir."

"Describe the redhead."

"He's a skinny guy, between twenty-five and thirty, and about an inch taller than she is. I'll give him one-twenty after a heavy meal. His hair's long, thick, curly and a mess. He'll be easy to shadow."

"You see any sign at all of a brunette?"

"Plenty of brunettes, sir, but none are within earshot. And none are close to the twosome."

"How about the sandy-haired guy in the suit?"

"Nowhere in sight."

"Can ya pick up any sounds?"

"I don't believe we've got much of an audio feed on that block. Even so, the crowds would tend to distort anything retrievable. As usual, the foot traffic is substantial."

"Are you taping all that?"

"Yes, sir."

"Email it to me. I'll try and get someone over there to tail those two."

"What about the third party, sir? You want me to—"

"I want you to stay right there and keep watch. If that other guy is involved, he shouldn't be far."

***

Jose Bribon knew right off that he found the two rogues Braithwaite had been lusting after.

Even from across the street, he could tell that the blond babe was going to be trouble. He could see it in the perfect body, as well as the thick honey-blond hair and the bodacious jugs. Even with the other skinny, leggy babes walking the street, this lady stood out. He had no idea what she'd done to get the big man after her, but whatever it was, it was serious.

"Baby," he muttered under his breath, "even without that price on your head, you could get me after your ass in a New York second…"

The redheaded dude with her wouldn't pose much of a problem. He was only slightly taller than the blonde, and his skinny body and pipe-stem arms conveyed the strong message that he was anything but an ass-kicker. Besides, Braithwaite had told him that the blonde was the problem child, and the redhead—or, as the big man had called him, the "stinkweed"—was merely tagging along.

This made things *so* much simpler.

He had to get the two of them alone. Jose was confident that he could guide them away from the traffic. Jose had a natural talent when conning people. His simple, well-rehearsed story of his being "lost in the glitter of Tinseltown" usually did the trick. All he had to do was approach them and ask directions, then feign confusion. Once he'd coaxed the two of them down one of the side streets, the rest would be easy. A simple freak accident might work to get the ball rolling. Or maybe a sidewalk ruckus involving a couple of passing tourists. The proven dispute over the vanishing wallet could also work here. Using his creative talents, Jose could make it materialize at the perfect moment. Or have two or three twenties appear on the sidewalk.

The redhead would not be difficult to overpower. Jose was confident that he could devise something to put the dude temporarily out of commission. Then he could concentrate on the blonde. Braithwaite hadn't wanted him to take them by himself, but if the opportunity presented itself, Jose knew he'd be a fool to pass it up.

The cheeks of his ass tightened.

This was gonna be ridiculously easy.

Getting in the big man's good graces would be the smartest thing he ever did.

Jose approached the curb. Just then, he saw that his task might not be as simple as he'd originally thought.

A trio of large dark-skinned punks had entered the scene, stopping just a few feet from the blonde and her partner. Jose could tell by the smirks on their faces that there would soon be serious trouble.

***

Owen Willis emailed a copy of Ralph Sykes' digital to Donovan Blake, one of the three detectives Willis' firm, S&J, used from time to time to help them with their more unusual cases.

Blake, a vet who'd been deployed in Iraq, had been trained in Military Intelligence as well as

Tactical Weapons. Three times divorced, he lived in a garden apartment just a few blocks north of Santa Monica Boulevard with his two cats, Tom and Jerry, and his silent movie collection. When he wasn't working, he enjoyed lounging on the couch in his boxers, drinking Guinness while watching Harold Lloyd movies on the widescreen with Tom and Jerry in his lap. His simple lifestyle made it convenient for him to be ready for any job at a moment's notice.

This afternoon, he was getting ready to drive out to Dempsey's, his favorite steak restaurant. He didn't indulge himself much these days, choosing to eat out three or four times a week in favor of fixing his own meals.

He was halfway to the front door when his cell buzzed.

"Did you get my email?" Owen Willis asked.

"About an hour ago."

"How soon can you be available?"

"I was about to grab some supper, but I'm a go right now, if you wish."

"I hate to cut into your personal time, but this job, well, it's kind of weird, and we'd like to put a lid on it as quickly as possible."

"Really?" Something about this didn't make it too high on the plausible meter. What he'd seen in the three-minute segment suggested someone with big money had been insulted and wanted some instant karma for self-gratification. "Three party crashers? A rush job?"

"Apparently our client thinks there might be more to it than what meets the eye."

This sounded like Willis could be playing patsy to one of the hundreds of Hollywood millionaires out here. "Really?"

"We'll figure this out before long. How quickly can you get to the FedEx store on Santa Monica?"

"I'm about ten minutes out. Since I'm already dressed, I can be there right away."

"There's a twenty percent bonus in this for ya if you can find them."

"All righty, then. I'm there…"

"One other detail you might be interested in. On the tape, we saw a blonde and a brunette."

"So did I." The blonde he'd seen had taken his breath away. In a place like this, a guy didn't forget a lady that fine very quickly.

"I just got word that the blonde is now with a small, slender redheaded man."

Blake stopped just short of pulling open the front door. He stood stock still, wondering if what he'd just heard the man right.

"Blake? Ya still there?"

"Did you just say what I thought you just said?"

"Did you hear me say that the blonde is now with a redheaded man?"

"What happened to the brunette?"

"No idea."

"If I saw what you saw, this brunette was just as much of a looker as the blonde. Gorgeous babes just don't disappear—not even out here. Not that quickly, anyway."

"Agreed."

"Then how the hell could this one just up and—"

"Just get your butt out there. We can figure this all out later, when we've got more facts to work with."

"You think it'll be that easy?"

"I'm hoping..."

***

"The money, bitch. You, too, sucka..."

The man, six-two or -three, was about twenty-five years old. He wore an oversized gray sweatshirt with the sleeves ripped off, exposing his muscular arms. His skin was fair, his Negroid features unmistakable. His head was covered by a white baseball cap with the black brim on sideways and pushed up, making him look silly. His baggy black sweatpants were pulled halfway down to his knees, displaying red undershorts. His athletic shoes looked new and top of the line.

His companions were about the same age, but thinner. All had dark features. One was wiry and about two inches taller than the first guy. The third, an inch or so shorter. Both wore the same brand of cap, and in the same manner. All three were nervous, watching the passing crowd, then each other. The one who had spoken gripped something small and metallic in his right fist. Tiffany couldn't tell if it was a switchblade or some other kind of weapon.

"The money, bitch." The punk eyed the crowds, who veered around them, moving away quickly. "You too, pee-wee." He glared at Chip.

214

"*Pee*-wee?" Chip frowned at Tiffany. "That's *cold*."

"The *mon*ey, suckas!"

"I know. We heard you the first two times." Tiffany was growing irritated. She didn't want to waste their time dealing with such nonsense.

The punk held out his left hand. "C'mon, bitch. Cough it up. You too, asshole."

Chip shrugged. "I guess asshole is slightly better than pee-wee."

"Shut the fuck *up*, moron!"

Chip shook his head. "Moron is pushing it, though. I think I like asshole better than pee-wee, or—"

"You tryin' to piss me off, dick-wipe?"

"Now it's *dick-wipe*?" Chip sighed. "This dude's getting way beyond personal, Tifferoo."

The punk turned back to Tiffany. "Cough it up, bitch."

Tiffany held out her arms. "Do you actually see a *purse* anywhere? A handbag, maybe? A clutch?" She shrugged. "Even if I had money, where would I be carrying it? These pants are tight. Judging by the looks I've been getting, I'm sure all three of you have already noticed."

"Want me to check for myself, bitch?"

Chip chuckled.

"Somethin' *funny*, asshole?" the punk growled.

"I'll let you find that one out all by yourself," Chip said, grinning.

"Somebody wants us to open a big can a whup-ass on a pee-wee," muttered the skinny one.

"A big can of *whup-ass*?" Chip asked Tiffany.

215

"That's punkspeak for "I'm gonna whip your ass," Tiffany explained flatly.

Chip nodded. "Good thing you cleared that one up for me. I was about to ask where they sell those."

"*Punk*speak?" the third one asked, scowling.

"You two tryin' to piss us off?" the leader asked. "Zat right, bitch?"

"You really shouldn't be calling me a bitch." Tiffany frowned. "It's kind of demeaning. And no, I don't want you or your friends touching me. *Or* my friend."

The other two snickered.

"The money, bitch!"

"*You want to keep on with this, Tiffers?*" Chip sent over. "*Or do you want* me *to do something?*"

"*Any suggestions?*"

"*How about I work a little magic here? Personally, I find these morons boring. And they all need a shower. And some serious dental hygiene.*"

She glanced at him. "*You're sure?*"

"*Didn't you see the overbite on that skinny one? And that other guy. What's with those gums? He looks like a can of clam chowder just exploded in his mouth—*"

"*I meant, your magic thing...*"

"*What about it?*"

She rolled her eyes. "*You know what I'm talking about.*"

"*Well, you're the one who always fixes things. I've been getting kinda rusty lately. Besides, we are a team, righterino?*"

216

Tiffany smiled. *"Work your stuff, then, Mr. Trickster. But make sure that whatever you, do it without bringing too much attention to us."*

"Sorely you jest?"

"There are entirely too many cellphones and iPads jumping around. I don't want any of this to show up on YouTube."

"I think I've got it. One fantastic but low-keyed and basically unremarkable miracle coming right up..."

She winked at him.

"You be *winkin'* at me, Momma?" The second punk moved closer.

"I was winking at *him*." She pointed to Chip. "I'd *never* wink at someone like you. And I could *never* be your *momma...*"

"C'mon, bitch." The first punk jerked his open hand closer. "Don't got all fuckin' day."

"You're wasting our time." Chip rested his fists on his hips. "Go shake down someone else. My buddy and I, we've got stuff to do. Important shit. Believe me, it's much more important than standing here, wasting terrific put-downs with you stupid, clueless grade school dropouts."

The three burst out in laughter.

"How 'bout that?" the second one said. "Rashawn found hisself a teensy-weensy whitey badass!"

"Whatcha gonna do now, Teensy?" The third punk motioned for Chip to move closer. "You gonna open up a big fuckin' can a whup-ass? All by yo'self?"

"All by myself," Chip replied, grinning impishly.

Something out of the corner of her eye caught Tiffany's attention. A slender gray-haired man stood at the curb, doing something with his cell phone. He kept glancing toward his right, where an electronic store advertised a twenty percent discount on all DVD players. His cell phone looked strange. It was silver and seemed to be reflecting off the sun. This was what had probably caught her eye. However, it wasn't what concerned her now.

There was something vaguely familiar about this man. She was certain she'd seen him before. In fact, just as she tried remembering—

An explosion of giant guffaws interrupted her thoughts.

Rashawn, shaking in anger, had moved toward Chip.

Chip bent over and began re-lacing his shoe. When he finished and stood up straight, he'd become more than a foot taller, with yard-wide shoulders and thick muscular arms.

***

Rashawn froze. His eyes had filled the sockets. His jaw dropped as he pulled his head back to gawk at the phenomenon he'd just witnessed. "W-What...h-how...the *fuck*?"

The other two backed up and gazed stupidly at Chip.

"Nice," Tiffany commented with a smile.

Chip chuckled. "You like, Tifferoosky? I thought maybe a sudden growth spurt would be a snazzy touch here."

218

"I like."

He smiled down at the three punks. "You dumbasses still interested in watching someone open a big fucking can of whup-ass?"

No response. The dazed stares continued.

"Wanna see me bend a horseshoe?" Chip held out his hands, which had doubled in size.

No response.

Chip studied his hands. "Oops. I guess I'll need a horseshoe for that." He turned. "Tifferoo? Do ya mind?"

"Not at all. Any specific size?"

"Any normal size would be just spiffy. I kinda think a Clydesdale shoe would be a slight overkill for this demonstration, don't you?"

"You're right. We don't want these gentlemen to think you're a showoff, do we?"

"Especially since you don't want us to show up on YouTube."

"Sound reasoning."

"By the way, you didn't happen to bring your handbag with you, did you?"

"Got it right here." Tiffany brought up her left arm. A pricey-looking black leather handbag had materialized in her hand. Two of the punks gasped at the sight. The third swallowed audibly. Tiffany opened the handbag and reached inside. When she pulled it out, a shiny silver horseshoe was trapped in her palm. "Here ya go."

Chip took it. "Now. Where was I? Oh, yes. How's this?" He gripped an end in each hand and began pulling the shoe apart.

Just moments before he'd separated the ends, the trio had already spun around. Squealing, they ran away hysterically, darting into traffic at the end of the block.

"Shucky-darn." Chip watched them. "They didn't stay for my show."

"Don't worry." Tiffany patted his shoulder. "We both know how talented you are."

"Thanks, Babykins. I guess I really don't need this after all." He held out the horseshoe.

Tiffany glanced at the handbag, which suddenly disappeared. "I guess I don't need it, either."

Chip dropped it on the pavement. It disappeared silently the moment it hit the ground. "Okay, then. Where were we?"

"Where we were before. Looking for Alan Richards."

"Where do you think we should start?"

"Personally, I would appreciate it if you went back to your original appearance."

"Really?"

"You don't want me getting a stiff neck looking up at you, do you?"

He sighed. "Just when I was getting used to being big and strong. And wonderfully intimidating."

"Just do it so no one notices, okay?"

He frowned. "Tifferoo, you take all the fun out of everything." He bent and fiddled with his shoelace. When he straightened, he'd returned to his former size. "Better?"

"Considerably."

"Then why do you have that perplexed look on your flawless face?"

"Your nose."

He crossed his eyes and wiggled his nose. "You mean this one? The one directly in the center—give or take one or two millimeters—of my devilishly handsome face?"

"That's the one."

"What's wrong with it?"

"It isn't pointed or upturned."

Chip produced a small pocket-sized mirror and held it close to his face. He blinked. "You're totally and completely right on the money. This thing looks almost normal!" He had one last glimpse, then made the mirror vanish. "What's happening to me, Tifferoo? I seem to be losing my impish accoutrements."

"I think it looks almost noble," she said.

"I've had this nose for centuries. It's always gone wherever I go, and not once went missing. It's never actually been considered noble, but I've learned to live with it, nonetheless. I'm kinda attached to it, so to speak."

"I just don't think it's anything to worry about."

"You really think I shouldn't be concerned that one day, I might actually look normal?"

She shrugged. "Why would you? You'll still be you, won't you?"

"I guess you're right about that…"

It was time to get back to more important matters. "Let's find a cab and—" Just then, she stopped.

221

"Tifferoo? Why the sudden brake action?"

She tilted her head and listened. "There's a demon headed our way."

***

Jose Bribon grinned.

Braithwaite had been right. These two were not to be taken lightly. Anyone who could shapeshift so easily deserved serious respect.

Respect is what I intend to give you two, Jose thought. He kept his leisurely pace down the block, where the two rogues were talking calmly just a hundred feet ahead, as though nothing out of the ordinary had happened.

Si. Respect. Lots and lots of it. Right up until the moment I hand your asses over to the big man!

***

Donovan Blake had been a detective in the L.A. area the last twelve years. He'd started working in the private sector after taking a bullet in Iraq and being forced to come home three months early. The bullet had slammed into his back, missing his lower spine by half an inch, thus preventing him from becoming a paraplegic. Aside from chronic back pain, he suffered no other noticeable effects from the wound.

However, after nearly a year of finding no work other than an occasional missing kid or deadbeat husband, he had to face the fact that he wouldn't be able to make ends meet in the L.A. area and might have to find some other way to earn his living.

His luck changed when he'd bumped into Ralph Sykes one afternoon in a Santa Monica bar.

After half an hour of exchanging war stories over a pitcher of Guinness, he decided to take on Sykes' offer of hitching up to the S&J stable.

Since that day, Donovan had worked regularly, doing mostly surveillance work and occasionally working with L.A. cops as well as the Beverly Hills squad in a shadow capacity to apprehend local felons. The hours were oftentimes long, but the paychecks made everything worth the trouble. He seldom had to risk his life, and since the bullet in his lower back didn't restrict his movements very much, he considered himself fortunate. At forty-two, he was reasonably healthy, enjoyed a good income, and lived in a respectable neighborhood.

This present job, however, was something he couldn't quite wrap his mind around.

A "rush job." For three party crashers.

Something about this reeked. To make matters even more confusing, the short segment Owen Willis had emailed him less than an hour ago suggested nothing criminal. It looked no more serious than something you expected to see at a high school dance.

Even so, who was he to quibble? The case appeared to be ridiculously simple. And, to make the situation even more favorable, Willis had offered him a twenty percent bonus.

Don, my man, he thought as he kept the Land Rover steady in the heavy late afternoon traffic, *you'd be a moron to question* any *of this.*

His cell buzzed. It was Owen Willis. "Where are you?"

223

"I'm about two blocks west of the FedEx store."

"You want the latest?"

"Affirmative."

"Well, it's kind of hard to explain, but my man just spotted them on one of the monitors across the street from the coffee shop halfway to North Fairfax. It seems the two of them are still there, on Santa Monica."

"What's hard to explain?"

"What we just saw from the tapes were three lowlifes showing up and attempting to work a shakedown on the blonde and her partner. The three were dark, obviously mixed blood, young, early twenties, and big—six feet on up. They walked right up to the two. The biggest held out his hand for their valuables. The blonde didn't comply. Neither did the guy with her."

"Okay…"

"For some reason we can't figure, some damned oddball reflection got in the way of the monitor and blocked everything. And I mean *everything*."

"Instrument malfunction?"

"Possibly."

"Then what's the problem?"

"Why did something like that happen at that precise moment? Kinda suspicious…"

"Sabotage?"

"Unlikely."

Donovan couldn't help smiling. Technology had never been his best friend, and he was never shy about letting his feelings be known. "What I've

224

learned about technology in the last twenty years is that even though it's the greatest thing in the world when it's working, it tends to be temperamental, illogical and totally frustrating at the most inconvenient times."

"Sounds like we're talking about my ex-wife."

Donovan smiled. "Even so, we've got to consider all possibles."

"You're definitely right about that. Unfortunately, that doesn't exactly help us."

"Well, then, I can't think of anything else that might explain—"

"The fact is, we don't know *what* the hell happened."

"Did the reception ever come back?"

"Damned right it did."

"When?"

"Right after the three perps fled the scene."

"They just…left?"

"For some reason we can't understand, they ran away. All three of 'em."

This was beginning to sound way the hell beyond bizarre. "Are the two still there?"

"The blonde and the redheaded man, yes."

"What about the brunette I saw in the segment?"

"We can't find her."

Yes, this was beginning to sound *very* bizarre.

"Any ideas?"

"None."

"What's your take on this?"

"The only thing that matters is that the blonde's still in sight. Go after her and do whatever you can to bring her back…or at least detain her in some way."

"What about the guy with her? You want him, too?"

"Definitely."

"How badly?"

"I'm not asking you to risk your life."

"Does he look formidable?"

"Anything but. But since this whole thing is strange, I wouldn't want to jump to any conclusions. If you can detain both without anyone getting hurt, then do it. Otherwise, try like hell not to take any unnecessary chances. And whatever you do, don't get anyone else involved."

"Copy that."

***

The demon was dark-haired and medium height, with heavy, brooding features. Not bad-looking, but since Tiffany knew he was a demon, his beaming smile—as well as his large, penetrating dark eyes—meant nothing but trouble.

She kept her gaze on him as he walked over and stopped about five feet away. "New in town?" he asked in a soft, low-pitched voice.

"How'd you know?" She quickly noticed the tiny red glint in his eyes.

The beaming smile remained. "Just a guess. I see you just met some of our local neighborhood crap."

Tiffany shrugged. "No problem. We convinced them to leave us alone."

"I saw that. They nearly killed themselves making a quick exit."

"I guess they decided to squeeze in their daily jogging regimen before the rush hour starts up," Chip said flatly.

The demon chuckled. "Good one."

"I've always been dynamite with the old one-liner."

"Dynamite's an understatement," Tiffany said flatly.

"Seriously, how'd you do it?" The demon seemed very interested. "These locals—especially the big boys with the pricey clothes and classic rides—would pay the serious bucks to learn your technique."

Tiffany could tell he was trying to probe her mind. To make it more difficult for him, she concentrated on the three thugs, forming their images in her thoughts as well as their crude comments, while keeping her personal evaluation of him from entering her consciousness. "We just convinced them that they were wasting their time and should be somewhere else, trying to fleece someone easier."

He tilted his head. "To me, it looked slightly more complicated. Why don't we get better acquainted? I know this really great restaurant less than a block away, serves the best chimichanga you've ever—"

"No, thanks." She turned away.

"No, wait! At least let me buy you guys a drink, or let me—"

"You funny or something?" Chip frowned at the man. "What's your angle?"

"My what?"

"Why bother? And why so interested? There's trash everywhere in this town. Every street and alley. This place is a zoo. I just saw two things pass us that you wouldn't exactly call human *or* mammal. What makes us so interesting?"

He didn't respond. As he gazed at Chip, he was no longer smiling.

Tiffany did some quick probing. Images of herself lying naked with the demon, also naked, kneeling over her, showed prominently.

"This isn't about those three at all, is it?" she asked.

He blinked. "Whaddya mean?"

"This is about me. And you. Us."

"H-Howzat?"

She'd obviously flustered him. It was time to get in there and amp it up. "You know. You and me. My naked body and yours, doing the big, juicy nasty. Tell me right now that you don't wanna get me in the sack, and I'll apologize right here."

"That's crude, lady. Really crude..." The images in the demon's head had brightened, growing clearer. He shifted his weight.

"Am I wrong?" She noticed the trembling in his limbs.

No reply.

"Tell me I'm wrong. Tell me you aren't interested in these." She cupped her hands beneath her breasts.

"L-Lady..."

"Tell me you don't want to get seriously involved in this." She parted her lips, closed her eyes, fluffed her hair and shook her head.

228

"That's doing quite a lot for me, too, Cupcake," Chip whispered breathlessly. "If you can just tone it down a notch or two? I really don't wanna humiliate myself even more than usual."

The demon's cheeks had grown ruddy. "Listen here…" He cleared his throat. "That ain't what this is all about. And you know it."

"What *is* it all about, then?"

The demon took a step back. Tiffany caught an image of a cell phone in the demon's thoughts. The demon talking. Stuttering. Shaking. A booming voice on the other end. The demon turning pale. Swallowing.

Breath Mint. It *had* to be him…

She had to stay in control. She could do this. She'd done it many times before. There was no reason why this should be any different.

"What's this about, then? That phone call?"

The demon's eyes filled the sockets. He swallowed with difficulty. "Ph-phone C-Call?"

"The one that just made you turn as white as the driven snow."

The demon didn't speak for several long, tense moments. Then he said, "You're good, girl. *Real* good."

"Where was the call from?"

The demon didn't respond.

Tiffany caught another image jumping around in there. She could see the display quite clearly. "Was it by any chance from Tampa, Florida?"

The demon continued trembling. "You really *are* good…"

Tiffany caught movement in the corner of her eye.

A tall, broad-shouldered guy dressed in sports clothes was crossing the street in their direction.

***

Donovan Blake parked the Land Rover in front of a furniture store on Santa Monica Boulevard, between North Fairfax and North Orange Grove.

Across the street, a Hispanic guy was approaching the blonde and her redheaded friend, who were standing at the end of the block. The Hispanic looked around five-eight, between one-sixty and one-seventy. He was dressed in a tank top, shorts, and athletic shoes. He wore his coal-black hair close to the scalp and carried a pair of sunglasses hooked to his tank top. As the Hispanic approached the two, Blake couldn't help noticing the look on the man's grinning face.

He was after something. It was obvious. Money? Some other form of shakedown?

But when the blonde turned in his direction, Blake knew exactly what it was. He found that he could not move.

That girl...she's drop-dead gorgeous...

Blake experienced a gush of warmth at the base of his neck. The digital clip Owen Willis had sent him didn't do this girl one bit of justice. This beauty was obviously a model, escort, high-priced call girl, or movie celeb. Looks like hers couldn't go unnoticed for very long—not in this town. Blake realized in that single instant that even though he'd been living in Tinsel Town most of his life, he'd never in his thirty-nine years glimpsed such a stunning woman.

Her gaze was hypnotic. As he focused on her large glittering blue eyes, he experienced a sense of comfort and brightness he hadn't known before. A beautiful sunrise. A rainbow after a storm. A pasture of breathtaking flowers. A calming waterfall. His very first kiss, experienced in junior high with Susan Wexler, the cheerleader who'd gotten knocked up the next year by Ray Dremmer, the school's football quarterback.

His first honeymoon with Aileen fifteen years ago, on Catalina Island.

More sunshine. A magnificent sunset. Laughter. Love. Cuddling. Warmth. Flowers glistening brightly after a summer shower.

What the hell is happening? he asked himself nervously. Why did he feel so happy? So carefree? So full of life and contentment?

Then, in that next instant, he realized that for the first time since he'd been shot, the steady lingering pain in his lower back had suddenly ebbed into a state of near nothingness.

My God...

Who *was* this woman? What on earth had she done to him? How could a simple glance in his direction alter his physical condition? What was this strange power she had over him?

Suddenly he had to know everything. Every single detail about this woman.

Fuck the job. Fuck the money. Fuck everything but the dazzling beauty staring back at him from across the street.

231

I have to meet her, talk to her, find out who she is...

Ignoring rush hour traffic and everything else going on around him, Donovan Blake stepped down off the curb and hurried across the street.

He was totally focused on the gorgeous young woman standing at the curb, watching him intently, as a small white compact zipped through the yellow light and slammed right into him.

***

Johnny Rock sat at his desk, gazing at his laptop.

That blonde *had* to be in the system...somewhere.

Ever since he'd seen her on the screen, some lingering memory had been knocked loose, forcing everything else into the background—everything, that is, except for finding out everything he could about her.

A woman like her shouldn't be difficult to locate. This town was overflowing with gorgeous babes. This lady, however, stood way the hell above all the rest. She had what ninety-nine percent of them couldn't have, even if they paid dearly for it.

Class. This babe was rolling in the stuff. It showed in the way she walked, the way she moved. She obviously knew what she had but also knew she didn't have to flaunt it. Her face was that of a goddess, her hair made of spun gold, and she boasted a body that would be the envy of any of the most successful swimsuit models on the planet. She undoubtedly knew deep down that every single male who had ever caught a single glimpse of her would want her and would risk everything to possess her. However, judging by her casual attitude, this valuable piece of information didn't seem to bother her, affect her, or cause her to react in any arrogant way.

And that last thought was what had turned his crank harder than anything he had ever experienced in his forty-plus years.

After more than an hour of feverishly trying to google the babe, Johnny went right back to the screen and watched the segment again. And again. And again.

He finally paused the film. Then, as he'd done twice before, zoomed it. The girl's image turned out grainy, but he could make out her features. And what he noticed once again was that this girl was—

No. She *wasn't* dead. She was on the screen. Walking around, looking gorgeous. *Alive*. She was *alive*.

This babe, dammit, is alive!

How the hell can you be so damned sure? the cursed voice in his head demanded.

Just months earlier, this same girl had been on this same screen. Walking around in her two-piece, smiling, waving, turning the heads of everyone who'd passed her way.

But *was* this the same girl? *Was* it? Or was he just deceiving himself?

You're spooked, he told himself. *For some stupid reason, you're telling yourself to believe something that makes no sense. Something that just doesn't happen, that defies all logic. Something that is totally impossible.*

He had to remind himself that this was Hollywood. The flesh and fantasy center of the world. The place where glitter, glamor, and big money ruled. Where people were beautiful. And flawless. And dazzling. And peddled dreams. And fantasies. And took the populace into new heights. In other words, Hollywood was the closest thing to "heaven" that anyone would ever be able to experience on this earth.

It was a multi-billion-dollar industry. A glistening factory that produced idols and prototypes of all sorts and shapes of heroes and heroines that could—and would—instantly propel the public into a state of Nirvana to escape the stress and pressure of everyday mediocrity.

They did their job, and did it very, very well. They produced all sorts of heroes, all sorts of heroines, and all sorts of fantasy worlds extremely capable of staggering one's imagination.

But one thing they could not produce was an endless stream of beauty. Although they realized they were limited, they persevered, nonetheless. They soon discovered that if they couldn't consistently create masterpieces, they might be able to settle with types.

They began making "molds." They took their best creations and, using these molds, employed minor adjustments to suit the growing demands of their public. The face and body of Marilyn Monroe morphed into dozens of clones over the next fifty years. In the seventies, Farrah Fawcett, elected to be

234

the accepted "mold," spawned the next wave of bright-eyed starlets. During the next few decades, the faces of Jennifer Aniston, Heather Locklear, Pamela Anderson, the Hallmark movie babes, and countless others were splashed all over the tabloids, embellishing every movie and TV set. Johnny couldn't remember the last time he'd seen a movie that didn't include a Morgan Fairchild or Jennifer Love Hewitt clone in the cast.

Suddenly exhausted, Johnny switched off the film and shifted in his seat. He had to chill. To sit back and let the a/c calm him. He needed a little port to relax, let the nerves settle and reboot themselves. He had some high-quality South American blow in one of his drawers but wasn't in the mood to go rummaging for it. He wasn't young anymore. He didn't need to lose his composure—let alone his libido—just from looking some babe he thought was dead.

This was ridiculous. He couldn't let any of this happen.

This gorgeous babe wasn't dead. She was very much alive and had nothing whatsoever to do with the girl he'd originally thought she was. This starlet looked like that babe. Just another "mold" issue. She wasn't the babe in question for the simple reason that the babe in question was dead and this one was very much alive. Case closed. Check, please...

I need to get a grip, he told himself. *I need to stop this bullshit and force myself to remember where the hell I am. I'm in my study, in my mansion. This is my kingdom, dammit. This is*

Hollywood. The Dream Factory has been spitting out bodacious babes for as long as I can remember. I need to stop the daydreaming and come to the realization that the beautiful, sexy woman on the screen has nothing whatsoever to do with the one I've been obsessing over. She's dead, this one is very much alive, and I really need to come to my senses before it's too fuckin' late!

And with that weighing heavily on his mind, he reached for his cell.

Hopefully, Nate McCormick would give him an up-to-date progress report.

***

The street had quickly become total chaos.

Traffic had come to a grinding stop. People emerging from stores glimpsed the turmoil in the street and rushed over to the curb. Cell phones and iPads appeared like magic. Two small boys scampered over and aimed their cell phones at the man lying in the middle of the street, just a couple of feet from the white Smart Car that had smashed into him. Others snuck closer and, holding out their cell phones, filmed the scene.

Squeezing between a middle-aged couple clutching bags of groceries, Tiffany stepped down from the curb. She eyed the poor man lying on his back and instantly grew angry at the unruly crowd. She briefly considered using her powers to cause a power surge to disable all technological devices—

Not a demon, she reminded herself, struggling to stay calm. *You never were, never will be.*

"Tifferoo?" Chip's voice drifted into her head. "*We need to get out of here. I mean, like right now.*

To be even more precise, this instant would be just perfectimundo."

"I can't. Not now, anyway."

"Please explain this sudden irritating sense of irrationality."

"I have to help this man."

"But what about our demon?"

"Is he still there?"

"Need you ask? You know they're not like a fart. They don't vanish into the atmosphere after a few seconds."

"Then he is still there?"

A short pause. *"Don't see him, but since we don't know his capabilities, he could have changed form."*

"Maybe, maybe not."

"What makes you say that?"

"Just a wild guess."

"Well, that sure makes me feel a hundred percent better..."

"I can't explain it. I just don't think he's gone far. Anyway, like I said, I've got to fix this."

"And as I just asked, very politely, I might add, why, pray tell?"

"I caused this."

"How can you possibly blame yourself? You weren't driving that little white ugmobile, were you? And you didn't pull him out into the street, did you?"

"He was staring at me when he crossed."

"Tifferoo, I hate to tell you this, mostly because you already know it, and have known it for

years...but just in the rare case that you might have forgotten...guys stare at you all the time."

"He was coming over to talk to me and wasn't paying attention to what he was doing."

"Been there. Believe me."

"I've really got to fix this."

"I hear sirens, Tiffers. It won't be long before we're in the middle of a large gaggle of mortals even more agitated, confused and messed up than they are normally. Can't you see what's going on around you? The cell phones? The iPads? The popcorn crowd settling in to watch this afternoon's matinee? Mark my words, Baby Cakes. In ten minutes, that clean-cut, well-dressed group with the microphones and the headsets will be here in full force, asking all sorts of stupid, ridiculous questions."

"I understand what you're saying."

"Then you must also realize that if you don't move right now, it's gonna be impossible to work your way out of there."

"There are a lot of people running around. It's a regular circus. I see that. I'm right in the middle of it."

"They're taking pictures of that poor schmuck. You're a gorgeous babe, but even so, I don't think they're too concerned about you right now..."

"Thank you. But I still have to do something."

"Do it quick. We don't have much time. Those sirens are getting louder."

"I can't just walk away and leave him lying here like this."

"Tifferoo? Tell me you're not gonna take too long to work your magic."

She bumped into another selfie-taker. Then, resisting the urge to knock the device out of his grasp and accidentally step on it, she hurried right over and knelt beside the fallen man.

***

The blackness consuming him began to dim soon after he'd opened his eyes and struggled to remember where he was and why he was lying on the hard pavement, numb with pain.

Just a moment later, a bright light replaced the darkness, and a warmth he'd never experienced before made everything feel as if he'd drifted into a cloud.

Was he dead?

The moment his head cleared, he remembered the bright blur that had slammed into him, turning everything a splashy white and silvery gray just before the darkness followed, enveloping him in a cold blanket.

But after he'd opened his eyes and saw the late afternoon sun searing down on him, he realized that he *wasn't* dead. He was alive.

He fought to recall what happened, why he was lying here, and why so many faces had crowded around him, looking down at him while everything glittered from the sea of cell phones winking brightly at him.

Then it came to him. The beautiful young blond woman was the reason for all this. The reason why he was lying here—why he'd turned off every

239

single impulse in his brain and concentrated on that striking face, those big, beautiful blue eyes...

Those same hauntingly gorgeous eyes suddenly appearing amongst the crowd of shocked faces and cell phones. Those same alluring baby blues that were somehow telling him that things were going to be okay...that he would survive this...and that once he was taken away, things would turn out just fine.

His thoughts muddled, he struggled to recall what had been going on before this...before whatever had happened to turn his life into the jumbled mess it had suddenly become.

But just as his mind finally cleared, those beautiful blue eyes moved closer. Something warm and soft touched his hand, and every bit of pain that had torn into him since he'd awakened had vanished. He closed his eyes and smiled at the wonderful feeling. He may not have died and gone to paradise, but this sensation seemed as close to ultimate nirvana as he could ever have imagined.

A moment later, a soft, sensuous, low-pitched voice penetrated his thoughts.

"You'll going to be all right," the voice said. *"You were struck by a car, but you're going to be just fine. You'll recover, and when you do, you'll discover that you will feel terrific. You'll have no more pain, and you'll feel much better than you've felt in a long time."*

"W-Who...*are* you?" He didn't even know if the words had come out of his mouth—or if he'd simply thought them.

"That doesn't matter," the voice replied. *"The only thing that matters is that you'll be just fine."*

240

He wanted to tell the gorgeous face smiling down at him that he had never seen such beauty. He wanted to tell her that she looked like an angel…

But he realized in that same moment that saying such a thing wasn't necessary. She suddenly smiled, which told him she knew what he was thinking. Her big blue eyes grew even larger, glistening even more. "Thank you," he heard her say, "and while you're recovering in the hospital, just remember that you should do something nice for someone else once you're back on your feet."

Just as he opened his mouth to reply, to tell her that for the first time in years, his back no longer hurt, he heard approaching sirens. He gathered his thoughts to say what was in his heart, to tell her that she'd somehow fixed his back as well as everything else…

But by the time he had his thoughts ready, the paramedics had arrived.

Two young men in white uniforms were kneeling beside him, carefully placing a padded gurney on the pavement to his right, while a young female with long black hair fixed in a tight weave began fiddling with an orange neck brace.

Suddenly edgy, he turned to his left.

The beautiful blond-haired angel had vanished.

***

The moment the paramedics had wheeled over the gurney, Tiffany slipped away. A cop moved in her direction while another veered off to the side, talking to his radio while blocking off the area with an orange cone. A third tried keeping the crowd away using his whistle and large flailing arms. The

241

cop approaching her had his notepad out in front of him. He was staring at her as he approached.

Tiffany knew right then that she was going to have to make a quick exit. *"Chip, do a change."*

"Moi?"

"You. Yes. Right now. As quickly as possible, if you get my drift."

"Want me to go back to being svelte, voluptuous and ravishing?"

"I don't really care, actually."

"No problemo. Later, Honey Bunny."

A sizeable crowd had formed behind her, most of them taking pictures and talking on their cells while others made silly faces doing selfies around the Smart Car. The cop continued moving in her direction. He was talking on his radio.

A man and woman standing close together clutched bags of groceries while watching the chaos. Tiffany approached them. Smiling at the man, she said, "I'm really sorry about this, but I've really got no choice."

The man blinked. "Huh?"

The bottom of his bag suddenly broke open, spilling its contents onto the street. A carton of eggs slapped to the pavement and broke open, the eggs cracking and making a slimy mess on the curb. Two long loaves of French bread bounced onto the street. One of them hopped over to the cop. A carton of milk slammed onto the cop's knee on its way down, breaking open and splashing milk.

Tiffany squeezed around the confused man and joined a crowd filming the spillage. Slipping in among them, she turned her hair brown and

242

changed her face and outfit while edging between parked cars. Then, elbowing past two small clots of folks waving cell phones at the frenzied activity, she hurried down the street to the end of the block, in search of Chip.

CHAPTER 5 - NATE McCORMICK

For more than thirty minutes, Nate McCormick sat at the intersection of Santa Monica and Wilcox Avenue, waiting for the cops to clean up the mess farther down. Although he couldn't tell what was going on, he saw clear signs that the area was being roped off. He turned on his scanner and heard Dispatch from the Los Angeles Police Department discussing the situation with one of the cops on the scene. Something had happened just two blocks ahead. From the conversation, Nate gathered that some idiot in a Smart Car had slammed into a jaywalker. No fatalities, but it looked like traffic would be hosed up for the next twenty or thirty minutes. Rerouting everyone was not yet being discussed.

Nate had an appointment in fifteen minutes with an old friend, Jacob Sharp, a forensic scientist working with the Police Department in the lab. Knowing he'd be late, Nate pressed his friend's number on the hands-free system and waited for Blue Tooth to put the call through.

A moment later, Jacob's high-pitched voice came on. "I'm glad you called. I was just about to call *you*."

"I'm calling to let you know that there's an accident on Santa Monica, and it looks like—"

"Are you going to be able to get here any time soon?"

"Judging by what I just heard on the scanner, I'll probably be at least half an hour."

"I'll be here in the lab for the next couple of hours, so don't sweat it and don't do anything stupid to get out of there."

Nate didn't like the tone of his friend's voice. Jacob sounded darker than usual—which made Nate slightly nervous. Jacob was normally a laid-back kind of guy. In his field of digital imagery, he'd seen just about every sort of horror, but years ago had managed to ease off from the panic mode and decided to take things easy. Nate had seen the man munching on a sandwich while analyzing graphic images of autopsy photos.

"What's wrong?" Nate asked his friend.

A pause. "I can't exactly explain it on the phone."

"It must be something really important if—"

"Important, yes. And weird. And also something I just can't explain. At least, not right now."

"Jake, what the hell's going on?"

"Like I said, you need to come in. I can't say—well, you'll just have to see this. Even then, you'll probably have the same doubts I've been having."

"Can't you just tell me what the hell you're trying to—"

"You won't believe me."

"Try me."

Silence.

Nate felt the back of his neck growing uncomfortably warm. "Jake? It isn't like you to ass around like this."

245

More silence. Then, a click, telling him he had another call. He read the display. *Johnny Rock*. Terrific. The big man would just have to wait. Whatever Jake had on the burner sounded serious.

"Jake?"

A sigh. "It's about the woman you're looking for. In the digitals you sent me."

"All right…"

"There isn't any other way to say this."

"Dammit, say it anyway."

"Well, in a word, the woman you're looking for—"

"What about her?"

"She's dead."

***

Nate finally answered on the fifth ring.

"What the hell's goin' on?" Johnny couldn't keep from being anxious. "Why take so damn long to answer?"

"Well, for one thing, I had another call. And I'm stuck in traffic."

"What the hell's that got to do with anything?"

"Nothing. Not really…"

Johnny didn't like what he was hearing— rather, *not* hearing. It sounded like Nate was stalling—which also told him that McCormick might be trying to keep something from him. "Once again…what's goin' on?"

"I don't really know. I've got an appointment with a friend of mine, works Forensics with the L.A. cops in their lab. I won't know anything until I talk to him."

"Forensics?"

"I sent him the digital images of the two women who crashed your party."

"Okay…" Johnny felt his pulse quicken. He took a deep breath and forced himself to chill. "Are ya sure that's *all* you wanna say?"

"Like I just said—"

"I know what ya just said. Tell me what ya *ain't* saying."

A pause. "I don't know what you mean."

"Dammit, Nate, you're holding somethin' back. Tell me you're not and everything'll be just fine."

He heard Nate sigh, which signaled even more red flags. "Like I just told you, I have to talk to my friend before I can give you anything solid."

"You're telling me you're *not* holdin' anything back?"

"I'm telling you I can't share anything with you until I know for sure."

Johnny knew right then that something serious was going down. Something very bad, most likely. Something Johnny wasn't sure he wanted to hear. And he was positive it had everything to do with the digital of the blonde. "Ya sound weird, Nate. Really weird. It ain't like you. Tell me why ya sound weird."

Another sigh, this one deeper. "It's like this. This accident is doing me in. I'm sitting here, there are people and vehicles all over the damned place, three different homeless people came up to me and asked me for money while another went behind my vehicle and took a leak, and I'm getting kind of antsy. I haven't eaten since breakfast, my reflux is kicking my ass, and—"

"Enough, all right?"

"You asked..."

Johnny wanted to get angry but knew that wouldn't help. Most important, it would only make things worse. And Nate was right—he *did* ask. And if Nate wasn't quite ready to let him know what he'd found out, maybe that was a *good* thing.

"Just be sure to call me when you have somethin', *capisc*?"

"You know I will."

***

Disguised as a brown-haired, plain-faced lady in a lime-green pullover sweater, baggy jeans, and fancy hand-stitched open-toed loafers, Tiffany crossed the street. After veering around small roving groups of chattering teens and two cops, she hurried down the busy block, heading west. She watched the halted traffic as well as the activity across the street while looking frantically for Chip.

Half a block straight ahead, she spotted the tall, slender brunette. Dressed in tight maroon pants, a white wraparound blouse and black spikes, Chip was heading west as well.

Tiffany smiled. Typical of him to assume the same shape as before. This was possibly the smartest thing he could do right now. This way, Tiffany could recognize him right off. But since she was still wary about being overheard, she decided to use a man's voice as a disguise.

"*I see you, girl,*" she sent across the street, keeping the same steady pace as she approached the end of the block. "*Nice outfit.*"

Chip nearly stumbled as he moved down the street. He didn't send back a reply right off, just glanced in her direction and gave a slight nod. Tiffany could tell he had already figured things out. "*I thought you'd appreciate it,*" he sent back in his sensuous low female voice.

"*Where do you want to meet? It's less hectic down the next block. The police aren't doing anything down there.*"

"*I spotted a coffeeshop at the next corner. We could meet there and share a cappuccino.*"

"*Sounds good. By the way, see anything we need to be worried about?*"

"*No, but if he's tied in with you know who, he won't be far.*"

"*Maybe we should try another couple of blocks. Keep an eye out, okay?*"

"*Gotcha.*"

***

The blonde disappeared in the crowds the same moment her redheaded partner vanished amongst hordes of tourists scrambling for their cell phones to film the street activity.

Changing into a skinny guy with curly gray hair tied in a long ponytail and dressed in a baggy hunting shirt, ragged jeans and a pair of beat-up running shoes, Jose Bribon moved over to the storefront of a health food store. For the next few minutes, he leaned against the brick wall and carefully studied the activity.

Small groups of mortals shuffled by, some jabbering away while others passed in silence. Some were old, others young. Most were female, the youngsters, male. A homeless guy picked up a smoldering cigar from the gutter, sniffed it, then stuck it in his mouth. A skinny homeless woman squatted in front of a pharmacy door. A couple in their early thirties were bent over, picking up their spilled groceries. A cop was talking to a middle-aged woman in the crowd. Two giggling teens had moved closer to the accident and took pictures on their cell phones. Another cop rushed over and yanked them away. Four tanned young babes strutted past. Jose struggled to keep his mind focused. This wasn't the time to let his libido take over.

It was obvious that the rogues had shapeshifted. Since the crowds had turned chaotic in the last five minutes, things had grown trickier. Jose knew right then that he'd have to use all his powers to locate them.

A plain-looking woman around thirty years old with mousey brown hair and baggy clothes walked past, glancing at him briefly before crossing the street.

Jose sensed some chatter going on somewhere near the woman, perhaps from the small crowd in front of her. He heard a man's voice. Jose caught a couple of random words

("*Where…want…meet…*")

but nothing tangible enough to make out what was going on. He also picked up snippets of conversation from others, making things even more confusing.

He kept up his concentration and heard another couple of words, this time

("could meet there...")

from a different voice, this one another male.

He fought hard to focus. Although he wasn't one hundred percent certain, he guessed that these voices could quite possibly belong to the rogues he was looking for. Since he couldn't penetrate their thoughts in such chaos, he decided that he should follow his gut.

Jose concentrated even harder, but entirely too many individual voices and thoughts were making his efforts impossible. Certain the rogues would move away from the commotion, he waited for another small group of mortals to go by, then fell in behind them.

Half a block later, two mortals leading his group veered right, entering a coffeehouse. Staying close with the pack, Jose focused on pulling more thoughts out of the air. He heard nothing—which told him that the two possibly knew who he was.

Even so, the fact that he couldn't interpret what he'd heard before irritated him. How were they able to keep their communication from him? It just didn't make sense.

One block later, the slim brunette walking forty feet ahead turned off and entered a Chinese restaurant.

Just then, he heard the male voice again

("I'm...into...restaurant...")

and realized that he could be on the right track.

251

Jose kept with the crowd. Half a block farther down, he went over to another storefront and stopped beside the large bay window. Then, leaning against the building, he watched the mousey-haired woman crossing the street before ducking into the Chinese restaurant.

***

Nate McCormick and Jacob Sharp huddled over the worktable in the Forensic lab in the large dimly lit room, staring at two images Jake had frozen, blown up, detailed, then reproduced on the screen in front of them. The images showed the same woman, obviously, although in one of them, her skin was slightly darker from what was most likely the result of a tanning lotion.

Even though Nate had to agree with the result, he couldn't believe what his friend was trying to tell him. It just didn't make sense. How could a woman show up at a pool party—or any other place—if she was obviously dead?

"You're sure about your findings?" Nate asked his friend. "Absolutely sure? Positive?"

"The pixels don't lie." Jake adjusted the zoom lens, making the second image slightly sharper. "Judging by how I've matched the images, this face belongs to the young woman who was pronounced dead six months ago at Encino Hospital Medical Center."

Dead. The woman was dead. But she was clearly on the screen at Johnny Rock's pool party just hours ago. And she was alive. And walking around. And looking ten times better than any of the other babes at the shindig.

"But how can this be? It just doesn't...I mean, what the hell?"

Jake had been working at the L.A. Police Department for years and had seen just about everything. He was the best in his field of photography and digital imagery and had enjoyed a remarkable reputation for the last twenty-odd years. He held numerous degrees in Forensic Science and was frequently asked to speak at colleges and universities. He was not the type who could be easily stumped.

However, in this case, he clearly had encountered something very bizarre, and was disturbed by the result.

"I wish I could tell you," he replied after considerable thought. "All I can say is that the evidence shows—"

"It shows what? That this young woman resembles this other young woman who was brought in dead six months ago from one of Johnny Rock's pool parties?"

"Not only *resembles*," Jake Sharp said, a prominent vertical line appearing between his bushy gray brows. "The pixels, as I said, don't lie. The faces are entirely too close. Too similar."

"Identical twins?"

"Impossible."

"How can you say that?"

Jake went back to the viewer and carefully increased the zoom on both images. He took his penlight and focused a silver beam on the image on the left, of the woman's left cheek, just half an inch from where her lips ended. "See that tiny mole?"

"Barely…"

"Now check this out." Jake switched to the second image, focusing, once again, on the woman's cheek. The mole was identical, and in the very same area. "See this?"

"So? They have the same mole."

"In the very same exact area?"

Nate didn't like what the man was implying but didn't want to admit to anything. Not yet, anyway. Not when he had to report all this to Johnny Rock, who would not appreciate Jake's findings. "Identical twins share the same DNA, don't they?"

"Correct."

"All right, then."

Jake didn't say anything right off. Then he sighed tiredly. "Do you happen to know the odds of identical twins having identical birthmarks?"

Nate could tell where his friend was going with this and didn't want to hear the explanation. He just shrugged.

"Identical twins, or monozygotic twins, form when a single fertilized egg splits in two and develops into two separate embryos, producing two babies. Since the two develop from the same egg, they have the same genetic origins and very often have extremely similar physical characteristics. This makes them look identical."

"Wouldn't this explain the mole?"

"Not necessarily."

"What the hell are you trying to say?"

"Identical twins aren't exactly alike in every way. Human beings are influenced by more than their genes. Entirely too many other factors come

254

into play. There's environment. There's also movement inside the womb. The delivery process itself. There are all sorts of other significant factors we aren't even aware of yet."

"Then you're saying that the odds of this birthmark showing in the same exact place on two different faces are…?"

"To put it bluntly? Astronomical."

Nate groaned. This sounded worse and worse. He knew he was going to have to face the fact that what Jake was suggesting was totally incredible, but also something both he and Johnny Rock would have to deal with. "Then what you're saying is that you're one hundred percent positive that these two images belong to the same woman?"

Jake looked grim. "I would stake my twenty-five-year reputation on the fact that this woman is the same person who was transported from Mr. Rock's pool party six months ago and pronounced dead long before she was brought into this building."

***

Tiffany eyed the dinner crowd. Although she couldn't sense the demon's presence in the room, she knew something wasn't quite right. If she'd learned anything since her death, it was that she should never underestimate the tenacity of a demon.

She kept her senses alert as she approached Chip's booth.

He glanced in her direction and winked, which looked strange due to the long, curly lashes. *"Whaddya think, Honey Bunny? Egg rolls? The moo goo gai pan on that dish over there looks appetizing—"*

"Be serious, now..."

"Serious? About what?"

She gave him a glare.

He shrugged. "*Just trying to stick a little levity into the —*"

"Would you really like me to tell you where you can stick your levity?"

"Oucherino. But I see where you're coming from."

She went back to studying the customers sitting at the tables she drew closer to Chip. "*He's close."*

"You see any sign of him in here?"

"Not right now." She reached his booth and sat down beside him.

Chip flicked some long black hair away from his face and gave the room another glance. "Did you see anyone hanging around outside?" he asked in a soft voice.

"Just a skinny guy with a long gray ponytail leaning against the wall about three shops down."

Chip shot a quick glance at the front door. He turned back to her and blinked. "Something's really bugging the tits off you. Which really saddens me—"

"Stop it."

He grinned sheepishly.

She began thinking about the gray-haired man she'd seen earlier that morning, after they'd left the diner. But since she hadn't sensed anything special coming from him, she guessed that he was probably just a poor homeless soul.

256

But it made her wonder once again why she couldn't get him out of her mind.

"So what's bugging you, dearest?"

"I'm not sure. Just a hunch. I'll let you know if something tangible comes up."

The slender red-haired waitress brought over two menus.

Tiffany spotted someone coming into the restaurant. The man was about forty, with long, reddish-brown hair and a scruffy beard. He was wearing a dark-blue tank top, red shorts and dirty brown sandals.

Tiffany took her menu from the waitress and waited until she'd whisked away before concentrating on the newcomer.

The darkness drifting over from the man grew heavier. He drew closer and took a booth three down from her and Chip. The darkness instantly turned foul.

She sent Chip a look that clearly said, "It's him."

Chip frowned and coughed. "Smells ripe. Where is he?"

"Three booths down."

He cleared his throat. "The dude who obviously doesn't know how to trim a beard?"

She nodded.

"What do we do?"

"Any suggestions?"

Chip sipped his ice water. "Not yet."

"Give me a couple of minutes."

"I just hope we have enough time to do some nifty stuff. To tell you the truth, I've been getting bored lately."

"How bored?"

"Bored enough to stand up right now and do my famous head-spin."

"I'd rather handle this without an audience. I know how this can end. In two minutes, there will be dozens of cell phones pointed at us. A minute later, a thousand hits will respond to at least a hundred tweets. Two minutes after that, the police will follow the media people here. By tomorrow, this restaurant will be featured on at least ten different channels and will enjoy a tremendous burst of business—"

"I getcha, Honey Bunny."

"Then you'll behave?"

He sighed tiredly. "As much as I hate to, I guess I'll act like a good little boy—"

"You're a girl now."

"Thanks *ever* so for the reminder."

***

Johnny Rock didn't care much for the expression on Nate McCormick's face when the detective came into his study at 7:00 that evening. Nate looked tired, worn-out. To make matters worse, he was pale—something you just didn't see in this part of the country.

"What's goin' on?" Johnny gestured for the detective to sit. "You look two shits to the wind."

"I've just been with one of my contacts at the L.A. Police Department. He's one of the top

Forensic scientists in the country, specializes in photography and digital imagery."

Johnny watched as Nate sat down. Nate was staring in his direction, but it was obvious that the detective wasn't looking at him. In fact, judging by the blank expression on the man's face, Johnny didn't think Nate was looking at anything at all.

But what bothered Johnny even more was that Nate had been to the Police Department. Johnny had always been careful to stay on the right side of the cops since coming to the West Coast but didn't like dealing with them. He was painfully aware that Nate frequently rubbed elbows with law enforcement and realized that the man's profession required such dealings from time to time. And although Johnny had always firmly believed that things would stay relatively peaceful if he kept his affairs clean, he still found his nerves automatically fraying at the ends whenever he sensed that his business was treading a little too close to the Boyle Heights area. It was his childhood memories, no doubt, rushing back to haunt him.

And the mere mention of a colleague on retainer going to the cops naturally raised red flags.

Johnny poured some port wine. This was no time to lose control. *Stay cool*, he reminded himself. *Find out what's going on. Then you can figure out what to do. But not just yet.* He offered some wine to Nate, who shook his head.

"Forensics? You mean those squinty little guys crawling around at crime scenes? The ones with the powders? The sprays? The little cases filled with liquids and chemicals?"

"Like I just said, my friend works with imagery."

Johnny sipped his wine and decided to get right to the point. "And just what were ya doin' there?"

Nate didn't speak right off. He was looking at his hands in his lap. Squeezing them, turning them, cracking the knuckles. He looked like someone noticing his hands for the very first time. He finally raised his eyes and focused them directly on Johnny. "I sent my friend the image of the young woman you emailed me. He did extensive tests on the images, then called me into the lab to share his findings. We spent more than an hour comparing the image to that of another female. This same young lady had attended one of your parties six months ago."

Johnny stiffened in his seat but made no reply. This was getting much too close to the bone. He sincerely hoped that his suspicions would not ring true. They couldn't. Suspicions such as this would make no sense. No *logical* sense…

Nate sat back in his chair. Johnny could clearly see the confusion on the detective's face, as well as a slight hint of fear in the way the man's right eyelid twitched.

Fear was not what Johnny wanted to see at all. Fear made this situation troublesome. It made him suspicious that he might have been right about all this after all. This was the one thing in the world he didn't want. Not at all.

He promised himself that he *couldn't* be right. He just *couldn't* be. Things like this just didn't

260

happen. And he was going to find out that he was all wrong if it was the last thing he ever did.

But it didn't help at all that Nate still wasn't saying anything. The man continued playing with his hands. This had to stop. It had to stop right now.

"Well? What exactly did your friend find out?"

"The pixels presented a problem when he first started examining them. But upon further inspection, he discovered something else. Something that made no sense."

Johnny's throat had suddenly become constricted. He could barely get the words out. "*What* made no sense?"

Nate took a moment before replying. "These two young women," he said in a soft voice, "they…turned out to be…well, one in the same."

Johnny tried his best not to lose his composure. He didn't want any part of what Nate had just said. The detective's statement merely substantiated what Johnny had already suspected.

But it made no sense. Not one bit of fucking sense!

Steady, he told himself. *You're a successful guy, for Christ's sake. You know practically every single wheeler-dealer in this state. You've been to every conceivable bigshot function in Hollywood and have the biggest guys in the country on speed dial.*

Don't let this beat you down. Find out more about it first. For all you know, Nate might be totally wrong about the whole thing.

"I hope you realize that this doesn't seem to be makin' any sense," he finally said in a weak voice.

"I could be clearer," Nate said. "But that depends on you."

"I'm payin' ya serious money to tell me exactly what's goin' on. Now grow a pair and *tell* me, for God's sake!"

"Maybe this would be a tad more obvious when I say that the images of these women lead to one very startling conclusion."

"And that is…?"

Nate sat up sharply. He took a deep breath and looked Johnny straight in the eye. Johnny could see fear and doubt, as well as a few other things he didn't want to see. "The photos of the two women matched. Perfectly."

Johnny felt his entire body turn cold. Yes, dammit. *Much* too close to the damn bone.

Johnny finished his drink. He met the detective's gaze and felt a sudden pang in his gut. He had to make this crystal clear. He was paying ten K for a couple of day's work, for God's sake. In other words, there could be no doubts. No ifs. No buts. "I wish you'd speak plain, man. I'm payin' you too much damn money to—"

"What I'm trying to say is this," Nate McCormick said in a soft whisper. "Judging by the two separate images you provided, my educated friend maintains that the woman who crashed your party earlier today is the same woman who was pronounced dead at another one of your parties six months ago."

***

262

Their waitress hurried over to their booth. "Decided what you'd like to have for dinner?" she asked, smiling.

"Please give us another minute," Tiffany said.

Groaning, the girl hurried away.

Chip sipped his ice water and put down the glass. "Now that we have a pretty nifty idea of what's going on," he asked, "what's next?"

Tiffany stabbed a thumb in the direction of the customer sitting three booths down. She mouthed the word, "Distraction."

Chip shrugged.

"I think we need to stretch our legs in a little while," she said softly.

"I guess I could use the exercise. Being a voluptuous babe takes a lot out of a guy."

"Tell me about it."

"Okay... As a voluptuous babe, I frequently find myself agonizing over the silliest—"

"I didn't really mean for you to go into a lengthy explanation."

"Honey Bunny, when have you ever known me to—"

"Every time you open your mouth."

"Besides that?"

"Stick to the subject."

"Which is?"

"Stretching our legs."

"Any ideas? We haven't seen as much of Hollywood as I wanted."

"What would you like to see?"

"How about Hollywood and Vine? I've heard that a shitload of big-name stars congregates in that section."

"What big-name stars are you talking about?"

He shrugged. "Gable. Bogart. That tall, lanky guy from Montana who always said, "Yep," and "Nope.""

"Wrong century," she said with a scowl.

"Well, I guess I'll always be a little old-fashioned."

Tiffany nodded.

"Let's talk food, then."

"Well, since we're sitting in a restaurant…"

"What would you like to have?" he asked. "The orange juice sounds to die for."

"I'm more interested in their egg rolls. I've heard a lot of things about the egg rolls in this place."

"Good things?"

She glared. "Would I want to come here if I'd heard *bad* things about their egg rolls?"

"Good point."

Tiffany focused for a few moments, did a quick probe into the brain of the demon, then smiled.

"Talk to me, Princess…"

"This guy," she mouthed. "He's a prankster."

"You mean, like me?"

She shook her head. "Not hardly. This guy hurts people."

"I've been known to do things like that."

"Not to the extent that this boy does."

Chip sighed. "Oh well. I guess that's why I'll always be small potatoes."

264

"I wouldn't want you any other way," she said with a wink.

"I'm flattered. And befuddled. And amazed. And bewildered. And—"

"Save it—please?"

"Well, since you were so polite…"

Tiffany stabbed a thumb at the front entrance and used her other hand to count out fifteen.

"Minutes?" Chip mouthed.

She whispered, "Seconds."

Chip didn't say anything right off. Tiffany could tell he was thinking this over.

Tiffany lowered her voice. "One thing, though. We can't cause any injuries."

"You mean—"

"That's exactly what I mean."

"But—"

"No buts about it."

Chip pouted. "Dammit…"

"Why the pout?"

"You should know that by now."

"You should be used to all this."

"I know. But I'm not."

"Then try."

"I can't promise anything…"

"Try anyway. We've been doing this quite a while, now…"

"I know. But it's hard being good when you really don't know how."

"Back to the plan. Any questions?"

"I guess I'll have to trust you."

"I've been pretty dependable up to now, haven't I?"

"That's beside the point."

"Then why do you have doubts?"

"It's this thing I have. My mother gave it to me."

"What's it called?"

He shrugged. "Doubt."

"That's silly."

Chip beamed. "My middle name, angel baby."

***

As Jose Bribon sipped his ice water, he watched the blonde and the brunette babe leaving the restaurant.

He put down his glass and tried focusing but could not pick up anything from either of them. He'd heard them talking earlier but hadn't been able to pick up on anything useful. There were just too many other disturbances. The four babes at the corner table had complicated the situation by engaging in endless chatter. The fat guy at the center table pigging out on wontons and egg foo young had also added confusion with his burping and loud belching. To make matters worse, the irritating, high-pitched gibberish from the toddler squirming around in the highchair in the next booth convinced him he wouldn't be able to focus sufficiently.

Even so, he could tell the rogues were up to something. They obviously knew he was here.

He slid out of the booth, got up, and bumped into a waitress balancing a tray of orders. The food slid off the tray just as she turned on her ankle and went down, banging Jose in the shoulder with the tray and forcing him down as well. Temporarily dazed, he got right back up. Another waitress rushed over to help her friend, bumping him in the side and knocking him down again.

Flustered and angry, Jose searched for an escape route. At that same moment, someone pulled back a chair, blocking his exit. Groaning, Jose got to his feet and struggled to squeeze between the two waitresses. A plate of egg rolls slid off the next table, dropping to the floor at his feet. An egg roll bounced toward him, wedging itself beneath his shoe, and he slipped and went down once again.

By this time, nearly a dozen people had joined in on the chaos, some helping the waitress while others grabbed their cell phones for selfies.

It took Jose several minutes to extricate himself from the bedlam. By the time he'd reached the front entrance and dashed outside, both the blonde and the brunette had vanished.

***

Once Nate McCormick had left, Johnny Rock opened his liquor cabinet, got out the $11,000 bottle of 1955 Glenfarclas he'd been saving for a special occasion, cracked it open and filled his glass. To hell with the port. Port was good for thinning out the blood. And for helping digest dinner. And for having something light to help kick back and mellow.

This situation called for the big guns. Something you needed to numb yourself into thinking that whatever you'd just heard didn't really happen. That what you'd just been told was wrong. And that what you'd suspected all along just wasn't so.

He kept telling himself that what Nate had told him just couldn't possibly be. What Nate had said defied logic. And understanding. And belief.

A dead woman coming back to life and showing up at the same mansion where she'd died six months earlier?

Just how the hell could anyone believe something like that?

He sat back, closed his eyes and tried hard to recall what had happened. Nothing came right off. Sighing, he brought the glass to his lips and drank an inch of the strong malt. It went down warm, tingling in his gut, settling the shaking in his limbs and numbing some of the tension. Not too shabby for one of the most expensive drinks in the world. He closed his eyes again and struggled to chill. To get past all this. To convince himself that he'd been blameless in this. And most of all, to persuade himself to believe that Nate McCormick—as well as McCormick's fancy Forensics buddy—had to be totally and utterly wrong about their discovery.

But after just a minute or so, he realized he was fooling himself. Nate's buddy was a professional who worked for the L.A. Police Department. A lab expert who dealt with digital images all the time. A man who sniffed things, dissected things, swabbed things, tested things, analyzed things, studied things until he practically went blind, then spent hours upon hours researching what he'd learned, deducting a solid conclusion from what the evidence had told him. All day long—five, maybe six or even seven days a week—for a quarter of a century. And what the man had come up with was something that had been proven scientifically, relying heavily on the latest technological advancements.

The images had matched. The woman who had shown up at his pool party earlier that day was the same woman who had passed out and died at a party he'd coordinated in this very same place six months ago.

Her name was Tiffany something. Yes. How could he forget? How could anyone forget the name of a stunningly beautiful woman who had died on his property just six months earlier?

From what Nate had said, the identical twin theory couldn't hold water. The possibility of the images of both women having the same exact mole in the same exact place was downright impossible. Johnny seriously wanted to consider it, for no other reason than to shoot down Nate's theory, as well as his lab friend's professional analysis. It was possible, wasn't it? Of course it was. Identical twins were walking around everywhere. Why couldn't this be one of those cases?

And what if one of the moles had actually been *painted* on? That was possible, too, wasn't it?

No. It wasn't.

A painted-on mole would have been too damn convenient. And, for a forensics expert, ridiculously easy to spot. And whenever Johnny even attempted to ponder that, his conscience came right back and told him he was being silly. There was *no* identical twin. Whatever happened was *not* logical—or even possible...

Though Johnny had never been the most superstitious guy in the world, he did believe in the Afterlife, God, Purgatory, Heaven and Hell, and ghosts. And although he had never once considered someone actually coming back from the dead, he knew that, like most everything else that happened in life, everything presented a distinct possibility. And if this possibility did happen, it was on him. And he'd be a damn fool to think otherwise.

The memories came back in a chilling rush. The party. The sudden commotion just a few minutes past the lunch hour. The frantic 911 call. And lastly, the arrival of the paramedics.

"Mr. Rock?" It was Stacy, his secretary back then. She'd opened his door and rushed in, unannounced—something she'd never done before. Her huge green eyes were filling the sockets when she blurted it out in a hysterical voice: "Something horrible's just happened out in the pool!"

"What is it?"

"It's one of your guests... She's...she's unconscious!"

He'd rushed out of his office, hurried down the spiral staircase and bolted outside in the matter of seconds—a dangerous feat for a man in his mid-forties and more than fifty pounds overweight.

He'd reached the scene just moments before the paramedics had arrived and began zoning out while watching two of his guards—as well as Lenny, one of his lifeguards—frantically administering mouth-to-mouth to the gorgeous, bikini-clad blond babe lying lifeless at poolside.

"What the fuck happened?" It was the only thing his brain could come up with at that moment. And all he could remember was that no one had an answer for him. At least, nothing that made any sense. Everyone was gawking at the unconscious girl, their eyes on her breasts, her thighs, and her thick, golden hair spread out like a glittering curtain on the pavement.

The only thing that finally made sense was the fact that less than an hour later, after the medical unit had taken her to the hospital, he'd brought up the tapes of the party and saw Alan Richards, that reality show hopeful working for one of the town's biggest film producers, standing off to the side, sipping a martini and looking like he was just a shot or two short of passing out.

And when he'd phoned Richards later and told him to come up to his office, the idiot shuffled unsteadily into the room two hours after the phone call and stood there like a drunken idiot, eyes glazed, jaw slack.

"What the fuck happened down there? I saw ya talkin' to that girl just before she collapsed. It's right there on the damned tape. What the fuck did ya do?" Johnny had wanted to wrap his hands around the idiot's neck and strangle him until those glazed eyeballs popped out of their sockets and rolled down his cheeks. Johnny had heard stories of Richards doing the date rape thing to get laid, but even though the idiot—as well as everyone else— had been warned against doing things like that at the estate, that everyone involved would be banned from all future pool parties and celebrity events if it

271

ever happened, and that everyone, no matter who, would be blackballed in L.A. if something like that ever did happen, Johnny realized that the asshole gazing blankly at him in his study just wasn't worth the bother it would take to get him on a charter plane to Hawaii and toss his worthless ass in the ocean on the way over.

"Did you put something in that poor girl's drink?"

A shrug.

"What the fuck does that *mean?"*

Another shrug.

"You were with her, you moron! Just before she fainted. I saw it on the screen. What in holy fuck did you do?"

The man's glossy eyes told him the worst. Richards had been much too drunk at the time and had no idea what he'd done. But at that same moment, Richards muttered in a slurred voice, "Wasn't my fault."

"What the hell d'ya mean by that*?"*

Richards gave a loose shrug. "You know we all do it, don'tcha?"

"No. I don't *know that. A few months back, I heard that one or two of you bozos had been doing it, and that's why I tightened security. I can't possibly have date rapes or date rape drugs associated with my shindigs!"*

Then, incredibly, Richards laughed.

It was right then that Johnny felt his blood pressure spiking, beginning to burst. "You think this is funny*?"*

272

"I think it's funny that you think you can stop it from happening. These babes are hot, man. I mean smoldering! What the hell's the big deal?"

"The big deal, you stupid idiot, is that what you gave that girl put her in cardiac arrest!"

Richards's eyes suddenly grew. To Johnny, it looked like he'd just sobered up. Apparently the idiot hadn't heard the latest. In a soft, unsteady voice, Richards said: "Mr. Rock...I might have spiked her drink, but I had no idea...I didn't know...this is a complete surprise—"

Johnny couldn't believe this man could be so stupid. "You had no idea what was in it?"

The man didn't reply. He began to shake.

"I want the name of the asshole you bought that stuff from. I want it now!"

Richards began shaking even worse. "I can't...you know I can't give that to you!"

"Can't? Or won't?"

"I have no idea who gave it to me!"

"You just—"

"I bought it from one of the guards at Paramount. I assumed it was the same stuff I've always—"

"You've done this before?"

"A couple of times..."

"Which guard?"

"The one at the front gate. The tall dude with the red buzzcut. But listen, I don't think—"

"You need to leave. Right now." It was all Johnny could do to keep his arms at his side. He'd grown up on the streets and had encountered some unsavory characters, but he'd never wanted to

273

*strangle a man so much before in his entire life.
"I've got some very important business to tend to.
I've got to get with the Paramount people so they
can fire their guards and hire a bunch of new ones
they can trust. Then I'm gonna bury you, you stupid
son of a bitch. I'm gonna make it where you won't
be able to find a job in this town if it bit you in your
worthless ass! Does that mean anything to you?
Did it penetrate that moronic pea-brain you've
been carryin' around all your pathetic life?"*

The man continued trembling.

*"Get the hell out of here! And if I ever see you
within five miles of this estate again, I'm gonna
personally have my guards bundle you up, drive
you out to the dock, put you on one of my boats,
take you out to sea, chop you up into a million bite-
size pieces and feed you to the fuckin' sharks!"*

And when that last image vanished into a cloud
of heated blackness, Johnny Rock finished his
drink, put down his glass, fell back in his chair and,
groaning deeply, collapsed into a deep sleep.

***

Once the taxi pulled away from the curb, Chip
asked, "How'd you ever live here, Tifferoo?"

"Whatever do you mean?"

"I've seen more weirdos in this place than
anywhere else. And that includes Hades City,
where I saw more maggots wiggling around than
actual residents."

"You don't remember seeing any strange
people in Florida? Or Pittsburgh? Or even in
Peoria?"

274

Chip scratched the back of his neck. "They just seem weirder here. And there are a lot more of them."

"How would that be?"

"I keep seeing people walking around and can't make out if they're male or female."

"This is Hollywood. Don't you think that should tell you something?"

"It tells me that the plastic surgeons around here are a confused bunch."

"Like I've told you before, this is a beauty culture. If you're not beautiful, you'll never make your mark here."

"What about all those tents we've seen? And all those people taking a leak in the street? And all those gross piles of—"

"Enough."

"Well? Don't they have bathrooms here? Or is that part of your so-called beauty culture?"

"Let's talk about that later."

"I guess that means you don't have a valid defense?"

"As I just said, later. Right now—"

"I know. Taking care of business."

Tiffany turned and stared at the eight-foot iron fence and the huge three-story mansion behind it. The memories drifted by, reminding her once again of her horror.

"So then, do we just walk right in and give them our best smiles?"

"I don't think smiles will work in our case."

"Really? I've been working on a killer dazzle for the last twenty minutes. How's this?" He flashed his silly grin.

"That doesn't do a thing for me."

"How about this?" His eyeballs began moving around in different directions.

Tiffany just shook her head.

"Nothing? Really? That usually puts the worst of 'em in a good mood."

"For one thing, I don't feel like smiling."

"You should've told me that before I used up so much energy."

"I'd think that you should know what sort of mood I'm in right now."

"Good point. So then, Plan Number Two will be…?"

That was a good question. She hadn't even thought she'd get the chance to come back. It didn't seem possible, did it? After all, she was dead, and it was all because of what had happened just beyond that fence. Her destiny—as well as her fate—had taken place less than a hundred feet away.

But right now, as her brain swam with the events that had happened such a short time ago, she realized that there was indeed an order to the universe. She'd been here just hours earlier, but this time, things felt much different. The last time, she'd met up with one of the rich monsters responsible for luring the girls away. He might not have been the guilty one, but he'd put her on the right track.

This time, she would encounter the man in charge. She'd find the monster who had murdered her, once and for all. She'd been given the chance

276

to come back. Now it was up to her to make things right.

And that was the most important thing of all.

"Tifferoo? Plan Number Two? In a nutshell, maybe? Even a condensed version would be just dandy right now. If you've got the time, that is…"

"I'm not really sure," she replied.

"You look kind of bummed out right now, if you know what I mean."

"I'll be fine once we get this done."

Chip moved closer to the fence and grabbed one of the bars. "Well, it's not electrified."

"It doesn't need to be. There are guards all over the place. Johnny Rock usually has six or eight of them working and moves them around whenever he's expecting guests. The fact that there's none here right now tells me he's got nothing planned for tonight. But the side gate is always locked."

Chip was gazing through the iron bars. "I see a couple of steroid freaks in tacky suits farther down, toward the front."

"I see them, too."

"I hope you don't want us overpowering them. They look, well, like they haven't been fed in a while. They can't hurt us, but I'm sure you don't want this making the eleven o'clock news."

A plan began developing in her mind. "Are you up to some invisible magic right now?"

Chip's grin beamed brightly in the orange haze of the streetlight. "Honey Buns, I thought you'd never ask."

***

Opening his eyes in the semidarkness of his study, Johnny Rock had the unsettling feeling that he wasn't alone.

The booze, no doubt. With what had been going on lately, it was a wonder he wasn't shitfaced drunk.

Squinting, he gazed at his empty glass on the blotter in front of him. Strange. He'd been a steady drinker for the last twenty-five years. It took him much more than a couple of inches of the world's best high-quality Scotch to knock him on his ass.

What the hell was different here?

That nonsense this afternoon?

The fact that his security system had picked up on someone who shouldn't have even been on the grounds because she had been dead for the last six months?

Or was it something else?

Something Nate McCormick had found out?

Was Johnny's world coming apart?

Was it his guilt coming back after what had happened, bringing back everything else with it?

He sat back in his seat, rubbed his eyes and tried to relax. There was entirely too much shit going on. Shit that made no sense. He was getting too old for such nonsense. Getting too old to be facing ghosts. And guilt. And dead babes. And things that came with no explanations.

He stared at his glass again. All he had to do was splash another couple of inches into it. He could use a decent nightcap. Then he could lie back, close his eyes and let the Scotch coax him into a quiet state of relaxing oblivion.

At least he didn't have to worry about the wife bothering him. Sophia had learned long ago that when her husband was in his study, it was best to let things be and go on with her life. And also keep the kids away.

Sophia, bless her, had never been one to stir the pot.

"Too goddamn old for this shit," he muttered to himself, and reached for the bottle.

At that same moment, he caught movement in the corner of his eye. The shadow of a woman with blond hair emerged from the darkness and came into view.

"W-What the *fuck*...?" He put the glass back down, sat straight up and swiveled in his seat. With a shaky hand, he groped for the desk lamp. The light clicked on, casting a hazy golden glow in the room, settling on the beautiful young woman standing before him, just five feet away.

It was the girl he'd seen earlier that afternoon.

The same young lady who had died at his pool party six months ago.

***

His dark eyes gawking at her, the terrified man sitting stiffly behind the desk did not move.

Tiffany sensed fear, terror, shame, humiliation, guilt, and several other things that had turned the man's skin pale. She'd expected to experience an overwhelming rage but realized in that instant that she could not feel any anger at all. She was gazing at a pathetic, trembling individual. A pitiful soul just seconds away from coming right out of his skin.

Which only made sense. After all, she was dead. And if she was reading his thoughts accurately, this man knew she was dead. But now, since she'd found him, she discovered that there was one very important reason why she experienced no rage. This man wasn't responsible for her death. And since she wasn't even sure that he knew what had actually happened, she could not hate him at all. Instead, she pitied him. He obviously felt responsible for her death, and even though he most likely hadn't been the one who had supplied the drug that had killed her, he felt genuine guilt for what had happened and would feel this way for the rest of his days.

But none of this was important right now. The only thing that mattered was finding Alan Richards, the man who *was* responsible.

"Do you remember me?" she asked Johnny Rock in a whisper.

After several long, tense moments, he nodded.

"Who am I?"

No response. He was obviously too terrified to speak.

Tiffany took another step closer. She had to stay in control. If she didn't hold it together, this man could go into cardiac arrest. He wasn't young, and obviously at least twenty-plus pounds overweight. And, glancing at the bottle of Scotch and empty glass on the desk, she guessed that he'd been drinking heavily.

"What do you remember?" she asked.

No response.

280

Tiffany took a moment to collect herself. It was difficult, but she managed a smile and sent a feeling of warmth to the man. A moment later, he sighed and relaxed in his chair.

"Please tell me what you remember."

Johnny Rock didn't reply.

"It might be better if you did one of your pokey-head thingys, Tifferoo," Chip sent over from his post at the door. *"This bad boy's obviously ready to freak. Or dump a large load in his boxers. Whatever he does won't be pretty, and it surely won't help us find your druggie guy."*

"You might be right," she sent back. *"I really don't want to hurt this man."*

"You really don't want to hurt anyone, *Honey Bunny."*

Tiffany turned back to Johnny Rock. *"Tell me what you remember,"* she sent into the man's mind.

His thoughts immediately turned chaotic with a flurry of activity out by his pool. Splashing. Laughing. People running around. Others standing around in small groups, holding umbrella drinks. Men in suits discussing business affairs.

Then the inevitable happened.

She saw herself lying on her back on the concrete beside the pool near the shallow end.

Her spirit turned cold.

Shuddering, she opened her eyes.

"Tifferoo?"

She barely heard him. She was struggling to keep from jumping back into the man's brain. *Do this the right way*, the tiny voice in the darkness of her thoughts whispered. *If you truly want to find your killer, you must go back there.*

"Tifferoosky?"

You must go back...

I can't—

You must!

"*You really can do it, young lady,*" coaxed another voice, this one soft and gentle, sounding vaguely familiar, like that of a sweet old man.

She closed her eyes once again. This time, when she sensed her consciousness drifting into the other man's head, she felt strangely relaxed and was surprised that the fear and the anger that had overcome her moments earlier had vanished.

"*I was given another chance,*" she sent to Johnny Rock. "*I came back to do a few things. These things were very bad, but I didn't do them. And because of this, there are bad spirits after me, and they're on a mission to send me away again. That doesn't matter, not really, because I intend to do only good things. In other words, I'm going to right a few wrongs. Do you understand?*"

The man trembled.

"*I'm not going to do anything to you. You're not a bad man. You don't need to be punished. You didn't do or say anything that led to my death, did you?*"

The man stopped trembling long enough to shake his head.

"*Did you know why I died?*"

A reluctant nod.

"*What did you do when you found out what happened?*"

282

It took several moments before the man responded. *"I...I confronted the bastard...the one who killed you. I...asked him what happened. I told him that...I told him that what he'd done was goddamn awful, that he shouldn't have done it."* Johnny Rock sighed deeply and looked down at his lap. *"I was so angry, I wanted to kill him. I...I threatened him, told him what I was gonna do. I felt so bad...so incredibly bad... I...I wanted to do something for you, but...but—"*

"But what?"

"I got your address from your agent. There were no relatives I could find. No friends. I...I had you cremated, and...and—"

"Where's the urn?"

"There's a cemetery on Santa Monica Boulevard. They call it the Hollywood Forever Cemetery. It's one of the oldest, and it tends to all sorts of stars and celebrities. I've had several crypts reserved there for my family. I put your ashes in one of them. I didn't...I couldn't think of anything else... I just couldn't stand someone like you dying without...without—"

He just sighed again and lowered his head.

Tiffany felt a stab of instant remorse for forcing this man through this torment. She knew right then that he wasn't a bad man at all. He wasn't exactly a *good* man, but he had a conscience, and this was what mattered most of all. She couldn't help feeling a warm connection with him for what he'd done.

"You did that? For me?"

He nodded.

283

"That was... very nice."

He shrugged. *"It was... the least I could do..."*

Tiffany felt sorry for him. He had mob connections and the reputation for dealing with shady people. But he was innocent in this case. This man had honestly tried to make the horrible situation right.

"I guess you know what I want most of all, don't you?" she asked.

Johnny Rock continued staring at his lap. The image of Alan Richards showed brightly in his thoughts. Richards had been in this very room, his eyes blood-shot, looking like he was ready to collapse. Tiffany could tell by the raging heat in Johnny's thoughts that he did in fact want to kill Richards.

After long, tense moments, Johnny Rock sighed tiredly. *"You want him. You want the asshole who did you in."*

"Where is he?"

A shrug.

"You have no idea?"

"I...I ruined him. His career tanked...right after you...after it happened. Last I heard, he went off the deep end and started drinkin'. No one would hire him, so he left town and went off by himself..."

"Where is he?"

Johnny Rock shook his head.

"Please tell me where he is."

"What will ya do if—"

"I don't know. But I have to find him."

Silence.

"Do you know where he is?"

284

Still no response.

"Please?"

Tiffany glimpsed a dark street fronted with abandoned buildings, cardboard boxes and tents lining the block, and trash covering the sidewalk. Sloppy-dressed figures staggered down the sidewalk, smoking weed. Others were bent over, sorting through the trash.

"Last I heard, he was seen somewhere on North Normandie." Johnny looked up at her. His dark, deep-set eyes were wet. *"A lady like you...you shouldn't...you really don't wanna go there—"*

"I'll be all right."

"You said you were...brought back?"

"Yes..."

"Then you really are...you were...you're not—
"

"I'm a spirit."

The man sat in silence, struggling to comprehend. *"You didn't deserve...what I mean is...I didn't want that to...you shouldn't have—"*

"I understand."

Johnny sighed deeply once again and lowered his head.

"Thank you so much for caring. I'll never forget what you did for me."

Another image of Richards showed up in the man's consciousness. Richards standing in front of Johnny's desk, his eyes glazed over as he said, *"I think it's funny that you think you can stop it from happening. These babes are hot, man. I mean smoldering! What the hell's the big deal?"*

What the hell was the big deal?

Another blast of hot, seething rage roared back. She fought it down.

"The big deal," Johnny had replied to Richards, *"is that what you gave that girl put her in cardiac arrest!"*

"Listen...I might have spiked her drink, but...I had no idea—"

Johnny Rock's brain dimmed into darkness as he slumped in his seat. His head fell back, and he slipped into a deep sleep.

CHAPTER 6 - THE TAXI DRIVER

The gray-haired cabby stopped at the intersection of Santa Monica Boulevard and North Normandie Avenue. It was late, and traffic was light. "Which way?" he asked in a soft voice while watching them in his mirror.

Tiffany didn't reply. She was still wondering why this man's voice sounded so familiar. Her thoughts raced. She thought for a moment that it hadn't been long since she'd last heard it, but the more she struggled to recall the details, the less she remembered.

"Confused?" the cabby asked during the silence.

"Just distracted," she told him.

"She's having a blond moment," Chip said with a grin.

"This is where you wanted me to bring you," the cabby said. "Any idea where you'd like to go from here?"

Tiffany forced herself to focus. According to Johnny Rock, Alan Richards was last seen in this area. However, Johnny hadn't given her any specific details. And since Tiffany had never come here when she was living in Hollywood, she didn't know which way they should go or what they should be looking for. They couldn't stop and ask; the figures they'd seen were prostitutes working their trade between buildings while others slouched at street corners, sharing joints, mugging one another, sleeping in tents and boxes, or panhandling.

"I'm really not sure," she told the cabby.

"This isn't exactly a really good place to be," the cabby replied. "Especially at this late hour. You're such a nice, personable young couple. I'd hate to see anything happen to you."

"Thank you."

"I'm at a loss for words," Chip said. "I don't think I've ever been referred to as personable before." He chuckled. "Personable. I like that. In fact—"

Tiffany elbowed him in the side. "You really don't have that loss-for-words thing down yet, do you?"

"May I ask what you're looking for?" the cabby asked. "Or who?"

Tiffany shrugged. "I'm looking for a certain man."

The cabby nodded.

"It's not what you think. This man…he was…he did something very bad to me. He was last seen somewhere around here. But I really have no idea where he might be."

The cabby continued watching her in his mirror. He shook his head. "I just can't understand why so many choose to be so cruel to one another."

"Neither can I," she said, feeling both sad and angry. "But that seems to be the way it is nowadays."

"What do *you* think, young man?" the cabby asked Chip.

Chip didn't reply; he was watching something across the street.

Tiffany elbowed him again. "This man asked you a question."

He frowned. "You don't have to be so physical, Tifferoo."

"Sometimes it's the only way I can get your attention."

"What was the question?"

The cabby smiled. "I was just telling this lovely lady that I just can't understand why so many choose to be so cruel to one another."

Chip nodded. "Oh…"

Tiffany glared. "Well?"

Chip shrugged. "The answer is very simple. People are assholes."

Tiffany shook her head. "Sorry," she told the cabby. "Someone dropped him on his head when he was a kid."

The cabby chuckled. "Tell me something, young lady."

"Yes?"

"When and if you find this person, what'll you do?"

The images came up automatically, making it more difficult for her to stay focused. "I honestly don't know. I'd like to think that I wouldn't do anything to hurt him."

"She won't," Chip said. "She's not the type. She's more of the spread-the-world-with-sunshine kind of babe."

Tiffany said nothing.

"I wouldn't want anything bad happening to such a beautiful, pleasant, soft-spoken young lady," the cabby said.

Even in the darkness of the cab, Tiffany could see his warm smile and gentle eyes in his mirror reflection. "Thank you, but I'm not so sure I could be very nice to this person. Not after what he did."

"I think your friend is right," the cabby said. "I don't think you're the type of person who hurts people."

Tiffany had no idea how to respond. The way the cabby had said it sounded almost as if he knew more than he was telling her. "You really don't know me."

"No. I don't. I can just tell."

"How?"

"By how you speak. The gentle way about you. And, of course, the incredible warmth in your beautiful eyes."

She couldn't reply. Once again, she felt strongly that she'd met this man before. She tried a second time to place his voice. She sensed that there was something she should be remembering. Something very important.

"Have we possibly…met before?" she finally asked.

The cabby paused before responding. "I honestly don't think so."

"Are you sure?"

He smiled. "I'd surely remember someone as beautiful and as special as you, young lady. You're not anything like the other young beauties I've picked up before."

The image of a park bench flashed in her mind and vanished quickly. Then, just before the confusion set in, a clear picture of Jimmy Russo blipped in her head.

Park bench. Jimmy Russo.

Could this actually be happening?

"I have this strange feeling that I might have seen you in Pittsburgh…"

"I'm flattered that you think you know me, young lady, but as I just said…" He shrugged.

The man's voice…

It seemed so *familiar*…

She struggled to clear her head, but too many things were going on. It had been a very busy, nerve-wracking day. She just couldn't be sure about anything anymore.

The cabby glanced at his side mirror and straightened in his seat. "I think we'd better make a decision shortly. There are four gentlemen, to use the term loosely, heading our way, and unless I'm mistaken, they're not coming over to ask for directions."

"I just wish I knew where we should go." Tiffany struggled to force her mind into the present. "The man I talked to told me North Normandie was the area where we might find the man I've been looking for. He didn't say anything else. I guess you could take us another block or so and drop us off. Then we'll just have to manage on our own."

The cabby pulled away from the curb, turned at the intersection and took the cab down two blocks, where the street turned into a solid wall of block buildings with tents, boxes and strewn trash covering the sidewalk. He pulled over to the curb, stopped and put the cab in park. Then turned in his seat. "I really don't feel comfortable, dropping you off here."

"It's all right," Tiffany said. "We can take care of ourselves."

"I'm sure of that. But before I leave, might I suggest something?"

"Sure."

He pointed to his left. "If you use that street entrance and walk down the first alley you come to, it'll keep you away from many of the more dangerous criminal elements in the area. Then you just might be able to find the person you've been looking for. That is, without either of you coming to any harm."

"How would you know that?" Chip asked.

He shrugged. "I drive a cab. Unfortunately, I'm... familiar with this area."

Tiffany waited for more of an explanation, but the man did not elaborate. "Hollywood's very large," she said.

"Actually, it's relatively small, but combined with L.A., yes, we're talking nearly five hundred square miles."

"And you know about that alley?" Chip asked.

"I've been driving around here a great many years, young man."

Tiffany could tell the cabby was deliberately being evasive. "How would you know about the person we're looking for?"

292

The man smiled. "How could I?"

"Then how would you know where we should—"

"It's just a suggestion. I'm fairly familiar with the crime element out here as well as the hot spots to avoid."

"We'll keep it in mind," Chip said after a short pause.

The cabby nodded.

"How much do we owe you?" Tiffany asked.

"Don't you worry about that, young lady. My treat."

Tiffany couldn't believe what the man had just said. Once again, her curiosity perked up. "Really? Truly?"

"It's always a joy for me, meeting a beautiful young lady who isn't full of herself and knows how to be nice to the people she meets."

"That's Tifferoosky for ya," Chip said, tapping her shoulder. "Nice to a fault and only full of herself whenever I become embarrassing."

"Oh, stop." She turned to him and frowned. This was not the time to be cute.

The cabby chuckled.

Chip opened the door and they got out.

Tiffany watched as the taxi pulled away. She couldn't stop wondering about what had just happened. There was something about that man... Something she just couldn't pin down.

I don't think you're the type of person who hurts people...

He'd said it as if he knew. As if he truly knew about her. And who she was.

But how could he? How could this total stranger possibly know *anything* about her?

Was he a stranger after all?

He drove a cab in Hollywood. He said he hadn't been in Pittsburgh. Why would he lie? He had no reason to. In other words, whatever he'd told her must have been the truth.

But what about that other minor but very important detail?

My treat...

She'd spent the last four years of her mortal life in Hollywood. And what she'd learned early on was that no one did anything for nothing. There was always a price—no matter what the service. And even the "good" guys—those who didn't appear to be walking through life lugging around a hefty price tag—were no different.

And she knew that a cabby—especially one working in an area filled with millionaires and celebrities—would not under any circumstances refuse a forty-dollar fare. Especially when driving his fare to a crime-filled area.

"Tifferoosky? Something bothering you?"

"I really don't know…"

"Was it the cabby?"

She shrugged.

"Weird dude, eh?"

"I really don't think *weird* would be the appropriate term for him."

"What, pray tell, *would* be the appropriate term?"

"I wish I could tell you."

294

"But something *is* working its way into that gorgeous noggin anyway?"

"I wish I knew what it was."

"You really think you've seen him before?"

Tiffany shrugged. "I'd bet on it. I think I've even talked to him before."

"Where?"

The image of the park bench in Pittsburgh blipped once again in her mind, vanishing just as quickly.

Was that the entire story? Or was there more to it?

"I honestly can't remember," she said, the frustration growing.

Chip didn't reply.

Tiffany began studying the street facing them. It was narrow and in need of immediate repair, the stores fronting it abandoned or in a severe state of vandalism. The sidewalk was muddled with discarded bags, Styrofoam cups, cigarette butts, paper scraps, and other debris. The smell of urine and fresh feces hung heavily in the air. Figures lurked in the shadows. Others sprawled in storefront doorways across the street.

"Johnny the Rockman was righterino," Chip said, taking in the scenery. "So was our *simpatico* cabby guy. This wouldn't exactly be a good place to raise our children."

"What would he…that man…be doing *here*?" she asked.

"What man, Honey Bunny? The cabby? Or your reality show killer?"

She glared. "Guess…"

"Maybe the boy decided to tone down his digs after he realized he'd completely tanked his future by slipping you that drink that sent you off to the morgue."

Chip could be right. But even though she'd only met Alan Richards a few minutes before he'd handed her that fatal drink, she didn't think he'd be the type to let himself—or his career—crumble. He'd spent a fortune on himself—his hair, his nails. His skin displayed clear evidence of exfoliation and tanning products. His clothes were Baroni, his shoes Armani. He had important contacts everywhere and boasted political connections in high places. Since Johnny Rock had gotten him blackballed or blacklisted for what he'd done to her, Richards would have made tracks—to New York, London, or Paris. Or paid someone big bucks to pay off the right palms to wipe his record clean. He might have even switched careers. Or had gone to great lengths to change his name and set up stakes in a different place.

She couldn't see a man as shallow as Alan Richards tossing his career away and scampering away like a frightened squirrel into this neck of the woods.

She turned to Chip. "Are you thinking what I'm thinking?"

He shrugged. "Are you thinking about that messy-looking clump of what looks like a half-eaten cheeseburger lying on the sidewalk over there at the end of the block?"

"No..."

"How about that big lump in the storefront doorway across the street that keeps moving around and moaning?"

"Not that, either."

"Then I guess I'm not thinking what you're thinking. What *are* you thinking, Tifferoo?"

"I'm thinking that we should start looking for the monster who killed me."

"I guess I should've figured that one out."

"Yes, you really should have."

"Er…sorry, Tifferoo."

"Stop apologizing and start paying attention, okay?"

"Gotcha."

Tiffany led the way down the dark, foul-smelling alley.

***

Tents and large packing boxes shoved against the walls of the buildings spanned as far as the eye could see. Dark figures lay inside or sat in the openings, smoking or nibbling on something. A rusty barrel piled with sticks and dirty rags blazed in the center of the alley. A short, skeletal figure in rags poked the fire with a broken wooden rake or mop handle, watching them. The figure was a middle-aged woman, her long, stringy white hair dangling limply below a soiled red babushka. Her eyes blazed at them. She held the wooden poker in her right hand, a large steak knife in her left.

"I'll bet she's not about to ask us to partake in a fireside chat," Chip whispered.

Tiffany didn't reply. She was much too focused on her search. For one brief moment she sensed a cold darkness but cast the feeling aside. This wasn't the time for distractions. She led the way, and they veered around several vagrants milling around, some nibbling on their meager dinner while others smoked weed or just hobbled around, mumbling.

When they reached the end of the block, Tiffany spotted a lonely figure sitting on the concrete floor, his lower back pressed against the brick building. He was wrapped in a filthy green blanket. As they were about to pass, the figure lowered his head and began rocking and mumbling incoherently.

The man's voice, merely a croak, sent a clear image to Tiffany, who stopped cold. She moved closer. The figure did not look up. She stared down at him, noting the long, filthy, matted brown hair barely visible in the faint haze of the corner streetlamp.

"Tifferoo?" Chip's voice drifted into her head. "What's going on?"

"I think…this may…be him," she whispered back.

"You're sure?"

"Not totally. But I have this feeling."

"What sort of feeling? Nausea? Indigestion? An urge to throw up? To tell you the truth, I've got the same feeling, and if we don't make tracks soon—"

"It's not that at all."

"Really? Seriously?"

"Seriously."

"What are you gonna do?"

"Something tell me I have to make sure."

298

"If it's really him, and he recognizes you, you know what's liable to happen, don'tcha?"

Chip was right. If this truly was the man who had killed her, her appearance would send him over the edge.

But what if he didn't recognize her? The pathetic figure hunched down on the concrete couldn't possibly be in possession of his faculties. She couldn't even tell if the man could see...or hear...or comprehend...*anything*.

"What if...what if he's too far gone to remember?" she whispered, more to herself than to Chip.

"Are you willing to take that chance?" he replied.

She'd come this far. It would be very wrong not to finish what she'd started.

With a deep sigh, she changed her appearance into a dark-haired, plain-faced woman in raggedy clothes.

She bent over. When her face was just a foot or so away, she ignored the stench of feces, urine and mildew emanating from the figure. "Alan?"

The figure stopped rocking.

"Alan Richards?"

The figure froze.

"Are you...Alan Richards?"

The man raised his head. Tiffany squatted down. When she saw his face, she nearly gasped.

Once fine-featured, bright, clean-shaven and good-looking, the figure before her gazed blankly at her with dead, blood-shot eyes. His beard was long and scraggly, matted with dried-up food, snot and dirt. His mouth, barely visible behind the beard, was swollen and covered with sores. Cuts and blisters marked his sunken cheeks, and large portions of his hair had been yanked out in clumps. The eyes that had once conveyed both arrogance and confidence had become glazed and lifeless remnants of one so close to utter despair that nothing could ever bring back its former light.

"Alan?" Tiffany could barely find her voice.

The man began rocking and mumbling again. He clutched the ends of his blanket, pulling it tighter around him.

Tiffany straightened. A tear drifted down her cheek.

"Tifferoo?" Chip stood close behind her. "*This* is the fancy dickhead that fed you that drink?"

She nodded.

Chip continued staring. "No offense, but he doesn't exactly look like a dude who could manage to hold a glass in his hand, let alone feed anyone a drink."

"Something terrible has obviously happened to him."

"What was your first clue?" Chip asked. "The filthy beard thing? The smelly, snot-covered blanket? Or was it the stylish torn-out hair look?"

She shook her head. "I...never expected this..."

"I guess you could say the other shoe finally dropped."

Tiffany couldn't take her eyes off the pathetic figure. She hadn't been prepared to see something like this. "I can't...I just can't get over this..."

"Pathetic, ain't he?"

She sighed.

"I don't think he would have recognized you after all."

"I don't think he'd recognize anyone."

"We came all this way, Tifferoo…"

"I know."

"You don't want to do anything really interesting, do you? Turning him into an oil slick— or coaxing him to wander out into the street and turn into roadkill—wouldn't pose much of a problemo… But that just ain't your style."

"I think he's just about as punished as anyone I've ever seen."

"I had the strong feeling you'd say something like that."

Justice had indeed taken care of itself. Or maybe it was Karma. Whatever it was, she saw no other reason for staying here. This man had killed her, yet she could no longer hate him. All she could find within herself was pity. And a profound sadness. And regret. For what he'd done to her…and, finally, to himself.

"I kinda think we're done here," she said, feeling a sense of great relief the moment the words left her mouth.

"Want *me* to do anything?"

"What would you do?"

"At first, I wanted to pull out more hair. Then I thought about producing a group of doves and have them drop a load on his head, like what we did to the demon dude in Pittsburgh."

"And now?"

Chip sighed. "Nothing, actually."

She smiled at him. "You'll always be a jokester, but admit it, you're no longer a demon, are you?"

"Watch your mouth, Honey Bunny." He glared as if he'd been insulted. "Just because I can't think of any nifty way to finish off a dead man at the moment…"

Tiffany held her smile. "Admit it. You're no longer bad. Or evil. Just funny and sarcastic."

"Babykins, when you say it like that—"

"That's how it comes out."

He groaned. "You teach your kids everything, then they grow up and turn on you…"

She watched the pathetic figure for a few more moments. The images came back, but this time, they didn't hurt nearly as much. The end was the same, but the hatred and the hurt that had stayed with her all this time had gone. The only thing she could feel right now was sympathy.

Was this closure? Or had something else happened to her since all this had come about? Something she hadn't realized until now?

Just then, the pathetic figure raised his head. Tiffany felt genuine remorse in that one expression. And humiliation. And guilt. She knew right then that everything had somehow made itself right. Even though she was dead, she knew that this man had seen the light and realized from that point on that his life would never be the same.

Tiffany instantly changed back to her former self. Then she closed her eyes. "*I forgive you,*" she sent to the tortured soul facing her. "*I forgive you*

302

and what you did, and I hope that one day, you will be able to forgive yourself."

The moment she sent her message, she sensed a sudden uplifting of the man's spirit. The self-torment that had plagued him had diminished, and a burst of warm relief washed over his consciousness. He relaxed, letting go of his blanket. He sighed deeply and whispered in a soft, broken voice, "Th-Thank you..."

She opened her eyes. An overwhelming sense of freedom had filled her being. And then she realized that for the first time since she'd left her mortal body, she could breathe freely once again.

"Tifferoo? We all finished now?"

She turned. And froze.

Chip's face appeared longer, more fine-featured. His red hair wasn't as unruly and his green eyes had become larger, deeper, more expressive.

"You're…good-looking," she said, surprised.

"You okay, Tifferoo?" he asked, just as surprised. "Or just lonely?"

"Why should I be lonely?"

"Well, it's been a while since you've wrinkled the sheets with that restaurant owner guy. What was his name?"

"You know what his name was. And *please* stop trying to antagonize me." She turned back to Alan Richards, who now lay on his back on the concrete, sleeping peacefully. Tiffany realized once again that she felt better than she had since the moment she'd died and woken up in the field

303

bordering the Meddaworld. "We need to leave," she said.

He shrugged. "Tired of the accommodations? The perks? The panoramic view of the city? The local discolor?"

She was just about to reply when she sensed more cold darkness touching her. She turned back to where the dark shadows were shuffling around in the alley.

"Tiffers? What's up?"

A flash of cold brushed her cheek, and she winced. "We really need to leave."

They hurried down the alley, past the roving nibblers and smokers, and soon passed the mean-eyed, white-haired lady poking the fire in the barrel.

"You never did tell me who you were before you died," Tiffany said, suddenly more curious than ever.

"What, pray tell, does that have to do with—"

"Call me funny. I just think that since this is finally all over, we should be more open to one another."

"Open?"

"Yes."

"To one another?"

"That's what I just said. What's wrong with that?"

"Nothing. But…"

"But what?"

"You really *are* funny. Oftentimes, hilarious. For a gorgeous babe, that is."

"*Such* the charmer…"

CHAPTER 7 - BACK TO THE PRESENT

It was nearly dawn by the time they reached the main street and found the cab sitting at the curb. Tiffany wasn't surprised to see the gray-haired man waiting for them as they approached his vehicle.

"Slow night?" Chip asked as they climbed in.

The cabby glanced at Chip's reflection in his mirror. "I always get more selective as the night progresses." He pulled away from the curb, turned left, went up North Normandie, then made a left onto Santa Monica Boulevard.

"We didn't say where we were going," Tiffany said.

The cabby nodded but didn't reply.

They rode for a while in silence. Although the streets were nearly deserted, they saw signs of activity as they rode down the block. Figures dressed in rags and baggy clothes lounged in shop doorways while others stood bent over at street corners, hacking away, or sharing joints with their friends. A bearded man in a bulky Army field jacket sat in a store entrance, cradling his Golden Retriever. He appeared to be sleeping soundly as they passed.

"Did you ever find your person?" the cabby asked. "The one you had the beef with?"

"Yes." Tiffany knew that the image of the ravaged figure she'd encountered earlier would be forever implanted in her memory. What the man had become. What fate had done to him.

"Did you get closure?"

She could tell that the cabby somehow knew what had happened. She had no idea how, but the moment she tried making sense out of it, the image that had blipped in her mind several times before came right back. This time it was much clearer, much more detailed, and stayed in her mind. The memory took place not long ago in Pittsburgh, where she'd encountered someone on a park bench. A gray-haired man wearing horrible shoes. An elderly man much like—

Oh my God...

"Well?" he asked again.

"I-I *think* so..." Her voice had suddenly become shaky.

"Something wrong?" the cabby asked.

"Have we...met before?"

"You've already asked me that."

"I know."

A sudden silence.

"Do you remember what you told me when I asked about this before?"

"Young lady, what really matters is what happened to you. Your encounter with the man you had your beef with. Nothing else is important. Closure is the essential element here. The only thing that really matters."

She took a breath. "I gave you a pair of shoes, didn't I? A nice, comfortable pair. I gave them to you because what you had on your feet was

306

disgusting. It happened in Pittsburgh, didn't it? Wasn't that you? Sitting on that park bench?"

The cabby suddenly veered to the right and slowed down, stopping at the curb in front of a tee shirt shop. He put the car in park and turned around. Tiffany could tell right then that this man was not a cabby. He was something much different.

"And when I gave you a nice pair of comfortable shoes, do you remember what I said?"

No reply.

"I said, life can suck when you're wearing bad shoes. Don't you remember?"

The cabby still didn't reply, but she could tell by the way he suddenly looked down that she'd hit pay dirt.

"Who are you, really?" she asked softly.

"I'll tell you, young lady, but not right now."

"When will you tell me?"

"When you don't need to ask me again."

"I don't understand."

"I'm pretty discombobulated about this myself," Chip threw in, scratching the back of his neck. "Are we going in that tee shirt shop? It's kind of early. I don't think anyone's in there yet, so it'll probably be locked. But we really don't need to shop, do we? Not at this stage of the game. I can probably come up with much better tee shirts than we can find in that place. And, judging by the display in the window, way better jeans. I never really cared for jeans with the knees cut out, anyway. I think it looks silly."

The man smiled.

"What is it you know about me?" she asked in a whisper.

"I know why you don't understand. I also know what it will take to get you to realize what's happening."

Before Tiffany could ask him the next question, the old man raised his arm.

The inside of the cab immediately grew darker, and in seconds they were enveloped in a warm cloud.

***

The three of them stood in lush grass in a beautiful pasture. Long rows of tall pine trees graced the hilly landscape, and flowers of every color embellished the greenery in a symphony of brilliance.

"Cool beans!" Wide-eyed, Chip eagerly scanned their surroundings. "Looks like Emerald City. Is there a wizard around here, somewhere?"

"Where *are* we?" Tiffany asked in awe.

"When you were first deprived of your mortality," the cabby said, "you came to this place. Do you remember?"

She could never forget the strange pasture. But that place was much different. The grass was a light gray, the flowers a dull white, the plants a washed-out brown. It had been a very sad, lonely place.

"Of *course* I remember. But this isn't the same place, is it? When I…when I woke up that first time, I saw—"

"Odd colors. They were all wrong—is this not correct?"

"Yes."

"Well, in case you haven't figured it out yet, we've come back."

Confusion ripped through her. Something was very odd about all this. "Why is everything the right color now? This place is gorgeous. Why does it look so different?"

The cabby smiled. "When you first came here, your spirit hadn't yet progressed to its next level. You had just left your body. You hadn't the time—not yet, anyway—to undergo the purification process."

"What's *that*?"

"Let's just say that you've since achieved it and have succeeded well beyond our expectations."

"What are you trying to say?"

The man smiled. "You've become a heavenly spirit, my dear. An angel, to be more precise."

"I could've told you that," Chip said dryly. "You can't be goody-goody all the time without something else really weird going on."

"Your spirit has also developed," the man said, turning to Chip, "and, I might add, much to our great surprise."

"*Moi*? Develop?" Chip frowned. "I figured something creepy was going on in my head. The jokes aren't nearly as good as they used to be. And they seem to be harder to come up with."

"Yes," the man said. "And just in case you haven't yet learned this, your humor has no place in this discussion."

Chip lowered his face.

The park bench image returned to Tiffany, much clearer this time than ever before. "It *was* you, wasn't it? You *were* sitting on that park bench in Pittsburgh, and I was going through a rough time. I'd just lost two very good friends. Tell me that was you. Please? I really need to know."

The cabby continued smiling. "My dear, you are a very special lady. Your friend, here, is also very special. The two of you must continue doing what you've been doing. Can you possibly understand what I'm trying to say?"

"I'm still trying to wrap my little mind around that heavenly spirit/angel thing whatchacallit," Chip said.

"Why won't you tell me if that was you sitting on the park bench?" Tiffany found this more important than anything else. "That really *was* you, wasn't it?"

The man smiled brightly. "I was sent to watch you because you were dealt a very bad hand."

"Sent from where?"

The man continued smiling. "I was also sent to observe you periodically to make sure that what I was told about you was accurate. And it was. You were sent to a place where you were never meant to be, and at the wrong time. However, your true spirit came through, and you triumphed. And now that you have accomplished what appeared to others as the impossible, you've managed to succeed in every aspect."

"Are you saying that I've been watched ever since I—"

"You—as well as your friend—have been watched the moment the two of you escaped the Dark World."

310

"Is *this* why my powers have been growing?"

"One of the many reasons. That, plus the fact that your spirit continued glowing bright and could never be dimmed, no matter what you were forced to endure."

"Why hasn't Chip's powers increased until recently?"

The cabby smiled. "Let's just say there was a great deal of skepticism in his case."

"I resemble that remark," Chip said.

The cabby shook his head.

"So then, what's next?" Tiffany asked. "Do we stay here, in the mortal world?"

"Continue what you've been doing," the cabby replied. "Since you both have been doing good work, you will no longer need supervision."

"What about all these demons we've had to face? And what about Breath Mint? He still wants us really badly."

The cabby blinked. "Breath Mint?"

"She means Braithwaite." Chip sighed tiredly. "For some reason, she can never remember the names of the big boys down there."

"Maybe it's because I don't *want* to," she replied defensively.

The cabby chuckled. "I wouldn't concern myself about that beast. Or any of the others."

"But they're up here," she insisted. "And they're doing great harm to a lot of people."

"They won't have any effect on you," the cabby replied. "You'll be able to do your work without interference from them."

"How is that possible?"

"For one thing, they won't be able to see or feel you anymore."

"Really?"

"Demons will no longer be able to recognize you. Or work their evil upon you."

"But…how can this be?"

"Don't you remember that you performed this same miracle in Pittsburgh, upon your two friends? This was even before you'd developed many of your powers."

"Ashley and Jimmy Russo? I wasn't even sure if it would work—"

"And also the man in Raven you loved so much?"

Her heart tugged at her when she thought of Lou Gates. Lou and his beautiful brown eyes, his warm smile. And, of course, his tender touch. "That was…very difficult," she said softly.

"It has worked, my dear. And this same thing will work for you while you're battling the dark spirits. This, of course, also applies to your droll friend."

"Droll?" Chip scratched the back of his neck. "I *used* to know what that meant…"

"This just doesn't seem possible." Tiffany found that she just couldn't grasp the concept. "In other words, we can see *them*, but they can't see *us*?"

"What they will see—and feel—is someone they should avoid. They won't know why, and if they do question themselves, they'll quickly discover that they won't care, and will move on to someone much more interesting. And vulnerable."

Tiffany shook her head. "I don't understand—"

"That doesn't matter, dear girl. Just believe me when I say that you'll be able to continue your good work and will no longer have to worry about evil spirits interfering."

"It just sounds too good to be true."

"Many things in this mortal world turn out that way, but only a chosen few seem to able to recognize such wonders."

"So then, are you finished with me? With us?"

Sadness appeared on the man's weary features. "I'm very sorry to say that I've got to leave both of you. My work here is done."

"We'll never see you again?"

A smile instantly replaced the sadness on the man's face. "I wouldn't say that, my dear. But it will be a while before we'll be able to get together again."

"Will we be doing this indefinitely?"

"Until the Rapture."

"That could be a long time," Chip said. "I don't know if I'll be able to cope with toning down my humor for very long."

"I kind of think your Tuscan upbringing—as well as your voracious habit for terrible, tasteless jokes—could use the vacation," the cabby said.

Tiffany turned to Chip. "Tuscan? Seriously?"

Chip sighed and looked down at his feet.

"Then you *are* Italian after all?"

Another sigh.

Tiffany turned back to the cabby to thank him and tell him they'd do their very best.

He'd vanished.

So did the beautiful pasture.

***

Jose Bribon had spent the evening searching endlessly for the two rogues. After losing them at the restaurant, he'd spent the next few hours patrolling the area, repeatedly checking out North Fairfax, then North Orange Grove, North Ogden, and finally North Genesee, but keeping close to Santa Monica, where he'd seen them last. He went into every shop, store and restaurant, looking at everything. Flower shops. Tanning salons. Tee shirt shops. Souvenir outlets. Furniture stores. Every eatery, including the kitchens, bathrooms and offices. Parking lots, as well as the vehicles themselves. Every person in every building and on the street was suspect. Using his powers, he sniffed and listened, taking in every smell, word, thought, and feeling emanating from those he encountered.

And found nothing.

Braithwaite couldn't know about this. If the super demon found out what had happened—that Jose had come so close, only to lose them…

He shuddered at the thought. But he was determined to make this right. Somehow, some way…

He was convinced those two were obviously no longer in the immediate area. But they had to be *some*where…

Downtown L.A? If they'd gone there, it would be extremely difficult to track them down again. The foot traffic as well as the street traffic would be horrendous.

This was going to take time. Even if he brought out his classic Porsche to scope for them, he could be facing several days, perhaps weeks, of constant hunting.

At around eight the next morning, Bribon realized with ultimate relief that he had reached the end of his search. Just as he left the doughnut shop after wolfing down two glazed and a cappuccino, he glimpsed the two rogues.

Since he'd been concentrating on the wandering crowds, he hadn't seen them right off. But only moments later, just as he was about to attempt his search at another block, he spotted them coming around the corner. They were talking to one another as they strolled leisurely down the street. They were dressed in the same outfits—which made them easier to identify.

As the two reached the end of the block, Bribon, hiding behind a small group of tourists, rushed across the street and fell into step just ten feet behind them. Concealed by a middle-aged foursome chattering away, he had an excellent view.

Half a block later, the rogues turned right at the corner and went up to the front entrance of Bongovissi's Cappuccino Shoppe.

Bribon waited outside the brick building. When he was confident the coast was clear, he quickly changed his appearance. As a short, dark-haired Hispanic woman in her late fifties, he covered his blocky figure in a long black skirt and a bulky gray sweatshirt. Confident that he was sufficiently camouflaged, he shuffled into the shop in a pair of beat-up black sneakers. The shades he'd slipped on would conceal his wandering eyes. Satisfied with his new disguise, he carefully scoped the dark, half-crowded room.

The rogues had selected a booth in the corner, overlooking the sidewalk. An empty booth directly behind them awaited him. Bribon nonchalantly passed their booth, sat down and grabbed a menu. Then, holding it out in front of him, he tried picking up on their conversation. They were talking softly, which made things difficult. Frustrated, he tried penetrating their thoughts. First, the blonde. Then, the redhead.

Nothing.

Confused, he moved his face closer to the menu.

Still nothing.

What the hell was going on?

Fighting down the frustration, he stared at the blond curls just three feet to his right. And flinched when a glint of bright light penetrated his thoughts.

What the fuck...?

Frowning at the sudden stab of pain in his right temple, he massaged it lightly and struggled to determine what was going on. No conversation? No thoughts? A glint of bright light? A sudden sharp burst of pain in his head?

What was happening? Were these the rogues he'd been looking for? If so, why wasn't he able to read them? And, more importantly, why had he encountered darkness, silence, and a bright light, followed by sudden pain?

Bribon rubbed his temples, then his eyes. Maybe he'd been overdoing it. That could be the problem. He'd been on constant alert too long and was tired. His powers were sluggish, his senses worn out.

But this had to be done.

He had to collect these two and deliver them personally to Braithwaite. Otherwise—

He didn't want to go there. Otherwise didn't exist. Otherwise was a place he had no knowledge of, nor wanted to. He was Nequam, the Rascal, and knew how to get mortals to do stupid, careless things. True, these two weren't mortals, but he still had powers that could be useful. He was sitting in the booth next to two rogue demons who needed to be collected and sent back to Braithwaite.

Just then, the blonde turned in his direction—

And suddenly Bribon knew that she wasn't the rogue. The female's face was totally different. Older, perhaps. Maybe five or ten years. And not nearly as gorgeous or stunning.

And when he glimpsed the redheaded guy once again, he realized that he'd been mistaken there, as well. Not nearly as goofy-looking, and the face wasn't shaped right.

Bribon sank in his seat. He'd blown it again.

How the hell could he have been so wrong about those two? How could he have wasted so much time sitting here? These were two mortals, after all. They'd resembled the two rogues at first...but now? They looked totally different.

However, that wasn't what was bothering him most of all.

317

He'd never had a problem reading mortals before. Mortals were notoriously easy to read. Especially the dim-witted ones, of which there were so many. So why not now?

He'd overdone it—that was the reason. His powers had waned, gradually becoming useless. He was tired and needed rest.

But that was no excuse. He had to find those two.

Braithwaite would not tolerate failure. And telling the super demon you had failed because you were tired would not go over very well. At all.

And with those thoughts filling his head, Bribon jumped up from the booth and bolted out of the eatery.

***

Tiffany couldn't help laughing when the short Hispanic woman ran out of the room.

"Something funny, Honey Bunny? Remembering some classic moment we shared?"

"No…"

"Some high-quality witticisms coming from the bestest of the best in the west?"

"Not that, either…"

Chip sighed. "What did I miss, then? I seem to be running out of first-class zingers here…"

"Believe it or not, that's him."

"Him?"

"Him."

"You mean—"

She nodded.

"That short, homely Hispanic woman you were watching? She's a *him*?"

"Yes. Definitely a him."

"You mean—"

"Our demon."

He glanced toward the entrance, after the figure had disappeared. "Seriously?"

"I wouldn't kid you now, would I?"

"To me, she looked like an illegal scrubwoman who spent entirely too much time selecting her ensemble from the local Goodwill box."

"It was him, nonetheless."

"Ya know, I did have a strange feeling about her—him—when she—he—sat down."

"You see? Your powers *are* developing, after all."

He had a swig of ice water from the pitcher on the setting in front of him. "I'll be damned."

"He was trying to read us." Tiffany sipped her vanilla cappuccino. "I felt that the moment he came in and sat down."

"That might explain the tingling sensation that went crazy in my head a few minutes ago."

"That was probably your brain resisting."

"Howzat?"

"Putting up some sort of a wall."

"Are you saying he couldn't read us?"

"Basically."

"And why not, pray tell?"

"Did you already forget what our cabby told us?"

"Other than the fact that he said I was droll?"

"Besides that."

"And that my jokes were bad and tasteless?"

319

"They are. But keep going. You might just hit it on the head. Eventually."

"It's really hard, keeping them fresh, you know. My public is very demanding. And since I've been developing—against my will, of course—into someone not quite as silly or funny—"

"Concentrate on the question. *Please*?"

Chip's brows pushed together. "Let's see. Something about your being special... Then I believe he also said I was special, too. Which knocked me for a loop, since I haven't been called special since that time in Peoria, when I turned myself into a floor lamp for those kids at the hospital—"

"Focus, now..."

He sighed. "All right, all right." He rubbed his temples. I also vaguely recall something about the old dude telling us we should continue what we've been doing..."

"Don't stop there..."

"He also said he'd been sent here to watch you because you were dealt a bad hand. And he also had to make sure that what he was told about you was accurate. He then mentioned something about others watching both of us since we left the Dark World."

"You actually *remembered* all that?"

Chip shrugged sheepishly. He pointed to his head. "Things occasionally work in here, ya know..."

"In other words, you were actually...paying *attention*?" Tiffany shook her head. "I can hardly believe this. Just when I thought you couldn't care less—"

"Watch it, Babykins. You're beginning to sound a tad insulting."

"You *never* seem to be paying attention. To *anything*."

"I ain't just a pretty face, you know…"

"But—"

"That old dude also said something about your spirit. He said it could never be dimmed, no matter what."

"Do you remember what he said about *your* powers increasing?"

Chip frowned. "Something about his being skeptical. Can you believe that? Anyone being skeptical? About *moi*?"

Tiffany had more cappuccino. "Sometimes you truly amaze me."

"I know that head-spin thing really brings down the house whenever I—"

"That's *not* what amazes me."

"My tongue-dropping thingy?"

She shook her head.

"The ear-wiggling?"

"No…"

He shrugged. "Like I just said—not just a pretty face."

Tiffany thought about the other things the gray-haired man had said. Things that hadn't made sense at the time. "I think I know now what he meant when he told us demons will no longer be able to recognize us. Or that they'll never be able to work their evil upon us."

321

"You mean because of what happened with the scrub woman demon thingy a few minutes ago?"

"What other explanation can there be?"

He had another huge swig of ice water. "Cool beans."

"I kinda like that new wrinkle, too."

After a brief silence, Chip said, "Do you really believe that bit about us being…" He glanced about the room and lowered his voice. "…angels?"

"I like it a lot better than the two of us being demons."

He shivered. "But this means we have to do *good* from now on—right?"

"That's what we've been doing, you know. Ever since we came back up."

He didn't reply.

"Look what we did to the wolf guy in Ohio. Then what happened in Florida, with those rich Arab guys. And how we rescued Ashley. Then what we pulled off in Pittsburgh, with Jimmy Russo. Then in Peoria, when those two demons were terrorizing my hometown. Get it?"

"I getcha." He moved closer and lowered his voice again. "I also remember what you did when that little girl's puppy was smeared by that van."

She sighed. "I told you about that. I didn't think her little dog actually died, so I—"

"I know, I know. But even so, it convinced me at the time that you're probably not exactly the right babe for anyone with more than a few active brain cells to mess with."

"Oh, stop."

***

322

Tiffany and Chip stumbled upon the demon once again twenty minutes later, when they left the cappuccino shop.

He had changed back into his former shape as a male—medium height, dark hair and eyes, blocky build—and seemed uneasy. He was standing at the street corner, in front of an electronics outlet. He stood quite still, his head tilted. He seemed to be listening to the two young girls in shorts and tee shirts standing directly in front of him. The girls were chattering away about some guy they'd just seen in the tee shirt shop around the corner. One of them was certain that she'd seen this guy in a movie. Her friend insisted that she'd seen him in one of the latest reality talent shows. They both agreed that it didn't matter. They had to return to that shop and see if he was still there if they wanted to have sex with him.

Tiffany listened to the exchange and sent a message

("you need to head north for two blocks if you want to see the blonde and her friend again")

directly into the demon's head.

Stiffening, the demon turned sharply in their direction. Tiffany stared straight ahead, at the slow-moving traffic. Chip picked his ear while studying the street sign.

The demon turned to his right, then his left. His head cocked, he waited for another message.

Tiffany sent over, "*Try the souvenir shop halfway down the block.*"

The light changed. The demon turned around sharply and ran across the street, heading north.

323

"Did you do that, Tifferoosky?" Chip was watching the fast-moving figure.

Tiffany just shrugged.

"Seriously? You just directed a demon away from us with one of your mind thingys, and all I get is a shrug?"

"I just planted an idea in his head to see if he was paying attention."

"He obviously was. I'm surprised he didn't question it."

"It worked, didn't it?"

"Well, you definitely slipped an angry hornet directly into that boy's undershorts."

They joined the crowd heading west.

"Something's on your mind, isn't it?" Chip asked a few minutes later, while staring at her.

"It's nothing we can do anything about."

"Care to share?"

"I've been sensing a lot of darkness here lately."

"Darkness?"

"More demons."

Chip stopped walking and began looking around. The crowd told him nothing. "Anything close, might I ask?"

Tiffany nodded. "I began sensing them more and more after the cabby dropped us off on North Normandie."

Chip blinked. "Darkness?"

She nodded.

"And cold?"

"How'd you know?"

"The same thing happened to me."

"There are many of them here," she said. "A lot more than the two of us can deal with."

Chip thought about that for a moment, then nodded. "Then let's do the smart thing."

"What's that?"

"Make tracks to Peoria."

Tiffany's thoughts looped as she gazed at him. Chip was right. They'd come here to finish what they'd started and didn't need to worry about cleaning up what would most likely turn into an impossible task. Demons would always exist among mortals. There would never be enough benevolent spirits to defeat them all. And even though it bothered her to walk away from what would most likely become utter chaos, she told herself that she and Chip would always help those they would be able to help. "Sounds good to me," she told him.

***

A block later, Tiffany noticed the troubled expression on Chip's face. "What's bothering you now?"

"Nothing really. I'm just a tad bewildered, I guess you could say."

"And why is that?"

"Possibly because I have no idea what we're doing. Or where we're doing it. Or why. Or how. Or when."

"Well, it's not like we have to be anywhere, right?"

"That really doesn't answer my question, Baby Cakes."

"Back to Peoria, I think."

"Peoria?" He frowned. "You mean Illinois?"

"That's the only Peoria I know of. Unless they stuck another one in another state while we weren't looking."

"I don't think they could do anything like that, Precious. They don't even seem to be able to handle much going on in the towns already there, let alone create anything new."

"Then it's the one we just left—or did you forget?"

"Did I forget what? Peoria? Or Illinois?"

Tiffany blinked. "Are you being a butthole again?"

"*Moi*? A butthole?"

"Silly question, wasn't it?"

His ears twitched. "Which one? The one about me forgetting Peoria? The Illinois issue? Or was it the butthole thingamajig?"

"Listen to me and read my lips. Peoria. Illinois. My mom. Got it?"

"Got what? All of that?"

She just sighed.

"I got it, Tifferoo. Peoria, Illinois. To see your mom again—rightomundo?"

"Why did you make me go through all that if you already knew what I was talking about?"

"You said I'm a butthole, and that's what buttholes do. Besides, if I didn't occasionally put you through the wringer, you'd think something was wrong."

"Occasionally?"

"Figure of speech."

"Got it. And yes, I'd think something was wrong."

"It's Peoria, then. To get back with your mom."

"I told her we'd be back as soon as we took care of business here."

"Then what?"

"I guess we'll cross that bridge when we get to it."

"They have actual *bridges* in Peoria?"

"You're being a butthole again…"

Chip nodded but said nothing. When he spoke again, he looked confused. "This is all over, then? *Finito*? Your revenge thing, so to speak?"

She hadn't really thought much of it before now. But now that it had been finally said aloud, she realized that her personal campaign had reached its end. She'd come full circle and had managed to finalize things even though she really hadn't done anything to help it along. Although this was a sort of letdown, she knew that, in spite of what had happened and what she'd initially planned to do to set things straight, fate had intervened, finishing the job for her. Stepdad was gone, and so were several other very bad spirits who, because of her efforts, were no longer hurting people. And this, more than anything, meant the world to her.

"It's over," she told Chip, and felt more at ease than ever before.

Chip shook his head. "I just don't know if I can behave myself, now that we have to be do-gooders from now on."

"That's why I'm here."

"Why's that, Honey Bunny?"

"To keep you in line."

"You always were a badass."

Tiffany shrugged. "*Someone's* got to be…"

***

They reached the Greyhound Bus Station on East Seventh Street half an hour later. As they waited in the long line for the driver to show, Tiffany turned to Chip. What the gray-haired cabby had said had been bothering her. She had to find out what was going on. After all, she and Chip been together for what seemed a lifetime, and she still didn't know anything about him. Not regarding his past, anyway.

"What's all this talk about Tuscany?"

Chip didn't reply.

The fact that he stayed silent told her she'd struck a nerve. "What? No cute one-liners? No corny cracks? No tacky Chipisms?"

Chip shrugged. "Bus rides make me nauseous."

"That's better."

"You like it when I'm nauseous?"

"I like it when you change the subject. It tells me that you don't want to talk about something. And when that happens, I know I'm on the right track."

"You really want to talk about me getting nauseous? The gazz? The farting?"

"I want you to tell me all about Tuscany."

"Tuscany?"

"Yes."

"The one in Italy?"

"I didn't know there were more than one."

328

"There probably aren't."

"All right, then."

"Okay...so then, what about it?"

"Tell me all about it. Everything, warts and all."

"What exactly would you like to know about my warts?"

"You're doing it again."

"Really?"

"Yes. Really."

Chip went silent.

"I'm waiting, now..."

"Be more specific, Tifferoo."

"First of all, I'd like to know why the cabby mentioned it. Then I'd like to know why he was looking at you directly when he mentioned it. And finally, what exactly did he mean by your bad habit?"

"Would you believe—"

"No."

"How about if I told you—"

"How about saving me your usual distraction crap and just tell me the truth for a change? That might be slightly easier, since I'm so used to your shtick by now that I know better than put any credence into whatever ploy you try to distract me with."

Chip's uncomfortable expression told her she'd hit pay dirt.

"Let's start this all over. Tell me about Tuscany. And this time, don't try to evade the issue."

He shrugged. "Everyone has to come from *some*where."

"Are you saying *that's* where you came from?"

"What's wrong with Tuscany? It's actually pretty—as well as colorful and serene—most of the time, anyway."

"I've never been there."

"You really need to see it, dearest. It's quite beautiful—especially in the spring and early summer. There are flowers all over the place, and—"

"You're changing the subject again."

"Really?"

"Yes."

"What exactly were we talking about?"

It was a struggle to keep from making a scene. She didn't want to humiliate him by probing his brain. She decided that reasoning with him would be much more productive. "We were discussing Tuscany."

"Tifferoo, you're a gorgeous babe and all, but when you get that wild hair—"

"Stop the crap and *talk* to me!" It was becoming increasingly difficult to keep her voice down.

"All right, all right..." He sighed. "So what did you want to talk about?"

"Tuscany!"

"You don't have to shout, you know..."

"I really think I do. At least, right, now."

He went silent and for a few moments looked like he was thinking of what he would say. "Ever hear of the dude Carlo Lorenzini?"

330

"Why? Should I?"

"The name everyone knew him by was Colladi. Carlo Colladi."

She thought that over. "That *seems* to ring a bell…"

"Ever hear of Pinocchio?"

"Of course."

"It was a book Colladi wrote, and it sold a shitload of copies. Then, about sixty or seventy years ago, they made it into a movie, and—"

"Yes, I've heard of Pinocchio." She couldn't believe him sometimes. "I saw the movie when I was a little girl. A lot of us kids saw that movie. So then, tell me…what does an old movie about a puppet have to do with you?"

"In a nutshell, we kinda…sorta…well, we knew one another."

Tiffany groaned. He was evading the issue again. "You *knew* Pinocchio? How could you? He was just a fictional character."

"I knew *Lorenzini*, silly girl. The dude who wrote the book. Remember? Try to keep up, now…"

"Really? How?"

"How what?"

Tiffany glared.

The driver, short and round, shuffled by, carrying a metal thermos and a small paper bag. He broke through the line, went up the steps of the bus and closed the door.

Chip sighed. "The way dudes write books, I imagine. He probably sat down and started making notes. Then he began writing, and the story came out after—"

"You know what I mean, so stop the crap!"

"I kinda bumped into him when he started working for the newspaper. I was a copy boy, and he—"

"You're gonna tell me where this is going before we get on the bus, aren't you?"

"I can't if you keep interrupting me."

"Then, by all means, please continue."

"I sorta ticked him off in those days. I was just a lad, of course, and full of fire. Like I said, I was working for the paper, too, because my momma kicked me out of the house and forced me to find a job."

"She actually kicked you out of the house?"

"She said I was too much for her, and if I continued staying with her, she'd eventually have a heart attack. Or she'd kill me before she had the chance to have one."

"What were you doing that made her think that way?"

"All sorts of cool shit. I peed on her flower garden a couple of dozen times." He chuckled. "We had this big dog, and I scooped up his load with a shovel and went over to one of our neighbors I didn't like, and—"

"Never mind. Just continue where you left off."

"Where was I?"

"I believe you were working for a newspaper."

"I was a copy boy. I did all sorts of stupid errands. That's where I met Lorenzini. I did errands for him, but he was such a serious butthole, so I—"

"You did things to him?"

"How'd you guess?"

"I know you."

"To make a long story short, I was kind of a handful in those days."

"In those days?"

"I used to do some crazy, stupid things—"

"What do you mean, *used* to?"

"You're beginning to give me a complex, angel. But yeah, I was always setting him off. I'd put things on his chair when he was out of his office. I'd smear butter or jam on his seat. Then I'd do interesting things to his inkwell. Then, when he started working again, he'd make a mess and spill it all over himself."

Tiffany shook her head. "*So* juvenile..."

"What do you expect? I was a silly teenager."

"News flash: you're still silly. But *please* get to the point."

"The point is, I'd do nasty things to him, and when he asked me what happened, I lied to him."

"Now *there's* a stretch..."

The bus door opened. Moments later, people started boarding the bus.

"But like I just said, he was kind of a jerk. You know, ordering me around, making me sweep the floor even when it didn't need it, sending me on stupid errands—"

"That was your job, you know."

"I know."

"In other words, he didn't like you."

"That was the pisser. He *did* like me. He even told me he was thinking of writing a children's book and wanted to base the main character on me."

"You're kidding."

"He said he had this idea of using an amiable rascal, just like me, in a series of—"

"You're...*Pinocchio*?"

"Not quite, my gorgeous but oftentimes misinformed friend and colleague. He just used my talent and my wit—as well as my gifted personality—and, of course, my delightful good looks—to create a loveable character."

"One who lied."

"Hey, nobody's perfect."

This was unbelievable. Tiffany could not get over this. "I've been spending my afterlife with *Pinocchio*, of all people?"

"Personally, I think the asshole should have asked my permission," Chip said after some thought.

"Why didn't he?"

Chip shrugged. "Well, I sorta died before he got his book published. That kinda put an ironic twist on the whole thing."

"How'd you die?"

"It was an accident."

Tiffany thought about all this. Something just wasn't adding up. "Those things you told me in Ohio. And Orlando. And Pittsburgh. And even Peoria."

"No offense, but you'll have to be more specific."

"That stuff you told me about Caligula. And about your being in Rome at the time. And the things you told me you did over here, nearly two centuries ago. And—"

"You know Caligula is down there in the Dark Place, don'tcha?"

"Well—"

"And that I've sorta bumped horns with him upon occasion?"

"Yes, but that still doesn't explain why—"

"Honey Buns, did you ever actually *read* Pinocchio?"

"Now what does *that* have to do with anything?"

"Why, pray tell, would someone like Lorenzini pattern a loveable character like Pinocchio after someone like me?"

He had a point. "Okay, okay... Tell me more about what you did to him."

"Well, he had a kind of serious garden thingy growing in his backyard, and he was keeping this Yellow Lady's Slipper off by itself. It was his prized possession." He paused. "Actually, I don't really want to go into this, but—"

"You did something to kill his special flower."

"What can I say? I was a real asshole back then."

"And when you died?"

"You know the answer to that, right?"

"I was just wondering what you were thinking when you died."

"I was thinking of that stupid flower. And feeling kinda bad about what I'd done. It was really a beautiful thing. He cried when he saw what I did to it. And wondering why I did what I did. And—"

"How'd you die, then?"

"I…kind of stumbled…"

"Stumbled?"

"You're actually paying attention, aren't you, Tiffers?"

"Answer the question."

"I sailed out his window. He went sort of radical on me and scared the shit out of me. You know how Italians get when something really ticks them off—"

"I know. So then, you took an unexpected plunge?"

"Right out the third-floor window."

"Ouch."

"Satisfied?"

"I'm glad you've mended your ways since."

He blinked. "Where'd you get *that*?"

"The things you've been doing. The times you've saved me since we've been up here."

"There's that, I guess…"

"Don't you agree?"

"Well, since Karma grabbed me by the short curlies right after I died, I probably need to consider the cold facts…"

"I know one thing. Since we ran into the gray-haired cabby and were told what we'll be doing from now on, I suggest you curb that urge."

"What urge?"

"You know what I'm talking about, so don't play dumb."

"I didn't think I was playing, Tifferoosky."

"And please try very hard to use your talents for good from now on."

336

"My talents?"

"Others might call them shortcomings."

"You mean my tongue-dropping thingy? My head spin? How about that twitching thing I do with my nose and ears that confuses so many mortals up here?"

"I suggest you start using your newer talents. They're the ones that really matter. At least, from now on, they will."

"I'll see what I can do."

"Thank you *so* much."

"You folks gettin' on or what?" yelled the driver from the bus. "I'm runnin' on a tight schedule, ya know…"

EPILOGUE

Hours later, just as the Greyhound Bus approached the Las Vegas outlets on I-15, the driver suddenly slowed, pulled off the road and braked to a stop.

Chip stood up in his seat.

"What's going on?" Tiffany asked.

"Looks like an accident. A messy one."

Tiffany straightened. They were only six seats back from the driver, but since so many of the passengers in front of them had already gotten up to gawk at the commotion, she couldn't see what was happening. She closed her eyes and used her powers to sense what had taken place. It took her only a few moments to realize what had just happened.

Chip sat back down.

"What do you think we should do?" she asked.

"You mean, besides taking a nap? It's a long way to Peoria, baby doll…"

"I honestly don't think we should be napping right now."

"I was afraid you'd say something like that."

She shrugged. "Did you already forget the angel thing?"

"I was trying to, but—"

"But what?"

"You obviously won't let me."

"Seriously?"

338

He sighed tiredly. "I guess I should already have figured that you've decided to do something really nice and meaningful here."

"Well, we can't just sit here while someone out there needs help. Can we?"

"What about the paramedics? The cops? They actually get paid for dealing with stuff like this."

"Did you see them out there while you were gawking?"

He didn't reply.

"All right, then…"

"I guess this is what it's gonna be like, isn't it?"

She nodded.

"From now on?"

"Until the Rapture."

They both got up. With gentle nudging, they managed to navigate their way through the crowd, to the front of the bus.

The driver caught them in his mirror and held out a beefy arm to block their way. "Sorry, folks. Everyone's gotta stay in the bus. State regulations."

Tiffany sensed frustration, fear, and uneasiness emanating from the driver. His nametag said *FIELDS*. She sensed that his first name was Charles, but everyone called him Bud. The image of a short, plump lady with thick glasses and a pretty smile having breakfast in a large old-fashioned kitchen with three kids—two boys and a girl, all around high school age—flashed brightly.

She gazed into his small, blinking gray eyes. "*Bud, you're a very good man, and you have a nice family who loves you. I don't think you'd want*

339

anyone to suffer before help arrives, so I suggest you let us get off so we can offer some assistance to the poor people out there."

Watching her guardedly, the driver lowered his arm, then pulled off his cap and scratched his bald head. He stuck his cap back on and stared nervously at her and Chip. Then, with a deep sigh, he reached out and pulled the door handle.

Tiffany and Chip left the bus.

Three cars—a blue Lexus, a copper Nissan, and a black Honda Civic—blocked the middle of the highway in various stages of damage. A middle-aged couple lay bleeding on the pavement, between the Lexus and the Honda.

Tiffany rushed over and got down on her knees. Just then, she heard Chip's voice in her head:

"What now, Tiffany? I'm still kind of new at this do-goody crap, ya know. I really don't think my usual tricks would do much good right now. It would provide some levity, but I guess it's kinda hard to laugh when you've got that irritating airbag thingamajig stuffed in your face."

She flinched. *"Did you just...did I just hear you call me Tiffany?"*

"It's your name, isn't it?"

"Yes..."

"Then what's the—"

"You never call me Tiffany!"

"I figure I should try and clean up my act just a smidge. Since I'm kind of an apprentice now. You know. Baby steps, so to speak. Don't wanna disappoint my public, do I?"

340

She smiled. *"I get it."*

"So then, to repeat what I just asked?"

"Do what you can."

"I don't know how much I can actually do here..."

She turned and winked at him. *"I do."*

"Really? In all seriosity?"

"Just don't do anything silly. You don't want to give that poor girl a heart attack before you help her out of that car, do you?"

"You're no fun at a party, baby cakes."

"You've only told me that a hundred times before."

"That's only because I've meant it a hundred times before."

Chip tended to the frightened young girl wedged behind her air bag in the Nissan. By taking her hands, he managed to pull her free, then helped lower her gently to the pavement.

Tiffany turned right back to the middle-aged couple. Then, applying a gentle hand to the man's bleeding leg, she felt warm relief when the bleeding gradually stopped. She suddenly found that she was happier than she'd ever been in her entire mortal life, when she had everything to live for. Everything, that is, but longevity. And when she thought of that, she remembered the gray-haired man. His image flashed in her mind, and she wondered who he really was and why he'd shown up so many times to help her.

She realized right then that she knew who he was all along. And the moment the realization came, she saw beautiful clouds. And a magnificent

341

waterfall. And heard wonderful music. And felt genuinely happy once again.

Her thoughts drifted back to Raven, Ohio. And the first time she'd talked to Chip at the City Dump. And then she recalled the first time she'd seen Lou Gates. And Ashley Parker. And Jimmy Russo. And, of course, the time they arrived in Peoria and discovered that Stepdad was dead, and that Momma was living all alone. And she realized right then that good things never ended, and that life went on forever, taking along with it every single blessed miracle that had ever happened in its natural course.

And when the middle-aged man lying on the pavement in front of her opened his eyes and smiled at her, then whispered to the attractive middle-aged lady lying beside him, "Nora, a beautiful angel has been sent to help us," Tiffany smiled, because at that very moment, she knew the man was right. And that she herself had been right.

About everything.

ALSO BY DAVID BERARDELLI

THE APPRENTICE
THE WAGON DRIVER
DEMONCHASER
DEMONCHASER II
STEPPING OUT OF MY GRAVE
DEMONCHASER III
IN ANOTHER REALM
BEYOND RECOGNITION
THE NIGHTMARE COLLECTOR
DEMONCHASER IV
HIDDEN
BEYOND GUILT
A RIPPLE IN TIME
YESTERDAY'S JOURNEY
ENLIGHTENMENT
REDEMPTION

www.ingramcontent.com/pod-product-compliance
Lightning Source LLC
Chambersburg PA
CBHW010829250626
47157CB00010B/3225